# Praise for Sloan McBride's *The Fury*

Rating: 4.5 Nymphs "...the pacing for this story is perfect, leading the reader on a rollercoaster thrill ride of demon fighting, cultural understanding and the blossoming of new and forbidden love...Add in great secondary characters, and you have all the things needed to propel this wonderful series into the future. I look forward to the next release. Read and enjoy!"

~ *Mystical Nymph, Literary Nymphs Reviews*

Rating: 85 "...*The Fury* is a cleanly written and enjoyable story..., the emotional component in the romance is presented well enough for me to accept that there is more between the main characters than merely hormones going wild, and the last few pages are really romantic to read indeed..."

~ *Mrs. Giggles*

Rating: 5 Hearts "...Fight/action scenes add some tense and thrilling moments. The love scenes were arousing and incredibly sexy. The dialogue was well-written and flowed smoothly. It had me laughing on more than one occasion. This is a superb and thoroughly entertaining start to what looks to be an awesome series. It grabbed me and held me from the first to last page..."

~ *Abi, The Romance Studio*

Rating: 4 Hearts "...THE FURY is the first book of a wonderful new series from author Sloan McBride called Time Walker. Full of intriguing characters, fast paced storyline and simmering sexual tension, this is an author who leaves you on the cusp of something wonderful with each page until the climatic ending is revealed..."

~ *Dawn, Love Romances & More Reviews*

# The Fury

*Time Walkers: Book One*

*Sloan McBride*

A SAMHAIN PUBLISHING, LTD. publication.

Samhain Publishing, Ltd.
577 Mulberry Street, Suite 1520
Macon, GA 31201
www.samhainpublishing.com

The Fury
Copyright © 2009 by Sloan McBride
Print ISBN: 978-1-60504-343-2
Digital ISBN: 978-1-60504-213-8

Editing by Angela James
Cover by Natalie Winters

First Samhain Publishing, Ltd. electronic publication: October 2008
First Samhain Publishing, Ltd. print publication: August 2009

# Dedication

To my daughter: Always believe in happily ever after and never give up on your dreams.

# Glossary

**Anunna:**    A fallen group of sky gods banished to the Underworld who can take on human form.

**Blethred:**    Life mate (soulmate)

**Démarr:**    Marriage ritual

**Doghume:**    Humans with special powers, i.e. psychic, wizards, witches, etc.

**Enki:**    Water God/God of Wisdom

**Eridu:**    The sea-house where Enki lives in the underwater City of Abzu.

**Galla:**    Kur's minions. They deal in death and destruction.

**Go'ras:**    Mind wipe

**Lahamas:**    Two dragon-like stone statues that guard the doorways of Eridu and act as messengers of Enki. (Leotis & Natalia)

**Melari:** Melari darts are coated with a strong sleeping drug. They are used by the minions to subdue targets so they can be transported to Kur.

**Nephilli:** ½ Human ½ God

**Percilious:** The wizard Enki enlisted to put a concealment spell around all the homes of his descendents.

**Reskar:** Loved one

**Shakaah:** (swear word)

**Tregorians:** The second level of galla, taller, with decomposing flesh and glowing yellow eyes. Stand 8-feet tall, long black robes, pale, ghostly coloring. Scaly finger, hidden faces, all the warmth leaves the area, one touch gives you euphoria and you forget about the danger you are in.

# Chapter One

The weather broke and a blanket of snow fell hard from the dismal clouds. Through random flakes, Reese Whittaker thought she saw two shadows by the building up ahead, but when she blinked, they disappeared. An eerie chill snaked up her spine.

She'd just left her archeology team at The Bistro. The back street had a couple of food places crowded with patrons and an occasional car drove by looking for a good parking spot. Music drifted from the pub on the corner every time someone opened the door, and two winos on the stoop were having a heated debate about fish.

She stopped at the corner before crossing the street. Even though this wasn't the hub of the city, Friday night brought out its share of party-goers and drunks, those who would not be paying attention to a lone woman stepping into the street.

Something buzzed past her ear and the speed limit sign next to her pinged, as if hit with a rock. Before she could react, a large male body flew through the air and tackled her to the ground.

Reese couldn't breathe. Every rock-hard inch of him pressed against her. She struggled, but her arms were held tight by his well-muscled chest. Was she being mugged? Would he waste time lying on top of her if he were a purse snatcher? *Oh, God!* Maybe he'd drag her behind the nearest dumpster and rape her, then leave her lying in the garbage ravaged or dead.

With a rush of adrenaline, she vowed she wouldn't go down without a fight. "Get off me!" She tried to scream but couldn't suck enough air into her lungs with him lying on top of her.

"Are you hurt?" he whispered softly in her ear with a deep voice.

Was he kidding? "A total stranger jumped on me and is crushing me into the cold pavement," she managed in staccato breaths.

His stubble scratched her cheek as he turned to look back the way she'd come from. Wicked chills congaed up her body.

She struggled again. "Get the hell off me!"

His jaw clenched as if he was warring with himself. Deftly jumping to his feet, he held out a hand to help her up. She grabbed it and he jerked her flush against his body with hard impact. Reese immediately stepped back but he still held her wrist. He reached down and picked up something from the street to examine it.

"Excuse me," she said, jerking the wrist still in his grasp.

He ignored her.

Mr. Personality was tall, at least six-four, dressed in black jeans, a black turtleneck and a leather duster that barely reached his calves. A strong jaw and high cheekbones suggested he was of Native American decent. In the dark, she couldn't tell what color his eyes were, but his body was lithe, solid muscle. He had a wild, dangerous look like Mel Gibson in the first *Lethal Weapon* movie.

"What's that?" She leaned closer to get a better look.

The stranger held some kind of dart between his fingers. "This is a *melari*."

"A *melari*?"

Her attacker gritted his teeth and shoved the object in his pocket. "Come on," he mumbled and started across the street, dragging her with him.

"Let me go," she yelled and tried to disengage her wrist from his grip. She raised her foot to kick him, but he side-stepped it, and she almost toppled over because he kept moving.

"Stop fighting me, woman, unless you want to die."

That statement hit her like arctic water on a winter day. "Don't hurt me," she pleaded.

He stopped and glared at her. "I'm not going to hurt you.

I'm here to protect you."

He had a funny way of showing it. "Protect me from what?"

Exasperation laced his sigh. "From the death squad that's after you." He pulled the dart from his pocket and waved it in front of her face. "What do you think this is for?"

She narrowed her gaze on him. A hormonal surge of courage pumped through her veins. "I don't know what that is, but the only thing I've seen threatening around here is you." She couldn't be sure but she thought she heard him growl.

An aura of danger surrounded him. He moved like a graceful predator and oozed raw sexuality. Her mouth suddenly went dry. She needed to find a way to get away from this he-man. Her attacker palmed the object and hid it away.

The sound of a car backfiring jolted her. He grabbed her shoulders and pushed her behind him. "Shit," the stranger said and touched his hand to his shoulder. "Which one is your vehicle?"

Reese saw blood seeping into his coat. No dart caused that wound; someone was shooting bullets at them.

Another gunshot pierced the night and shattered the window of a nearby car.

She screamed.

The stranger turned to her. "Which one, dammit?"

"That blue one there." She pointed to her Chevy Malibu.

Courage and strength poured from him along with his blood. They ran for her car, with him right on her heels. He grabbed the keys out of her hand. "Get in."

"Hey!" she protested, until a dart whizzed very close, banging into the car door.

Without another word, Reese scrambled into the passenger side as he revved the engine to life. He slammed his foot down on the gas and sped away.

Dagan skidded off the main road onto a darkened side street. He needed to check for an exit wound on his shoulder, and hoped the bullet hadn't lodged in the bone. They should be okay here for a few minutes.

He threw open the door and got out. The snow fell in heavy

flakes joining the previous snow accumulated on the wintry landscape. He eased off his coat. The cold air added a sting to his skin. With his left hand, Dagan tested the tender flesh of his shoulder.

Reese opened her door and stood to glare at him. "Okay, while the whole tackle-me-to-the-ground thing was interesting, and being shot at definitely got my attention, do you mind telling me what the hell is going on?"

He glanced over the top of the car and held her gaze for a moment. He'd already broken the rules by coming into contact with her, but he'd had no choice. "All in good time."

"Wha—"

"Come over here. I need you to see if there's an exit wound on my back."

At first, she looked as though she would refuse, but then she stomped around to the driver's side. She tentatively touched his shirt. He hoped the dome light inside the car provided enough light for her to see clearly.

"There's a big hole in the back of your shoulder. You're bleeding," she said dryly.

"Thanks, but I already knew that."

The next couple of seconds happened quickly. She pushed him against the back quarter panel of the car, jumped in the driver's seat, and threw the car in gear. He only had an instant to move before she ran over his foot.

He growled his frustration. With a flick of his wrist, a sudden gale-force wind exploded, swirling the snow into a blinding tornado. Dagan held his hand out and said, "Hold." The car screeched to a halt. He could hear Reese gunning the motor as she pressed on the gas, still attempting to get away. Wincing, he bent over to retrieve his coat and silently cursed the blue-eyed vixen. Calmly, he strolled to the car, opened the passenger door and got in. The wind disappeared as quickly as it had erupted and the snow went back to falling lazily to the ground.

"Get out of my car!" she yelled.

His dark brow lifted. He'd never understand humans. Her life was in mortal danger. Kur would be drawn to Reese because of her ancestry, an ancient bloodline from Kur's most hated enemy, Enki.

Dagan's oath and duty required that he protect her whether she wanted it or not, and by the gods, he planned to keep her alive. Whispering the obedience spell in the old language, Dagan smiled when her eyes glazed over. The sprinkle of freckles on her nose and cheeks were light but gave her an impish look. Her brows were thin and perfectly arched over enigmatic blue eyes clouded with confusion. She put the car in gear and started driving.

"Where are we going?" Reese turned the knob so the air coming out of the vents got warmer.

"Drive out of the city. We'll find a cheap motel to stay for the night."

"I'll go out of the city, but only so far as my house," she countered.

Dagan gave her a penetrating stare. "You'll do as I say."

She growled. "I could go to the police station so they can arrest your ass for kidnapping."

He couldn't help but laugh. She had a feisty streak. And, for some reason, she had been able to subvert the spell. This warranted some serious investigation.

"You think this is funny?" She frowned. "You fly out of nowhere, knocking me down and bruising my..." He glanced over at her. "Never mind." She sighed. "I only have your word that those people were actually after me."

She had a point.

Dagan took a minute to study her before saying, "They shot the *melari* dart at you before I appeared."

The truth of his words registered on her face as she absorbed what he'd said.

"I'm an archeologist. I don't know anything important or top secret. My job actually bores most people, unless they love digging around in dirt to find pieces of ancient civilizations. Why would I be in danger?"

"It's not what you know but who you are that puts you in jeopardy."

"You make no sense."

He gently trailed his fingertips down the sleeve of her coat.

He used his mental powers of persuasion to calm her nerves and minimize her fear.

"I can't be sure those demons are not following us. They may already know where you live and could be waiting." He felt her fear escalating again, and a glimpse of her disappointment had him saying, "I'll give you ten minutes at your place to grab some things." Maybe having some of her personal belongings would make this ordeal a little easier, if that were possible. "Then we'll find a motel. Once I'm sure you're safe, I will answer your questions."

Reese frowned, her brows dipping between her eyes. Waves of uncertainty coming off her battered him.

"Did you say demons just then? Demons, like in horror movies?"

"Not exactly like the movies, but demons they are."

"Have you visited a psychiatrist lately? I know a good one. I can give you her card," she offered dryly.

"I'm not crazy."

She gave him a yeah-right look, but said nothing more.

It grew darker as the Denver city lights disappeared behind them. They drove in silence the rest of the way but still her confusion tangled with his resolve.

After Reese pulled into her driveway, he stopped her from getting out.

"Wait." He scanned the darkened area. The snowfall had stopped. He detected no sign of the *galla.* "Your nearest neighbor is one point seven miles away?"

"How could you know that?"

He released her arm and got out of the car. Moving immediately to her side, he used his body as a shield to protect her. Once inside the house, he ordered her to stay put.

"But..."

He glared at her. "Stay!"

She narrowed her eyes and mumbled something under her breath, but stood still.

He returned after checking the rest of the house and gave her leave to move. "You never told me your name," she said while peeling off her wet coat.

"Dagan." He locked the door, moved to the large picture window, and lifted the curtain back a few inches to stare outside. Everything seemed quiet but he felt a strange vibration. Reese stood with her arms hugged around her body, staring into space. "Pack enough clothes for one night, maybe two," he urged, in hopes of getting her moving. They didn't have much time.

She glanced his direction then went down the hall.

Dagan upped the voltage on his senses, projecting invisible sensors which would register all movement, sound and activity. These would alert him should the Underworld soldiers be close by. Unfortunately, it also meant he could smell and feel Reese that much more. The little spitfire was very distracting.

He scanned the comfortable living area surrounding him. The tan walls were plain but rich in texture, and the dark wood floor gave them a warm glow. Simple furniture adorned the space, also with dark wood. Massive, framed oil paintings covered the walls, reverently preserved and cared after. Wooden shelves were sparse throughout the room and upon each were artifacts, ancient relics from Sumerian and Babylonian design. He recognized the markings.

One piece, a chalice, contained in a lighted glass case beckoned him with a singing in his blood. He knew this piece all too well. How had she come to acquire such a cherished and guarded secret of the deities? Did she realize the significance of the cup?

Beside the fireplace on either side were shelves built into the wall. Dagan walked toward them. On one side were pictures, he assumed of her family, because isn't that what humans usually did, put up pictures of family?

In an antique gold frame, which had recently been cleaned and polished, the first photograph had a young blond man with aristocratic features and a genuine smile. For some reason, Dagan felt as though he'd seen this man before, but how could that be? Leaning into him on the right sat a strikingly beautiful woman, her eyes the color of a Highland sky and her raven hair curling around her shoulder. The man's fingers were lost in the locks. Down in front, sitting on the floor, were two girls. Although they looked very much alike, he could tell there was a difference in their ages. *Reese and a sister.* Reese had the coloring of her father; the other looked more like her mother. He would need to find out where her family members were. If the *galla* found Reese, they might find the others as well.

Family, something he held no hope of having. He took his life as a time walker very seriously. Again, the two young girls drew his attention. He stared in wonder at the feisty, strong-willed Reese smiling back at him. His nerve endings crackled.

His advanced senses experienced every movement Reese made. A jolt lanced him when she reached into the cabinet and brushed her breast against the counter. His nostrils flared, and it took the greatest willpower not to storm into the kitchen, lift her up onto the counter and feast upon her sweet flesh. What in blazing hell was she doing in the kitchen?

"Damn."

Reese poked her head around the corner. "I'm grabbing some tea bags. Did you need something?"

The hair falling about her beautiful face begged him to push it back so he could trail hot kisses along her cheek and jaw. A fierce longing speared his gut. *You, naked on the floor, the couch or up against the wall.* "Nothing," he growled. "Get a move on."

She scowled at him and disappeared back behind the wall when a small explosion rocked the house.

Reese ran into the living room. "What was that?"

Why hadn't he felt the death squad's presence? He'd been too absorbed with foolish longings, his rising libido and the intense attraction to this human female. "Stay inside," he ordered as he crossed to the door, pulling his guns out.

"But..."

He pointed a finger at her, his expression stern. "Do as I say."

She darted to the door as Dagan hurtled himself off the porch and whirled around with guns in both hands. He shot two rounds, hitting what looked like shadows to Reese, but when they fell, she realized they were alive.

Heart pounding, she dashed to the railing to watch the macabre scene when three more came at Dagan from the other side and he easily dispatched them with deadly aim. Transfixed by terror, she barely heard the shuffling to her left. Her attention drawn from the fight, she saw one of the shadows coming toward her. It blended with the darkness which now settled as a backdrop for this nightmare. She needed some kind of weapon.

Running back into the house, she picked up a lamp from the end table near the door and held it like a tennis racket.

"Don't come near me or I'll brain you, sucker." She lifted the lamp a little higher.

The shadow creature laughed, if that's what you could call the cackling sound it made. It advanced like fog, creeping closer. When it got to the doorway, it reached out for her. Reese hauled off and crowned it with the base of the lamp. With a loud crack, its head fell sideways and it dropped. She kicked it to make sure it wasn't moving.

Another figure grabbed her from behind, wrenching her arms and making her drop the lamp. She stomped on its toes and kicked at what she thought were its legs but it did no good. The thing had a tight grip around her arms and jacked them higher behind her back.

She cried out.

More shadows of varied sizes dropped down from the porch roof. She screamed and frantically looked for Dagan. A crowd of the creatures huddled in the front yard with Dagan in the middle. He fought hard, like a seasoned veteran. Using his elbow, he knocked one in the face and shot it in the head. It withered and disintegrated. He holstered the gun, unsheathed a wicked-looking knife, and with an upward swing, he sliced through the shadow's throat, decapitating it. The figure disappeared with a fiery flash.

Reese struggled against the thing that held her, trying to loosen its grip so she could break free. "Dagan!"

Dagan leapt onto the porch. He reached around one body with his left hand and swiped the knife across its neck, killing it. The creature that held Reese turned her to face him. His eyes glowed bright red and in his hand, he held one of the darts. In a downward stroke, he stabbed toward her neck.

"Don't even think about it," Dagan yelled, as he kicked one in the stomach and punched the face of the soldier that held her.

The creature let go of her and stumbled back. Dagan withdrew two six-point metallic stars, and threw them at his target. With a pop, it disintegrated.

"Look out," Reese screamed.

From behind, the one that Dagan had kicked now jumped up and ran toward him. Dagan easily drew another gun from its holster and fired three times. The demon was gone. A loud moan floated from the one at Reese's feet. The creature she'd bonked with the lamp woke up and didn't look happy.

Dagan stabbed the creature through the middle and when it swung around to face him, he sliced off its head.

Wide-eyed, she stared at the black mess pooled on the porch and splattered across the walls. The substance smoked like a dying fire and had an acrid smell. Her body shivered. She hadn't paid any attention to the cold when she'd run out the door. The temperature had dropped considerably and her breath created puffs of swirling smoke.

"Come on." Dagan grabbed her arm and ran to the car.

"But my clothes, my coat," she yelped.

"We can't stay here. They'll be back." He opened the driver's side door. "Keys."

"They're in my purse in the house."

"Shit." He raced over, grabbed her shoulder, and shoved her toward the porch. "Let's go, quickly," he said and pulled his gun.

The hold he had on her wasn't bruising, but light. A frisson of electricity passed between them causing her fingers to tingle. She looked up to see if he'd noticed. His eyes were in constant motion around the entire area. If he'd felt the jolt, she couldn't tell from his actions or his face.

He rushed them inside and locked the door. "Get your purse," he said as he snatched her coat from the back of the chair where she'd laid it.

She hurried into the kitchen and grabbed her purse, taking a moment to breathe deeply. A sick feeling clawed at her stomach. When she got back to Dagan, he slipped her coat on her, took the keys, and clasped her hand.

"When we get out there, don't stop." He gave her a stern

look. "If I say run, you run to the car and lock yourself in. Understand?"

Reese gazed into eyes she now realized were green. The intensity in them made her nod her head in response to his order. At the moment, this gorgeous stranger was her lifeline.

# Chapter Two

Dagan drove like the fires of Hell were lapping at them. With the lateness of the hour and the deserted stretch of road, there was little chance a cop would pull them over. Reese stared out the window at the passing landscape but said nothing. Finally, he pulled off the road at a rundown-looking place called the Moonlight Motel, stopping in front of the registration office.

"Wait here. I'll check us in," he said, opening the door.

Dagan went into the office. Drab walls, torn carpet and chipped wood off the dilapidated desk showed the disrepair of the place. Not like the outside hadn't already spoken of what type of establishment he had found. The greasy-haired man behind the counter nodded when Dagan entered. Yellow teeth and hideous breath greeted him from thin lips. Beady black eyes gave him the once over before he asked Dagan his pleasure.

Dagan smiled at the pock-marked face. "Don't see any cars out there. Slow night?"

"Seems so. What can I do fer ya?"

Dagan glanced at the side board that held all the room keys and counted twelve. "I'd like the room on the end if you don't mind."

"Not a problem. It's twenty-five dollars a night." Again, his eyes raked over Dagan's form, apparently trying to decide why Dagan had stopped there.

"Okay." Dagan reached toward his pocket.

The old man turned and pulled the key to twelve off the board. When he whirled back around, Dagan held out his hand and touched the old man's forehead. With the mind sweep, the night clerk would not remember him ever being there. Using a little power of suggestion, the clerk would still see the key to unit twelve hanging on the board.

When he got back in the car he said, "There is no one else staying in the motel tonight, so I had him put us at the end." He drove them across the parking lot to the last unit. He unlocked the door to room twelve, went inside for a moment then motioned for Reese to follow.

While Dagan's superhero act had been impressive, she didn't know him and this whole scenario had become absurd. When he'd gone into the building, he'd taken the car keys with him, which had nixed Reese's chance for a fast escape. The temperature and the fact that she saw nothing else around kept her from trying to escape on foot. Pushing severe tiredness aside, she'd opened the glove compartment to search for a weapon of some sort. She found Kleenex, the car registration and a road map, but nothing viable for protection. She needed warmth and a grande-size cup of hot chocolate. Her feet were numb and her hands hurt.

It felt warmer when she entered the place. The antiquated heat register hissed and coughed.

"I'm going to put the car on the backside of the building out of sight. When I leave, lock the door and don't let anyone else in except me," Dagan instructed her. He tossed the key on the table.

The numbness had now spread to her entire body. It took great effort to turn and lock the door, certain she wouldn't let him back in. The phone, she'd decided, but couldn't keep a coherent thought. Her feet felt like anvils and dragged as she wandered to the double bed in the musty smelling dime-sized room.

A wave of exhaustion went through her. Her legs collapsed and she dropped to the edge of the bed.

She wanted to sleep.

She had to concentrate hard to stay awake so she focused on what looked like a palm tree on the filthy wallpaper. She didn't know how long she'd sat there until she heard someone calling her name.

"Reese. Reese. Come on, honey, look at me."

When she tilted her head, she saw Dagan bent over her, a worried expression on his face. *How did he get back inside the room?* He lifted her up, wrapped his arm around her waist, and pulled off her coat. Next, he sat her down and removed her shoes. He turned her, placed his hands on either side of her face, and using his thumbs, pulled down her lower eyelids to stare into her eyes.

"Dammit."

Dagan grabbed the bottom of her shirt and lifted it over her head. Gentle fingers caressed her neck, shoulders and arms.

"Your arm was nicked by the *melari* dart when the *galla* fell. They are coated with a potent sleeping drug. That's why you're so sluggish."

Sliding his hand under her knees Dagan picked her up and placed her head on a pillow. In a haze, she watched him go into the bathroom, come back to check the lone window then bolt the door.

In murmurs so rhythmic they sounded like song, he repeated a chant several times. His sultry voice made her want to curl herself around his body and purr.

She felt him slide the cover and bedspread over her before climbing into the squeaky bed and spooning up against her spine.

"What are you doing?" she managed through numb lips.

"Your body is like ice. My body heat will warm you and we both need rest. Go to sleep, Reese."

A thought that she should be outraged and embarrassed came to mind, but passed as she closed her eyes and got lost in the cocoon of warmth and sleep.


When he'd knocked on the door and Reese hadn't responded, a trickle of fear had clutched his throat. He used his powers to open the door and found her sitting on the bed in a kind of trance. Luckily, only some of the *melari* had gotten into her system. If more of the drug had been injected into her bloodstream, she would have become comatose. She should be fine in the morning.

It had been a while since he'd lain with a woman. Her even breaths told him she slept. She still had an occasional shiver, but the chill had at last left her body. The soft fragrance of the woman tempted him with a delicate aroma, but this was no fragile female. With his fingertips, he felt the rise and fall of the swell of her breasts, which shot sensations straight to his groin. The power in her blood, the ancestry in her DNA, sang to him. Dagan gritted his teeth. Thoughts of Reese beneath him, those soft blue eyes looking up with desire instead of anger or fear, while he sank himself deep inside her, caused his entire body to burn.

His powers hummed with vibrancy and her essence surrounded him, invading his keen senses. Her body called to him in ways he'd not thought possible. Having sex with her wasn't an option. As a time walker, he should be immune to her—oblivious.

But that was not happening.

For some reason, her blood drew him, seduced him. Things would be clearer after a few hours of sleep.

He hoped.

A beam of sunlight shot through the crack of curtains and into the dank motel room. Reese came awake with it momentarily blinding her. A thigh wedged between her legs, warm breaths caressed her neck and a large hand skimmed circles around her breast. For a brief instant, she imagined running her hands along Dagan's bulging chest, around his neck and letting her fingers play with his gorgeous dark hair. She couldn't breathe without smelling the flavor of him—warm, dark mocha. Reese tensed when she felt Dagan's bulging erection against her butt. The continual swirling of his fingers around her breast upped her heart rate and branded her with a high level of desire.

She glanced over her shoulder. Apparently, he was sleeping. "Hey, slick, wake up."

At first, he nuzzled her closer then snapped fully awake. When he realized where his hand lay, he jerked it back.

She twisted to look at him. "Tell me that's not a pistol nudging against my ass."

He rubbed his hands down his face then looked at her and winked. "It isn't."

She rolled to her back and pulled the covers up when he got out of the squeaky bed. Her mouth went dry and her gaze traveled hungrily down the length of his toned body. Warmth spread through her that had nothing to do with the temperature in the room. Her nipples grew so hard they hurt and she had a strong urge to rub something between her legs. Her face burned with embarrassment. She didn't even know this guy.

He tucked his shirt into the waist of his pants then shrugged into his dual holsters, pulling the guns out to check the magazines. She got a glimpse of his shoulder, but saw no visible signs of where the bullet had entered. *How odd.* He hooked steel stars to his belt and strapped a dagger to his right thigh.

"That's some hardware." And she wasn't just talking about the weapons.

He gave her a cocky grin as if he knew exactly what she'd been thinking. "You need to get up and take care of any necessities." He raked a lustful gaze over her covered breasts before saying, "Get dressed and meet me outside in ten minutes."

Under different circumstances, she might find this whole situation interesting and plead with Dagan to come back to bed so she could explore his incredible body. Unfortunately, it was all too real and she needed to remember that. She still didn't understand why anyone would be after her and she planned to grill her kidnapper/savior for answers.

Dagan started the car and turned the heater and blower on high. A good three inches of snow had fallen last night. He got out and scraped chunks of ice from the windows. By the time he got back into the vehicle, the heater had begun melting the remaining ice and warming the car to a more comfortable temperature. He checked the gas tank, which showed a half tank left. It should be enough to get Reese back to her house.

*"Dagan."*

*"Flame?"* Through the mind link, Flame's thoughts came in

loud and clear.

"*Where in hell and damnation are you?*"

"*I'm in Colorado, twenty-first century. A strong congregation of galla is here. I came to investigate.*"

"*Did you find them?*"

Flame, son of Utu and Dagan's best friend, was a time walker, like himself.

"*They were after a woman.*" A fiery woman with spunk, he thought, but he didn't let Flame hear it.

"*Did you stop them?*"

"*Yes, for the time being.*"

"*Where are you now?*"

"*They attacked us at her house, so after I dispatched them, I took her to a motel.*"

"*By all the gods, you mean she saw everything and you haven't wiped her yet?*"

"*No.*"

"*Well, wipe her clean and get back here. Pyre is having a conniption because you haven't picked up your weapons yet. You know how he is when he's anxious to show you something new he's created.*"

"*I will do it today once I get her back home and post a guard.*"

"*Okay. Stay true to the cause my friend.*"

"*Always.*"

Dagan grabbed the cell phone from his coat and dialed. "Rufus, it's Dagan."

"Do you know what time it is, purebred?" said the sleepy voice on the other end of the phone.

"Of course I do."

"Then why the hell are you calling me?"

"I need you to guard a human for me."

"Trouble?" the man asked, now more alert.

As a *doghume*, a human with special abilities who helped the time walkers in their quest, Rufus had worked with him on numerous occasions when he'd been in this century.

"I'm afraid so. Go to the house, make sure no sentries are waiting then stay out of sight."

"I'm getting dressed now. Give me the address."

Dagan recited the address to Rufus and hung up. At least that would help. The hard part would be performing the *go'ras* on Reese. He should never have touched her, but caressing her soft skin and holding her close while they slept made his fingers burn to play with her breasts again.

Red particles clumped together to form Feral, the captain of the squad Kur had sent to capture the Whittaker woman. The gaping hole in his chest was the last thing to close.

Kur, King of the Underworld, lounged in his throne room. He needed the *galla* to bring him some humans. He hated these times in between feedings when he got weaker. The weakness kept him secluded in Divinity, the ironic name he'd given his kingdom in the Underworld.

"What happened?" he asked Feral.

"A time walker...Dagan."

Anger lit across Kur's face and he jumped to his feet. "Dagan?" He growled. "Damn." The time walker's presence was unfortunate.

"It will make it harder to get to her."

"Harder, yes, but not impossible. How many did we lose?" Kur sauntered over to the massive table covered with exotic foods.

"I don't know yet." Feral rolled a gold coin across his knuckles.

"Failure is not an option."

Feral acted nonchalant, but Kur smelled the faint scent of fear. "I need her," he snarled.

A sneer marred Feral's face and he palmed the coin. "I will try again soon. I need to gather my force."

"Good, don't wait too long."

Feral bowed and left.

Kur roared his displeasure. He didn't find pure blood descendents very often and one from Enki was rare. Her life force would heighten his abilities and make him stronger than he'd been before. He would not allow Dagan to take away this opportunity, even if he had to go himself.

"Vile," he yelled.

"Yes, Lord."

A lithe blonde woman dressed in black leather pants and a red midriff shirt stood in the doorway. The low-cut collar showed her ample bosom and she forever contorted her body in ways that ensured he got a good glimpse of her breasts.

"I need some humans. I don't care where you get them, but I need them."

"Always happy to serve," she said and left to do his bidding.

Kur took deep breaths to calm down. Anger robbed him of energy he couldn't afford to lose. Conserving energy would be top priority until he got more humans and the prize, Reese Whittaker.

# Chapter Three

Dagan had the car ready and waiting when Reese came out of room twelve. The car was blessedly warm with the heater on full blast when she climbed inside. Two large cups of coffee and a bag of donuts sat on the dashboard. She didn't know where he'd gotten them since there were no other buildings in sight for miles. Her mother would have been appalled at the way she scarfed down the donut and slurped the coffee, but manners meant little to her at the moment. Her heaving stomach delighted in the food.

"Ready?" Dagan asked, before pulling onto the deserted road and heading back toward Denver.

The roads were wet but not icy. After last night's snowfall, the landscape looked like it had jumped off a Christmas card.

"I think I need to contact the police and tell them what happened. You can take me in and I'll fill out a report."

"No."

She glared at him. He wasn't the boss of her. "You're really starting to annoy me."

He barked out laughter. "That's funny, you started annoying me the minute I saw you."

"You're an ass."

"I'm an ass who's trying to save your life."

"Then let me call the police, tell them what happened."

"No, not yet."

"Oooooo, you're..." Reese wanted to choke him.

Dagan gave her a cocky smirk before concentrating again on the driving.

"I want to know what's going on, Dagan." She wrapped her arms around her waist. "Who are those *things*, and why are they chasing me?"

"There is not a lot I can explain right now other than to say that it has to do with your ancestry."

"That helps immensely. Everything is so much clearer now. Thanks," she added sarcastically.

"You're welcome." He smiled.

"So you're not going to tell me anything, are you?"

"No."

"I will call the cops at the first chance I get and report all this to them."

"What will you say, Reese?" he said in a softer tone. "Some shadows attacked and a strange man appeared out of nowhere to save me. I've been with him all night."

When he said it that way, it did sound far-fetched. The police would think she'd lost her mind.

Maybe she had.

Insanity didn't run in her family that she knew of. Yesterday had started out as a normal day. Should she try to sneak off long enough to call her colleagues, particularly Joe or Geoffrey? No. What could they do anyway? He hadn't harmed her. She'd wait it out and see what happened.

"Where are we going?"

He glanced over. "I'm taking you home."

"Really?" she said with enthusiasm. Uncertainty crept into her voice. "What about those creatures, the *galla*?"

His hand found hers on her thigh and grasped it. "I've sent someone to your house to check things out and make sure we don't have any surprises." He glanced over. "Don't worry."

She nodded. That was easy for him to say.

A few miles up the road, they stopped for gas. After he filled up the tank and Reese used the bathroom, they headed out again. The closer they got to Reese's house, the more urgent his need for information became. She sat there like a warrior princess. Her unsmiling face spoke of nervous tension, and

29

long, slender fingers had ripped pieces from one of the napkins that had come with the donuts. The remnants were scattered in her lap and on the floor.

"Reese." She jumped a little as if she'd been deep in thought. "When we were at your house last night, I noticed a picture with you and, I assume, your family."

"Yes?"

"Where are they now?"

A suspicious shadow crossed her face and she leveled those spitfire eyes on him. "Why do you want to know?"

He sighed dramatically. "After everything, do you not trust me even a little?"

She mulled it over.

Finally, coming to some decision, she huffed. Dagan clenched his hands on the steering wheel awaiting the information he hoped she would offer willingly.

"My sister, Riley, is in Europe right now."

"How long has she been there?"

"For about two years."

Europe for two years probably meant Riley was safe for the moment, but he'd send one of their operatives to check it out.

"My mother died three years ago."

He glanced at her and saw tears well in her eyes. "I'm sorry."

"Yes, everyone says that," she replied in a dry tone.

"And, what of your father?"

She stiffened. "He's here, I mean, in Denver, at his home."

Unexpected surprises didn't please him, especially when it meant another human faced immediate danger. She didn't say anymore.

When they were a couple of blocks from her house, Dagan pulled out his cell and called Rufus.

"It's clean. I've checked the house three times and have been moving around the grounds. Other than the nasty charred spots on the porch, you'd never know the shit-eaters had been here."

"Great."

"Am I playing watchdog after she gets home too?" Rufus snickered.

"Absolutely."

"Damn cold at night this time of year. Good thing I brought my parka."

"Quit whining," Dagan said and hung up.

Reese looked over at him. "Problem?"

"No. Your house is clear. No sign of the *galla* either inside or out."

"Good, that's good."

Dagan agreed but knew it wouldn't last. With the night came the creeping crud, i.e. the demons of death. He'd leave Reese in the capable hands of the *doghume*. He'd order another to stake out her father's home and keep watch. The thought of leaving her left him uneasy, which was another oddity that conflicted with his training. He had no choice but to do it.

There was no other way.

He pulled into her drive and parked. Scanning the area, he sent out feelers, but sensed none of Kur's minions.

Reese scrambled out of the car and grabbed her purse. "I can't wait to take a long, hot shower."

Dagan grunted. He felt a strange current of energy buzzing in his head the closer he got to the house. Still watching for intruders, he followed Reese up the stairs and inside. The sound got louder and stronger, playing with his internal senses like a live electrical wire bouncing around on pavement. This could have been the vibration he'd noticed last night. Of course, his senses were concentrating on movement of the *galla* at the time, and were absorbed by the proximity of Reese. Those distractions had demanded his focus, so he hadn't paid that much attention to the field of static electricity.

He grabbed her arm when she started to take her coat off. "Wait here."

"Oh for crying out loud," she said in an exasperated voice. "I thought you said everything was fine."

He turned a heated glare on her. "Wait here."

She stuck her left hip out and crossed her arms over her chest, glaring right back. She looked like Mount Cradacus

31

before it erupted, and he knew that eruption would spew toward him.

He wandered through each room, making sure there were no surprises. When he had walked the entire interior and checked all the locks and closets, he strolled back into the entryway and right up to the beautiful time bomb that waited there.

Her soft blue eyes were tiny flames now. It was a good thing he liked playing with fire or his ass would be cooked.

"Are you done?" she asked dryly.

He stared down at her upturned face, appreciating the gentle flush that turned her cheeks pink. She licked her lips and he wondered what she would taste like. Before he thought too much more about it, he placed his fingertips on her temples and began massaging them.

She straightened. "What are you do—"

Dagan closed his eyes and reached out with his mind to touch hers. There, he removed all traces of the *galla* and himself.

"You will wake up and go about your day," he whispered in her ear before gently lying her unconscious form down on the smoky green couch.

He removed her coat and cast one longing glance at her body before moving to the door. He needed to see Pyre about weapons, and a certain god about the unexpected energy field surrounding Reese's house.

Kur had just tossed aside the emptied body of a homeless man Vile had brought him when Feral strolled into the throne room. His footsteps echoed on the polished black marble floor.

Kur reached for the golden goblet filled with blood red Merlot before glancing in Feral's direction. The wine tasted like nectar on his lips. Adding his victim's blood to his wine gave it that sweeter taste. "What news do you bring me, Captain?"

Feral bowed before saying, "My scouts thought they had found her, but then her trail disappeared."

Kur growled and threw the sparkling goblet and its contents against the nearest black-draped wall. "That bastard,

Dagan, tests my temper." He stormed over to the long, ornate table of Roman design and splashed more liquid into another opulent cup. Downing the wine, he dropped the piece on the exquisite tablecloth staining it red. "I should have killed him all those years ago when I had the chance."

"My Lord?"

Waving his hand through the air, Kur said, "Never mind." He stepped over the human male's shell of a body. "Do you have a plan?"

"Of course. I have sentries posted in several areas she is known to frequent. My squad will be ready when she reappears, then we will strike."

"Excellent." Kur stepped close and glared at Feral. "Do not disappoint me."

"No, my lord."

"Very well, get it done. My body grows restless with need for the power."

"We will succeed."

"Go then."

Feral disappeared through the massive archway.

"Wretched!"

A beautiful brunette with a sheer, glowing, blue gown materialized before him.

"Yes, my king."

A wicked smile curved on his lips. He loved the way his people bowed and referred to him as king.

"Have some *galla* take this trash away, then come back here, and be naked when you do."

She curtsied, going low to the floor. Her gown pooled around her. "As you wish, my king."

Wretched left the room. The power from the meager human he had consumed thrummed through his body. When the female returned, he would bend her face-first over the throne and shove his already throbbing cock into her ass. Walking to where the withered body lay, Kur reached inside his black leather low-riders and pulled out his swelled cock. Energy was not the only benefit to sucking humans dry.

He laughed.

Closing his fingers around the straining shaft, he imagined how dark and tight Wretched's ass would feel clamping on him. He stroked harder and faster until his gray juice spurted over the lifeless form.

The henchmen appeared a few minutes later to remove the mess. Neither of them spoke to their master nor did they comment about the goo that coated the dead man's clothes.

Kur had not bothered to conceal his erection. Again, his cock filled and jerked with anticipation as Wretched appeared, gloriously nude. She proceeded toward the throne, where Kur ordered her to bend over, and then positioned himself.

Dagan materialized in the dank stone hallway of Mount Cradacus, the oldest and most active volcano of all time. Buried inside the hidden world of the Pantheon, it could not be seen by the human eye. The sulfuric, acrid air of the volcano violated his keen sense of smell. He strolled into the huge antechamber where Pyre and three others worked endlessly to create weapons to help the time walkers fight the minions of the Underworld and their leader.

"Hey, P, how's it hanging?" Dagan clasped hands with his brother-at-arms.

"Longer and stronger than you'll ever know, you purebred cur."

"Is that any way to talk to one of your oldest and dearest friends? Not to mention one of your best customers?" Dagan winked.

"I say it like it is."

Pyre's voice had grown raspy from working in this lethal environment for so long. Although he, too, was a purebred, when the call had come, Pyre begged the Goddess Inanna to allow him to serve by forging the weapons the army would need. He had always enjoyed working with his hands. The minerals that lay deep inside Mount Cradacus were perfect for molding. With the precise balance and tensile strength, the weapons were unbreakable and could penetrate any surface. Blades sharpened to perfection sliced through a *galla*'s form like butter, and bullets left huge holes in the enemy. Pyre was fully capable of fighting the battle, but chose to arm the soldiers with the right tools to win.

"So tell me what has you in such an uproar as to bring me to this vile place?"

"I've been working on a sword for you."

"A sword?"

Pyre walked away from the fiery pit where he forged the weapons and headed down a long, narrow, strangely cool tempered hallway. The walls twinkled with an abundance of minerals and stones.

Dagan followed his friend farther away from the fierce heat to a cooler clime.

"I wanted something you could swing with one hand, but would be light enough to carry under your coat." He stopped in a smaller antechamber where a wide variety of weapons hung from the wall and lay upon tables made of rock. Reaching up, he gently lifted a shiny blade from its hanger. Pyre held the object like a precious child and its silver coloring reflected bright in his eyes.

"It has a leaf-shaped blade and is double-edged. It's light." He swung it in demonstration. "The hilt is large enough to accommodate the size of your hand." He placed it back in the baldric and handed it to Dagan. "You hang it over your right shoulder across your back and it will go unseen under your coat."

Dagan unsheathed the sword and swung it through the air crisscross in front of his body. "It swings evenly."

Pyre nodded. "Just remember that it's double-edged so you don't slice off a finger."

"I'll remember." Dagan slid the baldric over his shoulder, brought his other arm through and adjusted his new weapon to sit between his shoulder blades. He then practiced bringing his hand behind his head, grabbing the hilt and pulling the sword free.

"If you can manage to do that every time without cutting off an ear, it will be a miracle," Pyre mumbled.

"It's a fine sword, P. Thanks."

"And the human? You did what you were supposed to do,

right?"

"Yes. It's done."

Pyre clapped his hands together. "Damn good then. She won't remember you, and you will do your job and be gone."

*Gone.* That thought didn't sit well with him.

"Go on and get out of here so I can continue my work."

Dagan faced Pyre. They both placed their fisted right hands over the left side of their chests and then took the same fisted hands and banged knuckles.

"To duty until peace," Dagan said.

"To disposal of the creature," Pyre replied.

Both men grinned.

# Chapter Four

Three hours later, Reese woke. She lifted slowly to a sitting position. The pounding in her head felt like someone was doing roadwork using several jackhammers. It took a while for her eyes to fully focus. Why was she lying on her couch? What time was it?

The filigree hands on the antique clock showed two-twenty. She must have laid down for a nap. But now, she needed to get to her office. Though she'd told the others not to come in until Monday, Reese had planned to spend today contacting potential investors. First, she needed drugs to get rid of the serious headache that threatened to keep her home. Strolling into the kitchen, she noticed two Styrofoam cups sitting on the counter, one half empty. Maybe she'd forgotten to pour out what she'd drank last night.

"That's strange." She shook her head and then cursed because shooting pains speared into her eyeballs.

Did she drink wine at The Bistro? Actually, she couldn't remember much of last night. Her archeological team had met to discuss a new dig on the Turkey/Iraqi border. It had grown dark and snow started to fall when she'd left, but after that, no memory at all.

She poured the cold coffee into one cup and put it in the microwave for one minute. The first gulp stopped her dead in her tracks. It tasted awful, too strong and bitter. What was going on?

At the end of the counter, the amber light blinked on her answering machine, letting her know she had a message. Reese pushed the button.

"Hello, Reese, this is Dr. Berticelli. Can you please call my office as soon as possible? I need to—"

She pressed the delete button. She didn't want to hear the rest. She'd heard it all before. She set the cup on the table and grabbed her jacket. "Maybe some fresh air will help the headache." Before she left though, she downed a couple of Tylenol.

Reese spent the rest of the day phoning people and sending e-mails. To her frustration, no one seemed interested in backing a full scale dig in an area so close to the Iraqi hot zone, and some were downright rude. A few alluded to the fact that the State Department had put the word out the area in question was under martial law. She slammed the receiver down on its cradle a little too hard after the latest rejection. The area being under martial law would provide an insurmountable obstacle.

Resigned to the fact that there could be nothing more accomplished today, Reese gathered her papers into a pile and shoved them to the side. The phone she'd abused moments before now glowed like a beacon. Her father's condition overshadowed the exciting news about the find. She knew what she had to do.

Lifting the receiver as though it were lead, Reese dialed Dr. Berticelli's private line and waited for her to pick up.

"Good afternoon," the older, well-seasoned psychiatrist intoned.

"Good afternoon," she replied in a nervous voice. "This is Reese Whittaker. I got your message. Do you have a few minutes to speak with me, or is this a bad time?"

"No, it's fine. Please give me a minute," the doctor said before placing her on hold.

Reese thrummed her fingers against the worn oak desk. She picked up the pencil and twirled it while staring at the oil painting which hung on the opposite wall, a chaotic piece that reminded her of her own life.

The doctor came back on the line. "Okay," she sighed. "Your father brought himself in here Thursday night. He wanted to be admitted to the hospital, but I refused."

"You did?"

"Yes."

Reese envisioned the thin, white-toothed smile on the doctor's face.

"He does not need to be admitted. He needs to be with family and friends. To get past the grief, he needs to work, at home in the yard, at his office, go to the grocery store. He needs to do normal things."

"He seems reluctant to do so, as you well know," Reese offered.

"Yes, that is unfortunate."

In a barely audible voice Reese said, "He loved her very much."

"I know, dear. But it has been three years and he is a virile, healthy man. Is there no way for you to get him out to be with other people?"

"He does go to work, but most times he's like a robot, going through the motions."

"Perhaps a dinner party or birthday party. It will help direct his thoughts in a positive direction."

"I'll speak to his vice president, see about throwing a cocktail dinner for their clients."

"That's a very good idea."

"I'll see what I can do, doc." Reese rubbed her eyes. "I'll keep you posted."

After her mother's death from cancer three years ago, Clive Whittaker, the once capable and dynamic owner of Whittaker Investments had nearly ceased to exist, heartsick over the loss of the woman he'd loved more than life. Her sister left for Europe after a year of trying to cope. She claimed it was to be with Steve or Tom, Dick or Harry, whoever the latest boy toy had been, but Reese knew that Riley had run. Tears stung her eyes. She needed to concentrate on something else or she'd fall into a sorrowful pit.

Reese grabbed her purse, exited the building, and headed toward her car. She'd call Tony Bloomfield, her father's partner, on Monday about the cocktail party.

A strange feeling of being watched made the hairs on her neck rise. Pulling out her keys, she pushed the unlock button, slid into the front seat, locked the doors, and threw the gearshift to drive. The thought of a long, hot shower brought a warm flutter to her heart and an ache between her legs, a sexual ache.

The tense forty-five minute drive home left her right shoulder and low back hurting. Deciding it was better to take the shower before making dinner, she headed straight for the bathroom when she got home. She twisted the faucets, got the water to the right temperature, and stepped under the hot spray. Yeah, that's what she needed to ease her muscles and dispel the bizarre thoughts that had plagued her all afternoon. Reaching for the soap, she leaned her head back to saturate her hair. She closed her eyes and imagined large, masculine hands rubbing it along her breasts and down her stomach, massaging her in all the right places. One hand moved between her legs and a soapy finger slipped through the fold. Her sensitive clit welcomed the attention and after several moments spasmed. The orgasm gripped Reese hard.

"I need to get laid," she whispered.

Or had she already?

Why couldn't she remember anything about last night? Hurriedly rinsing and toweling herself dry, Reese ran to her bedroom. She yanked the phone off its cradle and dialed Roberta's number.

Roberta Stonewater, a rotund African American taskmaster, was the glue that held the archeology team together and kept it functioning. She prepared all the tedious paperwork, knew whom to contact for just about anything they needed and could usually get it. There were bets on whether she was ex-CIA.

When she picked up Reese said, "Roberta, it's Reese."

"Hi, boss, what's up?"

"I know this is going to sound crazy but did I have any wine with dinner last night?"

"What?"

"Just humor me, please."

Roberta paused. "No, you drank some tea and then coffee, but no wine. What's going on?"

"I don't know, probably nothing. I've had a bad headache all day and strange things have happened."

"What kind of strange things?"

Reese wasn't about to tell her colleague that she'd had an intense orgasm while fantasizing in the shower. "Nothing. Don't worry about it, probably just too much caffeine. I'll see you on Monday, Roberta." She hung up before her co-worker could grill her.

She lay on the bed and pulled the comforter up to her neck. Rolling to her side, she closed her eyes and took long, slow breaths. An alluring scent of dark mocha tickled her nose and memory. She turned her face into the pillow. "This is getting really weird," she murmured and drifted to sleep.

In her dreams, a tall, gorgeous man in a brown duster, armed with weapons and a charming smile, tackled her. His bottle green eyes were mischievous and compelling. Things were hazy. A dark, evil presence surrounded them, but an aura of white light played around Mister Rough and Tough and that helped ease her fear. During the course of the dream, dark mist with red eyes clawed at her skin, pop-up balloons squeezed her in a tiny room made from a cardboard box, and her hero took her on a roller coaster ride which ended with lots and lots of incredible sex.

Reese's eyes flew open. Her brain registered some recognition and her aroused body acted as though her dream had been real. Granted, it had been a couple of years since she'd slept with a man but this imaginary guy cranked up her desire and sent it into overdrive.

She'd given up on relationships after a long string of failed attempts. They didn't last because of her occupation. At least that's what she told herself. Sometimes, she'd be gone for months at a time in some third world country. Most men couldn't handle the distance thing and ended up moving on. Of course, she'd never found one that sparked more than an iota of interest.

Her job was her life. Going on digs to unearth bits and pieces of ancient cultures drove her. The fascination or obsession with Sumer had been with her from a very young age. Thinking of her past brought a sense of loss and melancholy. She hugged the pillow to her chest and begged her subconscious mind to recall the dream. Rather than dwell on an inevitable phone call she didn't want to make to discuss a matter she had grown weary of dealing with.

Dagan shimmered to physical form, dripping wet, on the steps leading up to Eridu, the great sea-house and home of Enki. He hated coming to Abzu. He couldn't seem to stay dry in the underwater city. Cursing in the old language made him feel a little better, but not any dryer.

He climbed the endless stairs until he got to the top. There, he saw the two *Lahamas* guarding the doors as always.

"Hello, Leotis." He approached the dragon-like statue on the left.

"Dagan," the statue replied in a bored tone.

"Is he in?"

"The master is home. Do you request an audience?"

"Yes."

"Very well." The statue rose from its perch on a pillar made entirely of sea coral and strolled lazily to the doors which opened wide.

"You're looking well today, Natalia." Dagan walked over to the other statue. In truth, she looked the same, like drab, gray stone with little flecks of glimmering lights reflecting in the imitation sun's rays. Natalia ignored him. That too was usual for the beast.

Leotis returned. "You may enter."

Dagan strolled through the doors and the *Lahamas* jumped up to his seat, sparing one quick glance at Dagan before resuming his pose.

"Dagan, my boy." Enki's booming voice bounced off the walls.

The majestic deity moved toward him wearing flowing robes in a rainbow of colors and a big smile on his unmarked face. His blond hair streaked with silver had been cut short since the last time Dagan had seen him.

Dagan bowed.

"Stop that," Enki said and raised him while shaking his hand. "I saw your father the other day and he said he hadn't seen you in a while."

"*Galla* activity has increased lately, which keeps me busy." He adjusted his now dry duster. His clothes were dry as well.

"He would be glad to see you."

"And I him."

"Come." Enki led Dagan through the magnificent entry hall and into the huge amphitheatre room where he spent most of his time. On a large dais which had several sandstone steps leading to it sat Enki's throne. Even in the huge room, the ominous fixture drew attention. It had a plush cushion stretched across the seat, two large seahorse statues on either side, and a back made from an enormous clam shell that had pastel colors of the rainbow snaking through it.

Off to the right of the throne sat a gigantic canopy bed also raised up from the floor. The sheets were ivory and most likely silk, although Dagan had never dared touch them. This is where the god let his *water* flow into many willing and some unwilling females.

On the left sat tables laden with every kind of seafood. The table cloths were iridescent and glowed as he approached them. Everything sparkled in Enki's temple. Harps played in the background and the humid air carried the overwhelming smell of lobster and crab until it filled the large space.

"What brings you here, Dagan?"

The God of Wisdom sat patiently, studying his reaction to the question with a little too much intensity.

"My most recent encounter with Kur's henchmen took me to the twenty-first century and the state of Colorado." He didn't miss Enki's flinch when he'd mentioned Kur's name. The god tensed, all casualness gone, and listened more intently to what he had to say.

"Go on."

"They were after a young woman by the name of Reese Whittaker."

"*Shakaah!*" Enki swore and slammed his hands down on the arms of the throne. The whole place shook. "Did they capture her?"

"No. I managed to get there first...barely." Dagan moved closer, curious of the deity's reaction. "I felt a strange energy signature while at her home. It's not normal energy and pulses with a god's magic." He placed one booted foot on a sandstone step and crossed his arms over his knee. "I'd hoped you could shed light on this matter."

Enki nodded. "After Kur killed so many and swore to seek revenge on us all, especially me, I went to Percilious, the wizard, and had him cast a powerful concealment ward around the homes of all my descendents to hide them from Kur. I boosted the spell with my magic."

That must have taken a lot. Dagan stood and paced in front of the dais. "That would explain why they set off the explosion."

Enki frowned, his elegant features twisted. "Explosion?"

Dagan continued his march and voicing his thoughts. "So that we would come out of the house; they must have followed us."

"They cannot enter the house," Enki said. "She is safe as long as she is inside."

Dagan stopped and stared at Enki. "But she's vulnerable when she is anywhere else."

"Unfortunately, yes." Enki rubbed his eyes. "I could not protect every one of them all the time. There are too many."

Maybe if he'd quit spreading his seed so much, this wouldn't be a problem. But that would be like asking the Sun to stop shining and the different races on his world to stop committing genocide.

"Thank you." Dagan bowed before Enki. "That explains some things." On that matter anyway. "I'll take my leave."

In a soft voice that echoed through the hall Enki said, "Can you protect her, Dagan?"

Dagan stopped and glanced back at the man he'd known all his life. "It's my duty to protect her." And he would do whatever it took to ensure she did not fall into Kur's hands.

"Knowing how good you are at your job, I trust you will keep her safe."

If she would let him. Dagan bowed again out of respect and found his way to the door.

The sun sank low on the horizon when Dagan shimmered to form in the tree-lined drive across from Reese's house. Rufus stepped out from behind the bushes.

"She's in for the night I'm guessing. I've seen her in the kitchen cooking and she's wearing a short, silky-looking robe—"

Rufus's words were cut off abruptly when Dagan's hand encircled his throat and lifted him off his feet, pushing his back against the nearest tree. The *doghume*'s legs dangled in mid-air, his hands clutching at Dagan's wrist.

"You were to keep watch but not get close enough for her to see you," Dagan said through clenched teeth.

"I have binoculars, Dagan, bin-o-cu-lars." Rufus emphasized each syllable of the word to get his point across. His voice choked and raspy.

Dagan released him and he fell to the ground.

"Jeez, what's the matter with you?" The other man got up rubbing his throat. "Your eyes turned real dark, like you were going to kill me or something."

The roar of his anger and his blood were not lost on Dagan. The minute he'd thought another man had gotten anywhere near Reese, he lost control. That had never happened before. He hoped this would be over soon, but the thought of never seeing Reese again tore him apart inside. *Another anomaly.*

He held up a finger and Rufus instantly grew quiet. The night moved on the north side of Reese's house. Though they could not sense her inside because of the concealment ward, they knew she resided there.

"Do you have weapons?"

"Always," Rufus replied, still rubbing his throat.

"Good, they're here. You come from the south side and work your way around the back. I'll go to the north and meet them straight on."

Rufus nodded and pulled out twin daggers. He started away when Dagan called out in a whisper, "Watch your back, human."

Rufus saluted him and disappeared.

Reese stood at the porcelain sink washing some lettuce to make a salad when the hairs on her arms rose, as if she were surrounded by static electricity. Instinctively, she turned the water off and grabbed a large knife from the block to her right. All day her nerves had been on edge. She moved across the hardwood floor toward the back door but stopped long enough to grab the baseball bat out of her restaurant-sized pantry. She kept it there for protection. There were other items similarly placed throughout the house. For some reason she could not explain, she'd felt the need for such protection since she turned sixteen.

With the bat in one hand and the knife in the other, she slid her mules on, opened the back door with her fingertips and peered outside. The setting sun gave off enough twilight to show that no one stood on the small snow-covered porch or in the yard around the house. She reminded herself to shovel the porch off the next day. Relieved, she turned to go back inside, when a flash of movement caught the corner of her eye.

A young man with short brown hair seemed to be at war with smoke. The smoke or dark mist had arms and fought back.

Another delusion?

She started to yell out but decided it wasn't the best course. In her flimsy robe, she crept across the deck. Laying the knife on the edge of the porch, she grabbed the bat with both hands, moved down the steps, and snuck closer to the pair. Punches were thrown and kicks were blocked as the fighters circled in a violent dance. One move had the man facing her and his attacker's back in her line of sight. Swinging the bat like the best home run hitter, Reese nailed the whatever-it-was knocking it sideways to the ground. Stunned for only a moment, the young man smiled. "Thanks."

"You're welcome."

"Duck!"

She fell to the frozen ground. The stranger pulled a bizarre-looking knife from its place on his belt and threw it at the shadow, hitting it dead center of the chest. The thing disintegrated before her eyes. Left in its place was a puddle of black dust.

The man bent down, gripped her arms and helped her up. "Are you okay?"

"Yes, but what was that?"

"A burglar, I guess."

She arched a brow, letting him know she didn't buy his unconvincing story.

"Out for my evening stroll, I saw him approach your window, so I came to investigate." He flashed a white toothy grin. "That was awesome by the way. Where'd you learn to swing a bat like that?"

"Little League," she responded dryly. The stranger had slyly managed to shift the conversation.

"Cool."

Removing his jacket, he placed it around her shoulders and walked her toward the porch where she stopped to pick up her knife.

"You better get back inside now, miss. You must be freezing. I'll clean up out here."

"We need to call the police," she said through chattering teeth.

"Yeah, I'll take care of that." He smiled again.

"But—"

Just over the man's left shoulder, Reese saw another one of those things. "Look out," she screamed.

The stranger swerved to the right. With shivering fingers, Reese threw the knife, lodging it in the creature's throat. A gust of chilling wind blew its ashes into the night, leaving the cutlery to fall silently to the ground.

"Okay—" she faced the handsome stranger, "—you need to explain what the hell is going on, and don't hand me that burglar crap again." She grabbed the Louisville Slugger with both hands. "I still have my bat."

The stranger eyed her and the grip she had on the smooth wood. "Well, umm..."

"It's okay, Rufus," someone said from behind her. "I'll take it from here. Check the grounds."

"Good. No problem. Nice to have met you, Ms. Whittaker."

"How did you know my name?" she sputtered.

He retrieved her knife and handed it back to her on his way around the house. "Goodnight." With a salute, he faded into the darkness.

"But...your coat."

Heat filled the short space between her and the newcomer. Slowly, Reese turned to face the other man full ready to give him a piece of her mind before going inside to call the authorities.

Her breath caught.

Even in the twilight, she knew him. The handsome hero from her dreams, the one who made her sweat. Suddenly memories flooded her mind in a rushing wave—last night and this morning. Angrily, she slapped him.

"Bastard. You did something to me, didn't you?" She slapped him again then spun around and marched toward the house. Dagan stormed after her.

"You remember?"

Anger, embarrassment came out in a bitter laugh. "Leave." She stepped inside and tried to slam the door but he put his hand out to keep it from smashing into his face.

A bogie jumped on Dagan's back with enough force to knock them both to the slippery wooden deck.

"Stay inside, Reese. Lock yourself in." Dagan managed to yell the order before the demon struck him in the face with a vicious blow.

Reese wrapped her hand around the handle of a cast iron skillet sitting on the counter and raced outside to see two more rushing toward them. Scared to death, but unable to leave Dagan to do battle alone, she ran at the two new fiendish-looking creatures and whacked the first one in the head. It dropped to the ground like a stone. The second one turned on her and she swung at him but he deflected the blow. He laughed and produced what she thought was supposed to be a sneer, but it was hard to tell.

It grabbed at her, but she managed to hit it in the knee with her sturdy weapon. When it yowled and bent forward, she belted him on the back of the neck and he joined his cohort at her feet.

Searching the area with her eyes, she saw Dagan beat the one who had jumped him down, pull out his sword and cut off its head. A bright flash lit up the night turning it to what looked like black coal dust. Another one grabbed Dagan's lapel and pulled him over the railing.

"Finish him. I'll get the female," the one she assumed was the leader said.

The taller demon came after her and she ran. Reese heard gunshots as she bashed one *galla* in the head and turned to come face to face with a human. At least that's what she thought until he spoke.

"You've been a nasty piece of business, I must say," he sneered. "Now we're through and you're coming with me."

The vicious glint in his eyes sent a sliver of fear clattering through her. The stench from his mouth made her want to gag. "I don't think so."

Dagan leapt onto the porch. The smell of gunpowder and the loud report of the guns filled the night as he rapidly fired into the demon's body. It dropped to its knees and glared at Dagan.

"Tell your boss I'll be seeing him soon," Dagan promised.

The evil being hissed and melted away. He could have given the Wicked Witch of the West a run for her money in the melting department.

Dagan retrieved his sword and sheathed it. He strode toward her wearing a deep frown. She stared at the blackened remnants on the porch, door and side of the house which were fading as night fell.

"The next time I tell you to run, run, dammit."

Her gaze snapped to him. "You're not my keeper."

His intense stare locked on her. "You need a keeper."

Reese straightened and glared at him, a fist of anger returning. "They deserved it." She narrowed her eyes on him. "You deserved it too."

"Come on." Dagan grabbed her arm, pulled her inside, closed and locked the door.

She marched over to the pantry and pulled out a broom.

"What are you doing?"

Memories of what had just happened tap danced on her psyche, memories she shouldn't have—no one should have. "I'm going to sweep that rubbish off my porch." Her hands were shaking.

"Not tonight."

"I don't suppose you'd leave?"

Moving to her he said, "Not gonna happen."

Instantly, Reese dropped the broom and started slapping at the front of her shirt. Her eyes grew wider. "My chest is burning."

"Dammit." His bright green eyes turned black as the night. He tore off Rufus's coat, grabbed her shirt and pulled it over her head. Her body trembled.

Tossing the smoldering shirt into the sink, Dagan picked Reese up and ran to the bathroom. He set her into the bathtub, turned on the water, tossed his holster, sheaths for his knives and stars off, then stepped in with her.

Pushing her under the spray, he silently lathered his hands with the soap and began massaging her chest, arms, and down her stomach. "The *galla*'s blood is like acid."

He turned her around to rinse the soap off and undid her bra. "When I shot the last one some of its blood must have gotten on your clothes. That's why it burned."

Again, he lathered his hands and soaped her back, shoulders and arms. He threw the soggy bra on the floor and gently unbuttoned her pants and drew them down her wet legs and tossed everything into a heap. "Let me look at you, to make sure your skin is undamaged."

He turned her to face him and brushed callused hands over her skin. "Just a little redness. It didn't get all the way through your shirt enough to burn your skin, but let's wash you one more time to be sure."

She nodded but didn't speak.

He rubbed suds along her throat to her collarbone and her breasts. She couldn't hold the whimper that escaped her parted lips. The water trickled down the front of her body washing the suds away.

Reese opened her eyes, and for the first time since he'd lifted her into the tub, noticed the blood-stained rip in his shirt, the cuts on his lip and over his right eye, and a slash across his left forearm. "You're hurt."

She gently shoved his hand away.

"It's nothing."

"That thing's blood got on you, too." She slid the long-sleeved shirt down and pulled the T-shirt underneath up his arms and off, letting it drop as she examined his skin.

On his right forearm was a tattoo that looked like a starburst. A nasty, jagged, bright red mark cut across his right shoulder and down his chest to his left hip. It looked like a strip of sunburn. "Does it hurt?"

"No."

He lied, it had to hurt. Catching her bottom lip between her teeth, Reese danced her fingertips down his stomach.

His muscles contracted.

"It will heal quickly," he said through gritted teeth. His hands fisted at his sides.

Her fingers brushed the enormous bulge in his pants and he growled. Her eyes snapped to his battered face certain she'd find him smirking, but he stared unblinking at the wall and his tight jaw clenched.

Reese slapped her hands over her bare breasts and turned her back to him, suddenly aware of the intimate position.

The water had grown cold so Dagan reached his arms on either side of her to shut it off. He wrapped a beige towel around her shoulders and started drying her back.

She grabbed the edges and wrenched it out of his hands. "I can manage." Glancing over her shoulder, she gazed into his eyes, which were green again. "Can you explain what happened here?"

He grinned. "Reese, honey, you know what nearly happened here."

She felt the blush creep up her cheeks and she'd swear it traveled along her whole body. Shaking her head at his arrogant attitude she said, "I mean why I couldn't remember anything and suddenly it all came back?"

He sobered. "We need to talk."

"Yes, I think we do."

He stepped out of the tub and ran a towel along his chest and shoulders. The burned areas of his skin had turned soft white, like old scars, and were disappearing rapidly. She needed answers.

She glanced at the wet pile of clothes on the floor. This could be a problem. Joel, her cousin, did have some clothes here but she didn't think anything would completely cover this man's incredible body. He was huge. Her gaze traveled down, all of him.

"You should stop doing that or we'll not get any farther than the bedroom," he said in a husky voice.

Her head shot up to see him watching her watch him. His eyes had gotten darker. Sure that honor and chivalry would only go so far, and not wanting to push her luck, she looked directly into his eyes before saying, "Then get out of my bathroom." He hesitated. She turned her head away, knowing that looking at his semi-naked body again would be a bad idea. "Can you hand me another towel before you go?" she asked in what she hoped sounded like a steady voice.

He passed her another towel. "I'll go in the other room. I need to contact Rufus and tell him to have another look around."

Reese nodded. "Okay."

When she heard the click of the door latch, she withered to the floor of the tub. Her life had taken a bizarre turn. How would she protect herself against something that's not supposed to exist? And, what would she do about Dagan?

Dagan strode from the bedroom. He could not keep his thoughts from reaching back to those moments when his soap-slicked hands glided against skin so tan and supple he had to swallow a groan. A dull ache burned him from within as desire rushed to his already aching groin. His head filled with the music of his people, the ancient ritual drums pounded at his temples.

By all the gods, he should not continue on this course. It was forbidden for time walkers to have personal contact with humans unless absolutely necessary. But why had the *go'ras* not worked?

He remembered how she had stared up at him with those big blue eyes. The kind of eyes a man could get lost in for days and the same color as the blue satin panties covering her core. He groaned and reached into his soaking wet pants to readjust his erection.

# Chapter Five

How could she remember him when he had erased everything from her memory? This did not make any sense. He rubbed his cheek where she had slapped him. Flipping open his cell, he hit the three button. Rufus picked up on the first ring.

"Do you see anything?"

"No, not since you got rid of that last wave. I had started back but you were done before I could get there." A door slammed and the engine started. "She swings a frying pan as good as she does that bat."

"Yeah, she has been pretty amazing through all this." He sighed. "I have got a big problem though."

"Oh?"

"She remembered everything when she saw me again."

"No way. What'd she do?"

"She slapped me."

Rufus's laughter echoed through the phone. Dagan growled. Rufus would never let him live this down.

"You have your night gear?" Dagan said forcefully.

"I do."

Night gear consisted of several different things, the most important of which were night goggles. Pyre had modified them so that they picked up the faint electrical impulse generated by the *galla.*

"Keep your eyes open. They'll be back."

"Okay."

Dagan picked up Rufus's coat and willed it to his car. "I

also need you to get one of the others to head over to her father's house and keep watch."

"Did she give you an address?"

"No."

"Fine, I'll look it up. Anything else?"

"Yes, contact one of the sources in Europe. Riley Whittaker, Reese's sister is there. She will need to be looked after as well." He dug his fingers into his eyes and rubbed. "I'm not sure where in Europe she is, but she left two years past."

"No problem, I'll check phone records. I'm sure they've spoken. I can track her down that way."

"Okay, get on it," Dagan ordered.

"Right, and Dagan?"

"Yeah?"

"You better hide the bat."

Dagan snapped the phone shut, silencing more laughter.

*"Flame."*

*"Dagan, my man. What's up?"*

*"Have you ever heard of a* go'ras *not working on a human?"*

*"Are you serious?"*

*"I'm afraid so. She remembers everything."*

*"You're there again?"* Dagan winced at the tone of his friend's voice in his head.

*"I had Rufus watching the place. We had visitors."*

*"Did they get to her?"*

*"No."*

Flame popped into the room. "This is serious."

"No kidding."

"Did I hear you..." Reese walked into the room wearing a 49ers jersey that stopped mid thigh, tan stretch pants that molded to her body, red fluffy socks, and carrying some other clothes.

Flame whistled.

"Hello," she said then narrowed her eyes on Dagan, a familiar sight.

Turning to his friend, Flame chuckled. "Now I understand why you've taken an extra interest. She's got nice long legs and her face isn't bad to look at either."

Reese glared at Dagan. "I don't recall you saying anything about company and why is he talking like I'm not in the room? Did I suddenly become invisible?"

"Impossible!" both men said in unison.

Dagan smiled. "Reese, this is Flame. Flame, Reese Whittaker."

"Charmed," she said.

"My pleasure." Flame sauntered over, took her hand and kissed it, lingering a little longer than Dagan liked.

"That's enough, charm boy, get your ass over here." Dagan grabbed Flame by the arm and yanked him toward the fireplace.

Reese sat and watched the two men. Dagan stood at least two inches taller than the other man who was dressed in a pair of jeans that looked as though they'd been worn everyday for the last three years and were just now getting broke in. His black Jimmie Van Zant T-shirt had no sleeves and tucked into the pants giving her a fine view of his washboard abs. She noticed his right forearm held the same tattoo as Dagan's. It had to be significant. She stared hard at his blond hair, tipped in red and spiked. If you looked at it long enough, it seemed to sway and dance like fire. She wondered if Flame was his real name or an alias to go with the outfit.

"I can't tell you what I don't know, Dagan. I've never heard of the mind wipe not working on a human. This is beyond my knowledge. You will have to ask one of the Eight."

"If I go to one of them it will raise suspicion."

"Mind wipe?" Reese said in an accusing tone.

Neither offered a reply, but Flame looked over at her and winked.

"I'm thinking Nazi would be your best bet. Get him loaded enough and he'll tell you what you need to know."

"I guess it's worth a try."

Flame slapped his hand down on Dagan's shoulder. "Well, brother, you have your work cut out for you. I'll go talk to Rufus while I'm here about those other matters."

Flame gave her the once over. "I like the jersey, but I'm a Steelers fan." He grinned. "Goodnight, Reese," he said and opened the front door.

Stunned she yelped, "Where's your coat?" and got up to shut the door. "For God's sake it's freezing out there."

"I hadn't thought about the temperature when I popped in." A devilish gleam entered his eye. He snapped his fingers and a black leather duster appeared in his hand. "It's lined so I should be fine, doll. I appreciate your concern."

She didn't have time to question him about the little magic trick because he flew out the door. She turned to find Dagan loading wood into the fireplace, still wringing wet from the shower.

"I meant to get some matches but I've been abducted by a strange man and held captive."

"No need for matches." Ignoring her snide comment, he stood, snapped his fingers and flames shot up through the chimney.

"I'll bet you come in handy at bonfires."

"I have many good uses." He steadied his intense gaze on her, heating up her entire body like the fire he'd started.

Like a predator, Dagan moved toward her. Every inch of his sculpted form stalked her as prey. The primal gleam in his eyes had her fighting the urge to step back.

From what now seemed an incredible height Dagan said, "Get dressed, we're going out."

"What? I just got undressed."

This time she took a few steps back so she could see his face clearly. His hungry gaze made her quiver. Goose bumps herded across her already heated skin. She'd need to be more careful about the words she let escape from her mouth.

"While I'd like nothing more than to stay and debate your clothing choices..." his eyes changed, darkened, seemed to swirl, "...we need to go find a god to answer some questions."

"You can leave me here—"

A dark expression crossed his face. "No. You'll not be out of my sight again. Get dressed."

She'd had enough. He would not bully her and order her

around in her own home. She calmly strolled toward the kitchen to make some coffee. Before rounding the corner, she fixed her eyes on Dagan, shooting silent daggers with flaming tips in his direction. "I'm not going anywhere with you. I'm not leaving and you're not staying. I want answers here and now. Got me?" Then she disappeared. A low rumble sounding like thunder but what she knew to be Dagan's temper boiling over floated her way.

She reached up and got a bottle of Johnnie Walker Black out of the cabinet. She had a feeling the caffeine jolt would not be nearly enough to help her through the rest of this evening. After pulling two mugs down, she turned toward the refrigerator and stopped. Dagan stood in the doorway looking drop dead gorgeous, and her mouth went dry. Heat fused her body.

It would be a long night.

"Do you drink whiskey?" she asked, pulling her gaze from him.

"I'll drink any form of spirit you care to offer, Reese."

Yep, a long night indeed.

She filled the mugs with coffee and added two dollops of whiskey. Leaving the Johnnie Walker Black on the counter, she walked over, handed Dagan his cup and pushed past him to the living room. After snuggling into her favorite chair before the roaring fire she said "Okay, I want to know what the hell is going on. Who were those...things, and what do they want with me? And," she pointed a finger at him, "I'll warn you not to lie. I'm already pissed."

He cocked his head. "I'll tell you the truth," he said most earnestly.

With everything she'd seen tonight, she hoped he would. "Fine, begin then."

Dagan didn't speak at first. Instead, he chugged the coffee. Reese stared at the corded muscles in his neck and the bobbing Adam's apple as he swallowed. Even the simplest thing like taking a drink suffused her with hot, wicked imaginings. It was almost as if she knew him and yet she didn't. Like they were supposed to be here together, doing what?

His incredible eyes captured her attention. She took a shot of coffee which burned going down but settled nicely in her already tense stomach.

"You are descended from gods. Your bloodline is rich in heritage and power," he said.

"Gods? I'm descended from gods?"

"Yes."

"You're crazy. What gods?"

"A Pantheon of ancient gods known by many names in many cultures."

"Naturally," she replied dryly.

"Why do you think Sumerian and Babylonian mythology interests you so?" His right brow rose. "Because you're descended from those on high."

Certain now that he was a nutcase, Reese decided to get rid of him before something else happened. Besides, she knew the truth behind why she immersed herself in work, to keep her sanity, to keep from falling apart.

She had been swept away by his masculinity. That definitely couldn't happen again.

"You're directly descended from Enki, the water god, which is why Kur wants you so badly. Enki is his most hated enemy."

"I know the stories of the water god."

He inclined his head.

"How do you know this anyway?" She gestured skyward with her hands. "That was centuries ago. How can you possibly tell me that I'm descended from Enki?"

Dagan's eyes narrowed with intensity radiating from them. "I smell it in your blood, in your body's essence. It's what led me to you, and what draws Kur."

"This is absurd." She rose from the chair and went to the front door. "You need to go."

She felt his body before he said anything. "No. This fight isn't over."

"How do I know you didn't stage the whole thing? You could have arranged this charade to throw me off guard and gain my confidence."

"Then what?" he asked quietly.

"Then—I don't know what," she stammered. "Dammit." She

pulled away from him. "Who are you?"

She moved to stand before the fire then sat, deflated, on the floor. Suddenly, she felt very cold. "You asked about my family earlier."

He inclined his head but his eyes never left hers.

"Are they in danger?"

"Yes." He crouched beside her and picked up a lock of her hair to roll between his fingers. "I had Rufus send someone to keep an eye on your father's house and one of our operatives in Europe will be keeping watch over your sister."

He grasped her forearms so that she looked into his eyes. "They are very good at what they do, Reese. Your family will be protected."

She felt the tears welling but tried hard not to let them fall. One slipped out of the corner of her eye and cascaded down her cheek. "Thank you."

He helped her rise.

"I just find it hard to believe."

"Believe what you want or not, but tell me you didn't see the *galla* on your front porch. That you didn't feel the blood of the creature try to burn through your skin."

"Point taken." She offered him a slight smile, which was all her ragged nerves could handle at the moment.

"Now, go change so we can leave."

"Where are we going?" she asked as she removed her arms from his grasp.

"It's a bar on the east side."

"A bar?"

"Well, more of a nightclub really. You'll like it."

She doubted it. The woman in her scolded, the bookworm in her laughed. Still, she hadn't been dancing in a long time and it did sound intriguing. Who'd of thought you'd find a god in a nightclub? Better yet, who'd of thought gods really existed on this planet?

Reese flipped on the light in her bedroom and went through her walk-in closet to find something suitable to wear. The walls on either side were lined with racks of garments. They were divided by season then grouped for either work or casual. She passed over numerous business suits, ones she wore to make a good impression for the museums and collectors she dealt with. They were too straight-laced and not the kind of thing you wore to a nightclub. As she kept digging, she happened across a little black dress that she hadn't worn in forever. It would be the right thing to wear on a night like this unless they had trouble. The shoes would be a problem if she needed to run for her life.

With a sad sigh, she moved on down the row hoping to find something more suitable in case she met with unexpected trouble.

On the other side of the closet, she found a pair of black stretch jeans. "That'll do. Now what to wear with it?"

She slid hangers, discarding choices until she rested on a baby blue blouse that wrapped around her waist and dipped in a V between her breasts.

After plugging in the curling iron, she gathered her make up and went into the bathroom to fix her face. The deep blue and silver eyeshadow made her eyes shine and she lined them heavily. With a Kleenex, she dabbed and smudged the liner to give it a smoky look. Next, she blended the two tones of blusher into her skin. Last, she used a lip liner and rose-colored lipstick.

Perfect.

Her mood had brightened. Using the curling iron, she gave her hair a little lift and added extra-hold hairspray to guarantee it would keep for a while. She tugged and hefted the tight jeans over her hips. Well-placed soft cups molded her breasts and lifted them slightly. She circled her waist with the bottom of the blouse and tied a neat knot at her side before repositioning the slit. Teardrop diamond earrings made her ears sparkle. She finished off with a matching diamond pendant and her favorite Passion perfume. Black Timberland boots completed her ensemble, and fit the bill for both the weather conditions outside and a fast escape should it be called for.

Reese questioned her motive for the transformation. She could reason that it wasn't a giant leap, but she'd be lying. The feminine part of her wanted to get a rise out of Dagan and she couldn't wait to see the look on his face.

After Reese left the room, Dagan willed himself a change of clothes. He traded his duster for a bomber jacket but kept his boots. They were his favorites and he wanted to be comfortable tonight just in case they ran into more trouble. Amazingly enough, the sword that Pyre had made for him fit securely across his back and the loose-fitting jacket accommodated the weapon. His cell phone rang.

"Yeah."

"You going out?" Rufus asked.

"We're going to find Nazi. Did you handle the other things I asked?"

"Yes, it's done. I have Gideon watching Clive Whittaker and Angelique keeping an eye on the sister in France."

"Good."

"What are you doing with Reese?"

"I'm taking her with me. I don't trust her to stay put."

Amused, Rufus said, "Yeah, I'm sure that's the only reason."

"Stay close in case I need you to get Reese to safety, smartass."

"I'm your shadow," he said and hung up.

He bent to strap the dagger to his knee when Reese sauntered into the room.

"So you're going in armed?"

When he glanced up, his stomach plummeted. The black jeans fit her like a second skin, leaving little to the imagination. Her eyes were mesmerizing the way she had them done up, and if he didn't know any better, he'd swear the color changed. Her earrings glittered in the light and drew your attention to the column of her neck and the too much bare skin everywhere. *Damn.* She smiled and he lost all thought.

"Did you suddenly go mute?"

"What?"

"I said you're going armed?"

"Uh, yes. I never go anywhere unarmed." He adjusted his dagger. "It comes with the territory."

"Right."

She rifled through the small black purse she carried. At the door she turned. "Shall we?"

"I am not pleased with this news." Kur declared, his features spread tight with rage.

"He had another with him this time. We were not expecting it," the *galla* hissed.

Strolling by the table on which lay various knifes, swords and other sharp instruments, Kur glanced toward the covered alcove and winked at the bound and gagged Ereshkigal. Smiling, he picked up a twelve-inch long short-handled knife admiring the way it gleamed in the firelight. With practiced precision Kur swung around, beheading the *galla* from behind.

Ereshkigal screamed but the sound was muffled by the gag. The other *galla* dropped to their knees just as Feral strolled in with an amused grin on his face.

"I see you've gotten their report."

"Yes, and a sorry one it is."

The captain walked through the dark dust on the floor. "What are your instructions?"

Kur set the knife back on the table. "I think this merits some personal attention. I will go myself."

Feral bowed. "As you command. We will be close."

Waving his hand Kur said, "Leave me."

The rest of the *galla* who had been kneeling rose and hurried out of the room followed by their leader. Kur turned his attention to Ereshkigal.

"Alone at last, my queen." He snapped his fingers and classical music blared throughout the room.

She scrambled on tiptoes, trying to back away from him. Kur chuckled. "I have special plans for you. Something we both will enjoy."

He walked over to the table where various instruments used for pleasure and pain glowed in the dim candlelight, like a soft spring day. He picked up a pair of tongs then went to the fire and pulled out a long needle with a half-inch circumference. The tip glowed red hot and sizzled when he blew it softly.

Kur swaggered back over to where Ereshkigal hung. After

ripping the white shirt down the front to expose her nipples, he leaned forward and sucked one rosy tip into his mouth. He ran his tongue across it, pleased to see it harden and thrust out.

"That's it. I grow hard already."

He tugged the nipple with his teeth then bit it. She whined.

"That didn't hurt. I'm going to pierce your nipples today. Soon, you will wear rings through them that dangle and tease me. I will suck and pull on the rings while I'm fucking you. You will scream with ecstasy at my hands."

Tears fell from her eyes and she shook her head, silently pleading with him not to do what he'd promised.

"Don't worry, Ereshkigal, my sweet. It will be over before you know it."

He used the tongs to grab the nipple and pull it out before thrusting the searing tip of the needle through. She'd passed out before both breasts were finished. He gently washed her with cool water and antiseptic herbs. Two pure silver rings adorned with rubies and diamonds were slipped through the holes.

"Perfect."

Kur kissed each breast, but couldn't stop there. With reverent awe, he uncovered the rest of his wife's body. He kissed the valley between her breasts then continued down her flat stomach to the juncture between her thighs. He inhaled.

"So sweet," he murmured. Opening the soft folds, he proceeded to lave her slit. She awoke bucking against his mouth. This made him smile. "Soon, I will take you in every way possible and you will worship me and the things my cock will do to you."

He stood, unzipped his pants and released the aforementioned appendage. Turning sideways, he held his cock out to its full length for her to see. "This is all for you."

She fought the chains that held her. Kur laughed as he left the room planning the next move against Reese Whittaker and anticipating the power her life force would provide.

# Chapter Six

Dagan and Reese drove through the dark night in relative silence and in a sleek, silver-toned Porsche.

"One of my toys," Dagan explained.

Venturing through back streets and portions of the city she'd never been in, Reese wondered whom these people were associated with, and where, exactly, this bar could be located. He'd only said the east side. This was way east, almost to another state.

Insanity didn't run in her family that she knew of. And yet here she sat for the second day in a row with a man she did not know, allowing him to take her to strange places. At the first real opportunity, should she try to call Joe or Geoffrey? No. Besides, Geoffrey had gone camping. She needed to get through this night and figure something out in the morning. Of course, she still had the option of calling the police, but how would she explain bringing her attacker home? She didn't understand it herself.

"So tell me about these people you have guarding my father and sister. And what about Rufus? How does he fit in?"

"Are you going to batter me with questions all night?"

"Yes, until I get the answers I require."

Dagan sighed heavily. "Rufus is what we call a *doghume*. They are humans with extraordinary abilities."

"Humans?"

"Uh, huh. Then there are the *nephili*, who are half god and half human. It's sort of like your version of Hercules, only they have limited powers at certain times."

"What kind of powers?"

"It differs. Are you going to let me finish?"

She frowned at him.

"Last, we have the purebreds, which are those like me and Flame."

"And what's so special about you?" she asked, sliding an accusatory glance his way.

With a devilish grin he said, "We are the first born of gods and the best defense against the creature." He turned his concentration to the dark road.

Loud music drifted out the doors and across the parking lot as they pulled up. A Temptations song greeted them when they got out of the car. On the outside, the place looked like a huge warehouse made from old wooden boards salvaged from dilapidated buildings. An enormous sign hung above the door. She couldn't see it clearly, but as they drew closer, the words came into focus. Slow Burn. Underneath the name in gothic lettering it said, *Into the fires of hell ye be walkin.* Was that a warning?

Reese looked over at Dagan.

"What?"

"Interesting. Should I be worried about this place?"

"You have nothing to fear here," he assured her. "Neither Kur nor his followers can enter this place. It is protected by several powerful spells. That is why my kind can come here and relax without worry."

"Okay." She wasn't relieved at all, but she'd give him the benefit of the doubt.

"Dagan? I'll be damned." The burly man standing guard at the door had a deep burr to his voice.

"Hey, Seamus."

The bouncer looked like a brick building with arms the size of $CO_2$ canisters, the big ones. His dark skin shined and he had an enormous tattoo that started at the wrist on one hand, went up his arm, disappeared under his shirt and came out of the sleeve on the other side, stopping at his other wrist. She had no idea what the tattoo represented but it reminded her of ancient writing she'd seen on tablets in a museum a long time ago.

"Haven't seen you around these parts in about fifty years. You had one of those redheaded nymphs from Lysara as I recall."

Reese turned her questioning eyes in his direction. His arrogant demeanor kicked in and he winked at her.

"Yeah, Bethany liked this place too."

The other man turned his attention to her. "So who's this sexy number?" He moved up close to her and sniffed.

"I'm Reese." She moved back a step. "Are you sniffing me?"

Dagan laughed.

"Human?" Seamus asked.

"Yes," Dagan replied. "Reese, this is Seamus. He's a blood hound, literally."

"Nice to meet you," she said then frowned at Dagan.

Seamus took her hand and kissed it. "Pleasure. You have some powerful blood flowing through your veins, miss. Best watch who you hang out with."

"Thanks for the warning, Seamus, but you do see the company I'm keeping at the moment, right?" she all but yelled over the music.

Seamus broke into deep, resonating laughter.

"Come on." Dagan gently shoved her through the metal doors.

"So what did you mean he's a blood hound?"

"I'm not at liberty to say. I can't reveal all our secrets to a human."

She stopped walking and narrowed her eyes on him. He clasped her fingers in his and urged her forward.

When they got inside the place opened up and bodies gyrated to Beatles' music. A semi-circular purple stage stretched onto the dance floor about three feet. It had a long horizontal walkway with platforms on either side. On the raised platforms were three-sided cages where blond girls in white go-go boots danced. In front of the cages but down another level sat large green disks with stairs leading up to them so that showcase dancers could strut their stuff. Down another level lay the very crowded wooden dance floor. Beyond that were tables and chairs to sit, and on both sides of the seating area were bars that ran approximately sixteen to eighteen feet. Four different bartenders handled each side and they seemed to carry the burden of the crowd with ease.

"This is amazing," she said over the music blasting from several floor to ceiling speakers.

"I know, that's why we love coming here."

He shuffled her to the only empty table near the back.

The music changed again to a Marvin Gaye song and she said, "So tell me again why we're here."

"I need to see someone."

His vague answer irritated her. With everything they'd been through already, surely he didn't think anything he'd say would frighten her. Before she could ask anymore, he got up.

"Wait here," he ordered and left.

Reese's temper bristled. Did he really think she would sit like an obedient child while he mingled and ignored her?

She watched him walk toward the bar closest to her and approach a tall, slender brunette. The woman had extremely long legs, a pair of black boots that went up over her knees and a skirt that barely covered her butt. If her boobs were any bigger, Reese mused, the neon tube top would be irreparably misshapen. A waitress came to take her order. A few moments passed before she glanced to where Dagan had been standing. He had disappeared along with the brunette.

Reese tapped her finger to the beat of the music and sipped her amaretto sour. She'd been really looking forward to coming here. Okay, so the events of the last twenty-four hours had been bizarre and frightening and her bodyguard irritated the crap out of her, but it had been forever since she'd actually gone on a real date. She missed dancing.

Dagan had been gone for some time and she wondered if she should go look for him. Sighing, she turned her attention to the dance floor. A hot, good looking man approached her table.

"Would you care to dance, miss?"

His voice was smooth like Vermouth and carried a European accent. Penetrating blue eyes beckoned her and she couldn't resist. "Thank you, I'd like that." She took the hand he offered.

People parted as he led the way to the dance floor. Everyone stared at them as they passed. The band changed the tempo to something slow and the man pulled her close. He wound his left arm around her waist to the small of her back with fingertips splayed across her backside. The previously overrun floor now seemed deserted, or maybe she'd lost all concept of anyone else in the room. How could that be? She fought the urge to lay her head on his shoulder and let him negotiate the dance floor carrying her along. His movements were intoxicating and seductive and yet he'd not spoken to her since he'd asked her to dance.

In a charismatic voice, he whispered in her ear. "What's your name?"

"Reese."

"'Tis beautiful and so are you." He smiled and she felt a sudden need to kiss him. This was the second man in the last two days who had that kind of effect on her. She needed to get a grip.

"I think you'll be taking your hands off her now, Abu."

Reese stiffened at the steely voice. She turned to see Dagan glaring at the man holding her.

"We're having a nice time, Dagan. I hesitate to let it end so soon."

His cordial tone didn't fool Reese, the warning had been crystal clear. Abu pulled her closer to the hard muscle and strength coiled in his body, ready to strike. If he and Dagan knew each other she'd bet him to be another form of mythical being and this could get ugly, real quick. She tried to pull away but Abu wouldn't release her.

Dagan's nostrils flared and his eyes darkened. Abu smiled, but not with humor. His eyes changed color, first to dark blue then silver, like a kaleidoscope. She had to do something. Using all her strength, Reese stomped down with her heel and dug it into Abu's foot.

"*Shakaah*," he yelled and shoved her away.

Reese straightened up, readjusted her blouse and slung her hair back so she could glare at both of them. They treated her like some kind of possession and were acting childish.

"Number one—," she pointed at Abu who was rubbing his

foot, "—I'm not a piece of meat and I'm certainly not someone who chooses to be in the middle of all this male insecurity." She turned on Dagan who still glared at Abu. "And you are a piece of work. He and I were dancing. You have no right to stop me from dancing with him or anyone else?"

"You are under my protection."

Abu chuckled and Dagan stepped forward. Reese put her hand on his chest.

"You need to stop. This is ridiculous."

Abu reached around her waist and pulled her flush against him. He leaned down and nuzzled his nose against her neck. "You are fiery and brazen. I like that in a woman." He gently bit her shoulder. "Your blood sings to me, Reese. I want to taste it."

Her eyes flew wide. Dagan leapt toward Abu and grabbed him by the throat, using his other hand to snatch Abu's ponytail and yank it.

"Don't touch her ever again."

"You know there are better ways to get my attention," another voice called out in a lilting accent.

Dagan and Abu both turned in the direction of the sound. The onlookers parted to admit a well-built mountain of a man. Were there no normal people in this place?

Dagan let go of Abu. He grabbed Reese by the arm and walked toward the other man. "Where in the name of Nammu have you been? I was just getting ready to kick your brother's ass."

The new man laughed. "You two never give up. It's been what, several thousand years? You'd think you could just let things go."

"Not likely." Abu fixed his gaze on Reese. "Until we meet again." He bowed, turned and disappeared in the throng of people.

The music started playing and the mob broke up.

"Come on," the blond guy said, and led them to the opposite bar at the very end, away from the music as much as possible.

"So what brings you here, Dagan? And who's your pretty friend?"

Dagan ordered a whiskey straight up for himself and another amaretto sour for Reese.

"Nazi, this is Reese Whittaker. Reese, meet Nazi. He's who I came to see."

"Nice to meet you, Reese. Please excuse my brother. He's used to taking what he wants."

"Nazi." She inclined her head. "Another one with no last name?"

"Obviously."

"Yeah, well, your brother was a complete gentleman. Dagan, however—" she focused her glare on him, "—has a lot to learn about manners."

Dagan snorted.

"You are so right, but don't let Abu fool you. He would have taken you out back and fed on you for a while."

She coughed and Dagan patted her back. "Nazi."

"Why don't I take Ms. Whittaker out of your hair, boys?"

Reese turned watery eyes to see the same woman Dagan had spoken with earlier.

"Don't worry." The woman cuddled up to Dagan. "I won't let anything happen to her. Come on, sweetie."

She waited for Reese to pick up her drink and follow her away from the bar. "Damn tired of getting tossed around like a salad," Reese murmured as she followed the beautiful woman, whom she hated on principal.

"Don't sweat it, hon. You'd think that as long as they've been around they would realize that the female of the species," the woman smiled, "any species, is the better part of the deal."

Reese nodded.

"I'm Ninti. Nazi and Abu are my brothers."

"I feel for you."

Ninti chuckled. "You're spunky. Beware of Abu. He'll snatch you up the first chance he gets."

Nazi and Abu were so totally different, not only in looks, but in personality and demeanor as well. *Vampires.* Did vampires exist? Not too long ago, she had no proof that gods existed. She wasn't taking anything for granted.

"Let's play some pool."

Reese took a long drink from her glass. "Okay, lead on." She glanced back to where Dagan spoke to Nazi and wondered why she couldn't be around for the discussion.

"What brings you here, Time Walker?"

Dagan ordered them both another drink then rested his forearms on the bar. How would he find out what he needed to know without making Nazi suspicious? He'd never been very good at subterfuge.

"I'd venture to say your dilemma has something to do with the human female. The power radiates from her blood and her body. Kur will definitely zone in on her for just that reason. It is Enki's bloodline." Nazi downed his drink and snapped his fingers to get the bartender's attention.

"This isn't about Reese Whittaker. I had to bring her along until I get rid of the vermin trailing her."

"I see. So why have you come here to seek me out?"

Dagan threw back the whiskey and ordered another shot with a beer chaser. He glanced toward the stage to collect his thoughts. The band had begun their next tune.

Taking a deep breath, he cleared his mind and faced Nazi. "Have you ever heard of a *go'ras* not working?"

Nazi's head whipped around. He stared at Dagan, who did his best to concentrate on the shot and beer, which had just arrived. "There is no instance I can recall where a *go'ras* did not work. It is powerful magick. Why do you ask?"

Dagan shrugged. "Curiosity."

Nazi lifted a light brow. "And you say this has nothing to do with the woman?"

Dagan resisted the urge to run his hands through his hair or wipe the small trickle of sweat from his brow. "No, nothing to do with her."

Nazi turned hard, skeptical eyes toward him. "This is a strange question coming from you, a time walker. I wonder whether you're being truthful with me." He held his hand out with his palm facing Dagan.

Dagan had erected a barrier to keep the God of the Mind

from reading his true thoughts. He hoped it worked. One did not generally hide anything from this particular god. His heart rate increased as Nazi probed, and he fought to remain nonchalant while being scanned. Every ounce of energy he could spare went to strengthening the barrier.

Nazi lowered his hand. "I get nothing from you, which in itself is unusual. You're blocking me."

"I told you the truth." Dagan turned and ordered another beer.

"You know Abu's behavior was a little bizarre even for him this evening."

"He and I have come to blows for things far less than a woman."

"True," Nazi agreed. "I'm sure you were too caught up in the situation to notice that his eyes had changed and his aura had deepened as well."

Dagan faced Nazi. "What does that have to do with anything?"

"The power in her is stronger than any I have felt in centuries. When you draw near, her aura changes and power surges through her body."

Dagan frowned. He'd never intended to be anything more than a time walker. But, in the last forty-eight hours, things in his predestined world had tipped—toward Reese.

With an unspoken hunger, Dagan watched Reese dancing with Ninti on one of the raised circular spaces. In those black pants that did nothing to hide her delectable form, her body swayed to the music. His temperature rose by leaps and bounds and his cock thickened.

"I don't need to be in your mind to know your thoughts." Nazi's words tore Dagan's gaze away from the woman who tormented him.

"What do you mean?"

"With the power she holds it will be difficult not to get drawn in by her. Kur will not give up this prize easily."

"I know."

A gorgeous redhead walked by, catching Nazi's eye. "Well, I wish you luck."

"Yeah, thanks."

Nazi caught up with the redhead and put his arm around her shoulders. Dagan shook his head.

He stared at Reese. Something unusual had happened when he'd touched her in the shower and she'd touched him. Fires the likes of those in Mount Cradacus fueled his body's reaction to the female. The torture of caressing her soft skin had nearly caused him to combust. Tonight when he'd seen Abu touch her so intimately, a red haze had clouded his mind. If he didn't know any better, he'd think it was the *fury.*

The *go'ras* should have rid her of any knowledge of him. That it didn't created a new set of problems.

Dagan gathered Reese and her things for them to go.


The drive back to her house seemed to take forever. Over the past few days, she'd strained to hold onto a small thread of sanity; add in Dagan and some ancient demon out to kill her and she had the makings for a full blown psychiatric meltdown.

When they arrived at her house, Dagan said, "Go inside. Make sure all the windows and doors are locked. I'll be there in a moment."

"Where are you going?"

"I'm going to speak with Rufus."

She raised a questioning brow. "Rufus?"

Dagan nodded. "He's out there keeping watch."

Grinding her teeth together, through tight lips she said, "What do you mean he's out there?"

He shot her a droll glare. "He has been out there all day and this evening at Slow Burn, keeping in the shadows."

"Why in God's name would he be doing that?"

"Because I told him to."

She crossed her arms and frowned. "A bodyguard?"

"Exactly."

When she opened her mouth to fling harsh words at him, he got out of the car, leaned his head in and smiled. "Yell at me later."

*Count to ten, count to twenty.*

A nervous itch raked up her spine as she climbed the front porch steps and faced the scorched spots on the wood. She chalked the shiver that raced across her skin to the chill in the air. Stepping inside the front door, she flipped on the light. A whirlwind blasted by her nearly knocking her to the floor. Spinning, she found an enigmatic man standing in her living room. Uninvited.

"Hello, Reese."

The tone of his voice caressed her like that of a lover, his smile cold and calculating. His short, elegantly styled hair was a cross between blond and white. She allowed her gaze to travel over a well-toned body encased in black leather to rest on glittering, intense amber eyes.

"Who the hell are you and how did you get into my house?"

He laughed. "I must say, the strong invisibility ward did its job well. I knew I wouldn't find it on my own, so I waited for you to come home. When you opened the door, I took the opportunity to rush in before you could close me out again."

The stranger waved his hand and the front door slammed shut.

"What do you want?" Reese angled toward the fireplace, putting greater distance between them. If she could play for time, Dagan would show up.

"He's busy," the stranger said, as if he'd read her mind. "I could have you before he breaks through the door."

Her gaze wandered around the room, searching for the best escape route.

"Running is futile. I am meant to have you, Reese. Surely you realize that."

"I don't realize anything. I'm guessing you're Kur."

He inclined his head.

"You won't get me without a fight," she stated with bravado.

His amber eyes swirled like molten lava. "I wouldn't have it any other way. The fight makes it more intoxicating." Kur reached out his hand. "Come to me."

His silky voice echoed in her head. The command to come toward him replayed over and over. Against her will, her right foot stepped forward, then her left. She struggled to gain control of her body, but she was losing.

"That's right. Come to me so I can inhale the sweet scent of your blood. My enemy's blood."

Reese fought to keep her senses. She reached inside her purse and wrapped fingers around the Beretta she'd put there before leaving for the nightclub. Gripping the pistol with both hands, she dropped the bag and pointed the barrel at Kur's heart.

He lifted a blond brow. "Your will is strong. That is interesting." Kur smiled. "Give me the weapon." He held out his other hand. "Place it here in my hand and let me kiss you."

She released the safety. Her hands were shaking but she didn't take time to worry about it. If she did, she'd be dead.

Anger crossed Kur's face and he took a step toward her. She pulled the trigger. The sound reverberated through the room. The impact caused Reese to step back but she recovered and took aim again.

"*Felkah,*" Kur screamed. He pulled a bloody hand away from his shoulder. "You shot me."

"And I'll do it again."

He laughed. "I bet you would. The nice thing about being me is that the injuries heal quickly." Kur glanced at his wounded shoulder and then back at her. "Even the nasty ones."

He took another step toward her and she screamed. Fragments of the splintered front door flew everywhere. One lodged in Kur's thigh and he cursed loudly. Reese's hopeful gaze fell on Dagan's powerful form.

"Are you the welcome wagon?" Kur sneered and pulled a piece of wood from his leg.

"Hardly, I'm your ticket back to the Underworld, permanently." Dagan raised his arm, reached behind him and drew his sword.

"Ah, I see Pyre has been busy." Kur carefully removed his jacket and dropped it on the floor. A long scabbard hung at his side from which he pulled a thick bladed sword. He glared at Dagan. "I seem to remember being here before."

"Not quite. The last time you had five others with you." Dagan rolled his wrist swinging the sword. It made swooshing sounds as it cut through the air. "This time it's just you and me."

Kur smiled. "Let the fun begin."

The first clang of blades startled Reese. She didn't know what to do. Should she raise her weapon again and shoot Kur? No, she wouldn't be able to get a clean shot. She might hit Dagan. Where was her bat when she needed it?

The men knocked over lamps and smashed tables in the ferocious battle. The seasoned warriors took pieces of each other. Dagan's muscular arms delivered powerful strokes. Kur countered with fine moves and backward spins. She could have been watching a well-staged movie scene.

Kur slipped on some of his own blood and stumbled forward. This gave Dagan the opportunity to slice him across the shoulders, close to his neck. Kur whirled around and cut Dagan's forearm. Weakened, Kur struggled to stand straight and his blows were less forceful.

Two minions appeared in the shattered doorway. Reese swung around, pointing the gun in their direction. From out of the darkness, a whirring sound came just before a jewel-handled dagger imbedded itself in the back of one of the *galla's* heads.

The second one growled and spun around. He was larger than the dead one and skilled. Rufus wielded a Simitar and sliced toward his middle, but he managed to scoot back enough to avoid it.

"You'll have to do better than that, *doghume*," the demon growled. Reese recognized his voice from before.

Rufus smiled. "Oh, don't worry." He lunged forward and nicked his opponent's left shoulder. The other roared and ran toward Rufus. Reese held her breath.

The demon's roar was enough distraction to give Dagan the upper hand in his battle. He stabbed Kur in the right thigh which left a gaping hole to match the bloody one in his other thigh. Kur stumbled back against the wall. Propping himself up with a blood-covered hand, he puckered his lips and blew Reese a kiss. Turning his glowing eyes on Dagan he said, "This isn't over, Time Walker."

"I'll be waiting," Dagan responded before Kur evaporated

into mist and disappeared.

At the same moment, Rufus managed to stab the one he was fighting in the stomach. The creature fell to the ground, passed out and disappeared.

Dagan nodded at Rufus then rushed to her side. "Are you all right?"

Her legs gave out and she withered to the floor, but not before Dagan wrapped her in his bloody arms and went down with her. She shivered. Grabbing onto him she laid her head on his shoulder. She didn't care that the blood would ruin her clothes. She needed his strength and his warmth to chase away the terror.

# Chapter Seven

"Did he touch you at all?"

"N-no, he didn't touch me." Her body shook as she gazed at him with a slight smile. "I shot him."

Dagan snorted. "Damn straight."

Her eyes did a slow survey of the room. "You tore up my living room."

He laid his cheek on the top of her head. "After everything we've been through tonight, you're angry because some furniture is broken?"

"And the door," she added.

"Okay, okay. By the gods, you're exasperating." He hugged her closer. The shivering had ceased, but he wanted a few more moments of holding her.

Even in this state, she drew him like a tiger on a blood scent. His cock enlarged and his heart sped up. He wanted to remove his clothes, strip her naked and hold her until the shaking passed, hers and his.

This was wrong on so many levels. The *sukkal* would peel the skin from his body using whips and chains, beating him to a bloody pulp.

The sounds of Rufus cleaning up filtered through to him. "Why don't you go take a shower and get yourself pulled together? We'll take care of things in here."

"I can help."

He placed a finger on her lips. "No, you go get cleaned up."

She frowned. "You're ordering me around again."

He frowned back. "And this time, you're going to do as I say."

He rose, lifting her along with him, and gently shoved her toward the hallway to the bedroom. Reluctant steps turned into a slow walk, but she complied.

When he heard her close the bedroom door, he went in search of Rufus. He found him in the kitchen. "She'll need nourishment."

"I'm already on it. I'll get some stew cooking on the stove. She had all the makings for it." He faced Dagan. "How's she doing?"

He ran a still bloodied hand through his matted hair. "She says Kur didn't touch her. She seems to be holding up okay, considering she'd just faced the creature."

"She's kind of amazing."

An amazing lunatic. Dagan waved his hand, repairing the front door. He snapped his fingers and a fire roared to life in the fireplace.

A tapping drew his attention back to Rufus, who tasted the stew. He nodded as though pleased with the concoction. He glanced at Dagan's war torn appearance. "You might want to get cleaned up yourself."

The *doghume* was right. He walked over and rummaged through the cabinets. He found the Johnnie Black. "Try to get her to eat and drink something when she comes in. I don't see any brandy, so you can use whiskey."

"Am I supposed to get her drunk?" Rufus chuckled.

"Not if you want to live," Dagan growled.

"Just kidding, my man." He put his hands up in silent surrender. "I know she's yours."

That statement hit Dagan hard.

He had no rights over humans other than to save their asses from the demons of the Underworld. As a purebred, the son of two gods, the people worshipped him, but as a time walker, he gave up those rights. Besides, he didn't feel comfortable having humans worship him.

"I'll check everything in the house to make sure you're locked up tight before I go. I'll make a sweep of the area too." He grabbed Rufus by the shirt front. "Guard her like your life depends on it."

Rufus peeled Dagan's fingers from his shirt. "I know how to do my job, purebred. I've never failed before and I don't intend to start now."

Dagan registered the anger on the *doghume*'s face. He had insulted him, unintentionally. It would have to wait. He had more important things to worry about.

Dagan appeared inside the gates of the massive garden at Dilmun. His mother, Ninmah, the Earth-Mother Goddess, loved to work with the dark, rich soil. As a result, the garden was the most impressive thing anyone had ever seen. Flowers of every color and type lived all year long. On their planet, Bylari, a home he'd never known but had heard talk of often enough, one year was equivalent to four thousand Earth years. The flowers never lived very long. He supposed that's why his mother loved this planet so much.

He stood behind a huge palm tree watching the beautiful woman tend the garden. She never used gloves. He'd asked her about it once and she'd said that she loved to feel the dirt sift through her fingers. It reminded her of the flourishing life they had found here. They call Enki the God of Wisdom, but Dagan questioned that. His mother had more wisdom than anyone he'd ever known, and Enki had proven repeatedly that his wisdom could be fooled by a pretty face or a tight ass. He was also the God of Waters, and populations boomed because of it.

"Why do you hide there, my son?" Ninmah called in a soft voice.

He took a deep breath then walked toward her. "I do not hide, my lady, just admiring the beauty of your garden."

"I do spend a lot of time here, so I hope it is beautiful enough."

"Never enough for you." He smiled and reached down to help her up.

"So true."

She stood only five foot eight so he gazed down at her. A smudge of dirt on her nose made him chuckle and he swept it away before placing a chaste kiss on her forehead.

"What brings you here? I thought you were off *hunting*." Her beautifully arched brow rose and she gave his appearance the once over. "And are these the kind of clothes you hunt in now?"

He glanced down at his body. He hadn't changed from the clothes he'd worn to Slow Burn. They were ripped and bloody.

"Humanity is rubbing off on you. Perhaps you should come home and spend a while with us."

His chin lifted. "This is part of the attire I wore this evening and I *was* hunting." Hunting for answers, but he didn't add that part.

"So why are you here in this disheveled state?"

Dagan lowered his head. How to ask her what he needed to know? Would she turn him over to the others for punishment and send someone else to protect Reese? He couldn't live with that outcome though he chose to tell her the truth. He needed someone to trust and if he couldn't trust his mother, who then?

"Mother, I have a problem."

"Only one?" She turned and made her way to the stone bench in the middle of the landscape. "Come sit, and tell me what troubles you."

He did as she bade him.

"Who is she?" Ninmah asked before he spoke.

Dagan glanced at her. "Who?"

"That was my question."

She saw through him as well. First Flame then Pyre, now his mother. Was he really that transparent?

"Her name is Reese. I went to the twenty-first century because I sensed a formidable force of *galla*. They are watching her. When I got close enough, I knew why. She is a direct descendent of Enki and her power is strong."

She nodded as she listened. "I am sure Kur is eager to have her."

"As am I."

Ninmah's head snapped up. "What?"

He rose and walked a few feet away. Now for the hard part. Maybe he shouldn't have come.

"Tell me what you have done, Dagan."

He felt like a mere child instead of a man who had lived centuries. His mother sat staring at him and waiting for the response he knew he had to give. He'd already come this far.

Sighing, he went back to her.

"I have protected her from two attacks already. The last one, Kur himself showed up."

"Did he touch her?"

"No, but he promised he'd be back." He knelt at her feet. "I need to ask you something."

She caressed his hair and then his cheek. "Ask me anything, my son. I will always be here for you."

The thought comforted him, but he didn't know how long that would last once she knew the truth behind the visit.

"Have you ever heard of a *go'ras* not working?"

Frowning in concentration, Ninmah shook her head. "I am aware of no time where a mind erasure did not work."

That didn't please him.

"Why would I be drawn to her with so much force that I can barely control it at times?"

She thought for a brief second. "There is only one reason any of us, especially the males, lose control." She stood. "When you have found your *blethred*."

Dagan fingered his dark hair still stained with blood. "How can that be? She is human."

His mother walked away mumbling to herself. He stayed put. With her in deep thought, he'd dare not interrupt.

"This has never happened before." She tapped her finger to her chin. "The longer we are here and interact with the human race, the stranger things become. This is not the first time something bizarre has happened."

He resented that she felt his attraction to Reese was bizarre. "What should I do?"

"Have you mated with her?"

Embarrassed at the direction this conversation tilted, Dagan ducked his head. He didn't want to discuss his sexual relations or the lack thereof with his mother.

"Answer me," Ninmah ordered as she grabbed his arm.

He cleared his throat. He'd thought about it once or twice, or fifteen or sixteen times. He'd lost count. "No."

She nodded. "See that you do not." She released him. "This will have to be reported to the others."

He cringed. That meant another beating or something worse. You never knew what type of torture the Pantheon would come up with next.

She waved away his concern. "Do not fret. You will not be beaten for this. You cannot help it if she is your *blethred*. Let any among us, especially the Council, demand flesh for this outrage."

Outrage would surely develop. He had no doubt of that. She faded to peach-colored mist and left him alone in the garden.

This trip confirmed what deep down he'd suspected. Reese Whittaker was his *blethred*, a life mate with whom he would share everything—his blood, his heart, his soul, his life force—as dictated by the custom of his people. Once tied to her, he would know everything about her, every minute of every day for the rest of her natural human life.

"Damn." What more could happen? He needed to focus on the hunt and stay away from Reese Whittaker.


Kur's strength waned. It took him longer to materialize in Divinity. He collapsed immediately to the floor and roared his frustration. The sound bounced off the walls. Vile rushed into the room.

"What's happened?" she asked as she helped him onto the throne and proceeded to remove his shirt.

"I need humans." He hissed when the material pulled along the gouges. "Dammit."

"Sorry, my king. I'll have them brought right away. I'll get something to clean you up."

When Vile left, Kur slammed his fists against the stone. "You will taste my wrath, you purebred son of a bitch."

Vile returned with warm herbal water and cloth to cleanse his wounds. His anger simmered as she knelt before him and smoothed the cloth over cuts that weren't healing as fast as they should because of his weakened state.

"I've sent for some humans."

"Good." He closed his eyes.

His skin twitched every time the cloth touched it. The next thing he felt were tentative touches, Vile's fingertips caressing his mangled flesh. It warmed him and tingles rushed through his entire body. Though he'd been drained of energy from the fight, his body still reacted to the female. His cock stiffened and Vile purred.

Kur opened his eyes to see her staring at his groin. He chuckled. Moving his hands to his zipper, he slowly lowered it to allow his cock to spring free.

"Wrap your mouth around it, Vile."

Her eyes darkened and she leaned forward. Her hot mouth closed over his cock and she purred again, sending trickles of sensation through his body.

"Yes, I like that." He spread his legs wider. Soon, he would regain his strength and the war would begin.

# Chapter Eight

An enticing aroma assaulted her nose and her stomach growled. *Dagan must be making dinner.*

Reese jumped in the shower. After using her favorite body wash, lotion and spray, she felt like herself again. When she opened the door and moved into the bedroom, she stared at the fire ablaze in the weathered hearth built into the stone wall that had not been used in a couple of decades. Along the way, someone had sealed the chimney with concrete. Having it reopened had been on her list of things to do when she got around to it. *How could... Who could have...?*

*Dagan.*

Her bedroom felt like a tropical sauna so she put on a pair of leggings and a blue T-shirt. In the mirror, she stared at her reflection, not recognizing the person staring back. Red circles rimmed her eyelids and dark circles marred her pale skin. Stress and terror took its toll on a person. She definitely looked like death warmed over, as her grandmother used to say.

Determined to feel as normal as possible, she fluffed her hair and smoothed some cotton candy lip gloss her cousin had given her over her partially chapped lips. She opened the door and headed for the cooler kitchen.

Rounding the corner into the doorway she said, "Dagan, I—"

"Good evening, Ms. Whittaker."

"Rufus, what are you doing here?"

"Making stew. Are you hungry?"

Although she felt a little self-conscious and exposed, her

stomach picked that instant to growl loudly. She chuckled. "I guess I am. It smells wonderful."

"Have a seat," he said, and pulled out a chair for her. "I'll get you a bowl."

"You really don't have to wait on me. It is my house."

"True, but you were having a hard time earlier and it's my pleasure to do what I can to help."

He moved to the stove and ladled the stew into a bowl which he then laid on the table in front of her. Going back to the cabinet, he pulled down two glasses and the whiskey.

"I was ordered to make sure you drink this." He smiled.

"Ordered?"

"Yes, ma'am."

"Why do you let him order you around?"

"It's complicated." He went back to turn off the burner and get himself a portion.

"I've got nothing but time. Explain it to me." She swallowed a spoonful of the spicy broth and meat. "Ummmm, delicious."

"I'm from an Irish family and if I didn't learn anything else, I learned how to cook stew."

She wiped her mouth with the napkin that he'd placed next to her bowl. "So tell me what it is you do."

His brows came together in a frown. "You know too much already."

"Exactly," she said. "So it wouldn't matter if I knew the whole story now, would it?"

"It's not for me to say."

"Bullshit."

His eyes widened and he laughed. "You're a piece of work, Reese. A perfect match for Dagan."

"I'm not a match for anyone unless I say so."

"Pardon me, I didn't mean to speak out of turn."

"Don't hand me that bull, Rufus. I'm a good judge of character and you don't strike me as a man who worries about being politically correct."

He laughed again. "You're so right."

"Then tell me what goes on here that you've been left to watch over me...again." She took another spoonful of stew.

Rufus sighed. "When the call went out for the army to go after Kur, there were many who took the oath."

After throwing back a shot of whiskey, she said, "The oath?"

"Yes, those who stepped forward swore an oath to the Goddess Inanna."

"Inanna is the one who requested the army to fight the beast."

He nodded. "There are different levels, if you will." He too swallowed a shot of Johnnie Black. "The first are the purebreds, the sons and daughters of the gods."

"Like Dagan."

"Yes."

"He told me about these. Then there are the *nephili*, those born of humans who mated with gods which was not unheard of in mythology." Reese sat back against the chair, her head felt light.

"Then there are the *doghume*, which are full humans who have special or enhanced abilities."

Her right brow rose. "And what is your...special talent?"

He chuckled and reached out to brush his fingers over the knuckles of her hand as it rested on the table. "I have many...uh talents, but for the subject of this conversation, I have a very high IQ and the ability to work any and all kinds of technology with the utmost skill and accuracy."

"And all that talent will be laid to rest if you touch her one more time."

Reese's head snapped up to see Dagan poised in the doorway as though he would really attack Rufus. Rufus's hand disappeared from the table and rested on his thigh.

Her anger boiled. How dare he come into her home issuing orders? She and Rufus were having a nice conversation and he had done nothing untoward.

Dagan's eyes were that intense, deep green again as they glared at her.

"Don't take that tone with me," she said and rose from the

chair to take her bowl and rinse it out.

"You are done for the night," Dagan told Rufus. "Secure the perimeter and then go catch some shut-eye. Be back here by five-thirty a.m. The seal will hold until then."

"Okay, I'm gone," Rufus said. Before he left, he walked over to her. "You take care, Reese. Be safe."

She smiled at his sincere face as he winked and kissed her cheek. He was trying to get under Dagan's skin.

Dagan growled and fisted his hands.

She played along. "Thanks, Rufus. This evening had definite high points."

Rufus bowed and walked out of the room via the doorway opposite the one Dagan blocked.

Dagan glowered at her. "What was that supposed to mean?"

Reese turned her most innocent look on him. "What?"

"Don't try to hand me that innocent look. What did the two of you do here tonight?" He stalked toward her. "When I left you were like the North Pole all blue and shivering and shit."

"Do gods really talk like that? Like humans do, cause you sound like an arrogant, egotistical, jealous male. A human male. That's interesting. Do you think it's because you spend so much time here on Earth, mingling with humans or do you just like our language? Or maybe you like the whole intimidation thing."

She pushed past the tower of vibrating man and went into the living room.

"Reese, dammit. What happened while I was gone?"

Sitting down in her cozy chair, she picked up the romance novel she'd been reading for the last week. "I started feeling better," she said then focused on her book.

Another growl from deep in his throat floated across the room. Reese hid a smile. It served him right. He acted as though she owed him an explanation, which she didn't.

Dagan stormed past her chair and locked the front door.

Reese looked up in time to see him raise his hand and murmur words in the language she now knew to be his native tongue. She knew he was putting another seal on the house which meant they were in for the night...together.

His nostrils flared and her scent permeated every pore in his skin. Deep breaths helped slow the erratic beating of his heart; he needed to calm down. Strolling back into the kitchen he decided he could eat. It had been hours since he'd had nourishment and although his strength and skill did not require it, his stomach did. Grabbing the bottle of Johnnie Black off the counter with one hand, he took the steaming bowl in the other and sat at the table. He thought it best to keep his distance from Reese because in this mood, he couldn't be sure he wouldn't rip the clothes she wore from her body and mate with her in a matter of seconds. No, he needed to relax and calm down.

Dagan ate half the contents before grabbing the whiskey bottle by the neck and chugging it. Unfortunately, alcohol didn't affect his system the way it did humans. Getting shit-faced sounded good.

Two deep breaths, more food shoveled into his mouth, then chug. He needed to concentrate on those things his body required.

As he lifted the dripping spoon, he froze. Humming? A soft sweet melody drifted on the air from the other room. Closing his eyes, Dagan opened his senses fully. Her scent carelessly knocked him backwards. He breathed it in. The heat surged through his body like smoldering rock flowing through a lava tunnel. The *fury* escalated.

In this uncomfortably hard, small chair his body hardened and burned. He shoved the bowl aside and grabbed the neck of the bottle, bringing it to his mouth for a long swig. It did little to douse the tempered ache turning his gut out. The need grew more intense as the seconds ticked by. Her voice intoxicated him even more than the liquor.

Unable to stand it any longer, Dagan shoved away from the table and stood. In determined strides, he marched into the room where she sat. With a startled jolt, she looked up as he stormed toward her. The music stopped. Her scent grew stronger the closer he got and lust tore through him at a level he'd never experienced.

She must have known how close to the brink he teetered

because she said, "Don't start with me again." She rose from the chair, laid her book down and rushed past him, heading toward the kitchen.

Lifting the remaining whiskey-laced coffee to her lips, Reese peered at Dagan over the cup while she drank. Warmth flooded her body and the alcohol ignited her nerve endings on its way down to her stomach. Unsure of whether the reaction was due to the whiskey or the relative stranger, who claimed to be the first born son of a Sumerian god, standing there watching her, devouring her.

"You're doing it again," he murmured in a husky voice.

"Doing what?"

"Sizing me up, turning me on."

She coughed and practically spilled the coffee. "Sorry."

Hurriedly, she started clearing the dishes and rinsing them to put in the dishwasher. "So, you are the first born son of the air god?"

"Yes."

"Does he approve of what you're doing?"

Dagan stood just behind her. She turned and he handed her his bowl. A frown of concentration wrinkled his face. Even in that state, he managed to appear sinful and inviting. Her body tingled again.

"I'm sworn to protect humans. It's my duty."

"So you said." She filled the sink with warm soapy water to wash the pots and pans. "Why is it your duty to protect humans?"

"Perhaps I should explain how this all started."

His lips curled in a faint smile and her heart flipped. "Okay."

There was a brief silence, as if he considered what or how much to tell her.

"We are Naruki from the planet Bylari."

A gasp wrenched from her throat as Reese fumbled the plate she held and it fell to the floor, shattering into pieces.

"Did you just say you came from another planet?"

"No, I was born here." He gave a lift to his shoulders. "But my people came from Bylari about five hundred thousand years ago."

Sure, why not? The shock ebbed as the curious side of her pushed to the forefront. "So you're aliens?"

Dagan rolled his eyes heavenward. "I'm not really a green, slimy creature with tentacles, if that's what you mean. What you see is what you get."

She bent to pick up the large pieces of the broken plate. Standing, she let a reluctant smile touch her lips. "I'm sorry. Momentary brain stutter, which tends to happen when I find out I'm speaking with a..." she blew her cheeks out, "...*being* from another world."

He crossed his massive arms over his chest. "I'm the same *being* you've been dealing with since we first met."

Cautiously walking over to the large pantry, she dropped the broken bits into the trash can and brought the broom and pan back to finish cleaning up the mess. Stopping in front of Dagan's stiff form, she gazed up to his face. "I'm sorry, Dagan. Please continue."

He relaxed his stance. "From what my father has told me, my people left Bylari to escape the ravages of a war that had done untold damage to the planet. In the first ship were the males and Nammu, she who gave birth to all the gods."

"But you're not gods," Reese offered in a clear voice.

"To the humans we are. We live for thousands of years and we have powers that you cannot comprehend."

He took the dustpan and broom from her to discard the remaining shards of the plate. She turned back to the sink and the dishes.

"When they happened upon Earth, they were taken with the beauty of the planet and the abundant resources it offered, so they decided to make this their new home. The males did everything needed to survive in their lives. They farmed, they fished and built magnificent palaces in which to live. They were happy in their existence."

"Okay." She rinsed a pot and put it in the strainer.

"They sent word to the second ship which had left later and soon, the females arrived."

"Ah, the plot thickens." Reese smiled at him over her shoulder.

"The males became lazy and distracted by the females."

"As is wont to happen when women come around." She winked at him. A hungry, wicked look crossed his face and made her sweat. Of course, the rising temperature of her body could be due to the fact that she had her hands in warm water. She stole a glance. Nope, it was definitely him.

He came closer and whispered in her ear, "There is the ring of truth in that."

He'd come up behind her so stealthily, she hadn't felt him move. "So what happened next?" she asked breathlessly.

He hopped up onto the counter to watch her and finish the story.

"The gods were starving and in need of many necessities, but were too lazy and preoccupied to continue. So, they begged Nammu to create servants for them. Those that could tend the fields, maintain the structures and keep the gods in the lifestyle they wanted."

"Man?"

"Yes," he said as he ran a fingertip down her arm.

Chills raced across her skin and she swallowed several times trying to concentrate, washing the same dish over and over.

"Nammu went to Enki."

"The God of Wisdom," she offered.

"Intrigued by the idea, Enki saw no harm in it, so he arranged a party."

Reese finished the dishes and released the water. After wiping her hands on the towel, she walked over to stand by the table, keeping as much distance between them as possible. "I take it something happened."

"That's the truth of it."

His eyes darkened as she ran her hands up her arms.

"With the combined energy of all, Ninmah created man from blocks of clay, and Nammu breathed life into them. The attempt had been successful. The servants were provided with everything required for their survival. In turn, they built temples to honor the gods who'd made them. They gave offerings of livestock and crops. This made the deities happy and they continued their lounging and loving."

"I see," she said and moved farther away from him. "So the Naruki created mankind to serve them as gods with a mutual agreement they both honored."

"Yes."

"What about Kur? Not much has been found regarding the creature."

His eyes clouded. "In his drunken stupor and after having witnessed the creation of another species, Enki decided he wanted to create one himself." Dagan jumped down from the counter and paced the kitchen. "Unfortunately, without the others and the knowledge to create as Nammu, what he created was a weak, feeble, useless creature."

"That's terrible."

"Enki held compassion for it and begged Ninmah, my beloved mother, to take care of Kur. She agreed and did her best to help the creature. Unfortunately, even the Earth-Mother Goddess couldn't correct or change the defects in its genealogy. She summoned servants in a small village to watch over it for the rest of its days."

Dagan's pacing and intensity filled her with a sense of unease. She grabbed his arm and the static charge voltage of a bug zapper surged through her body, making the hair on her arms stand up. She jumped back. It surprised him as well.

"Was it awful?" she whispered while shaking her hand to get feeling back in her fingers.

He moved away. "Over time, Kur responded in small ways to those who cared for him. Being self-aware, he knew the story of his origin. Although able to function to a small degree, he hated his existence.

"One day a young woman brought food to his room. He had been contemplating revenge against Enki. His rage turned on the girl and he drained her life force which in turn made him stronger, more powerful than he had ever been before."

"He liked it."

Dagan nodded. "So much so that he murdered the entire village."

"Oh my God." Reese wrapped her arms around her body as if to stave off the evil.

"Kur went on a rampage and killed many across the land. Before the gods could stop him, he kidnapped the Goddess Ereshkigal and escaped to the Underworld."

Entranced, yet still unsure about the sanity of this ordeal, Reese aptly listened to the fascinating story.

"The teachings I've had were that An, the sky god and Enlil ordered Ereshkigal to the Underworld to be Queen of the House of Death."

He sighed. "There have been numerous attempts over the centuries to get her back, but none have been successful. He holds her deep in the bowels of the Underworld. We have no proof that she lives, but the Goddess Inanna will not give up hope."

"This is all interesting to be sure, but what does it have to do with me, a twenty-first century archeologist?"

Dagan caressed her cheek with his fingers. He fought the increasing urges to explore the contours of her face, the nuances of her body. "Enki's blood flows within you. The power of it pulls at Kur, who is still bent on revenge."

Reese shivered. A small whimper left her lips and Dagan pulled her into his arms.

"Don't worry," he said. "I'll protect you."

"Will he stop?"

"No."

"Then how will you protect me?" She glided away from him. "You can't be with me for the rest of my life and he lives on forever."

"As do I."

Reese shook her head. "I must learn more about Kur and those creatures. I want to know everything."

Dagan ran his fingers through his hair. Would she ever stop with the questions?

"Look." He held up a hand to cease her litany. "It's been a long day. I'm sure you'd like to get some rest and I'm beat. How about saving the interrogation until the morning?"

Her disappointment washed him with a gush of guilt, but it would pass.

Her eyes were like the lapis lazuli that swirled around the city of his birth. Her unique scent radiated from her skin and mixed with her sex, invading his superior and heightened senses. He closed the distance between them. His body burned with the *fury*.

Quick as lightning, he slid his hand under her hair, grabbed the nape of her neck and pulled her lips to his. She moaned.

Reese broke the kiss. "Stop."

He did, but it took great restraint. In an attempt to calm the storm erupting in the cells of his body, Dagan inhaled through his nose, exhaled through his mouth and bore holes in the wall behind where Reese stood.

Reese readjusted her clothing, which had twisted in his embrace. "I don't even know you. I've let you in my home, although why is anyone's guess, and you fill my head with fairytales." She pointed a finger at him. "Despite how intrigued I might be, it doesn't give you an open invitation to take liberties."

Nervous energy ignited her.

"You'll leave when the seal is broken, or whatever." She paced the area behind the sofa. "And—" She stopped and narrowed her eyes. "Don't you dare touch me again. Are we clear?"

He leaned his shoulder against the doorjamb and crossed his arms. "I agree. We should not touch again. It could be catastrophic." More for him than her, especially if his people found out.

"Good," she said and marched off toward the bedroom.

Dagan roamed the house checking doors, windows and any other possible entries into the home before settling uncomfortably on the floor with a pillow and blanket Reese had thrown at him.

He hadn't slept and all his senses were on alert so he knew when she'd re-entered the room.

"What happens tomorrow?" She looked at the clock on mantel. "I mean today."

"The seal will disappear at sunrise and I will hunt."

"Hunt?"

He sighed. Obviously, his hope for peace until morning was short-lived. He rolled to his side and propped his cheek on his upturned palm. "I will search out Kur's minions, his watchdogs. They'll either be sent back to the Underworld or destroyed so they can do you no harm."

She shivered. "What will I be doing while you're hunting?"

"You'll stay here and I'll seal the house again. You're safe as long as you're inside."

She lifted her brow and her voice. "Uh, no, and I'll go so far as to say, hell no. I can't stay here forever and I won't. I'm meeting my team Monday to start work on a proposal."

The determined glint in her eyes told him she was serious and that made him angry. "And what will you do if the death squad manages to get to you and I'm not around?"

In the dim lighting, he watched her shift from one foot to the other and imagined the wheels turning in her mind.

"I'll do what I have to." Reese rolled her shoulders. "Besides, you can't be sure how long they've been here. For all we know, I've been watched for weeks."

"Not likely."

Planting her hands on her hips she said, "How can you be so sure?"

He sat up. "Because I would have felt them and been here as well. Kur sends the *galla* to different breaks on the timeline to search out descendants of the gods. They must have happened on this point in time and sensed your presence."

She flicked her wrist as if swatting a gnat. "Regardless, how do I explain you to my colleagues? A big, dark Sumerian warrior following me everywhere I go?" She shook her head. "Oh, don't worry about him. He's my bodyguard to save me from the evil Lord of Hell, nothing to be concerned about."

The tone of his voice hardened. "Lord of Hell? He would probably like that title." Dagan glanced toward the window. "I should get ready, dawn will break soon." He shifted to his

97

hands and knees before unrolling his body to a standing position.

"Right," she murmured.

Dagan zipped his pants and sat to put his boots on.

*"Are you awake yet?"* Pyre's voice echoed in his head.

*"You know I'm awake."* He walked past the window and saw the sun just breaking the horizon. *"What do you* want?"

Pyre chuckled. *"Did you get up on the wrong side of the woman?"*

*"Is there a wrong side to a woman?"* Dagan asked.

He looked at his ruined shirt and tossed it in the trash. Since the seal was no longer in place, he held his hand out, palm up, and a new shirt materialized.

*"Not that I have found."*

*"Pyre, I'm in no mood. Kindly tell me what you want,"* he said as he slipped the new shirt on.

*"What are your plans? The seal will break when sunlight hits it."*

*"That happened five minutes ago. I'm readying myself now."*

*"What will you do with the female?"*

So Flame had spoken to him. *"What can I do with her? She can't stay locked away forever."* Although he wished it were so.

*"Do you need help?"*

*"So far Rufus and I have been handling it. I'll call if I need you."*

The *galla* and Kur he could handle. It was the human female that turned him inside out.

When Reese came back down the hall dressed in tight jeans, a yellow turtleneck and Winnie the Pooh sweatshirt, he swallowed hard. He fought every urge to tell her not to go out. She would do what she damn well pleased whether he wanted it or not. *Stubborn.*

"So what are your plans for today?"

"I have some errands to run." She pulled her purse up from the floor, checked her wallet to see how much money she had, then dug deeper for the car keys.

He stayed silent.

"What, no argument from the big bad warrior about how I should stay inside and lock all the doors?"

"It would do no good," he said in a strained voice.

"Damn straight, fella."

She didn't dare look at him. She wanted to rush into his arms and beg him to keep her safe, but she wouldn't do that either.

"Be careful."

That stopped her. She turned to him narrowing suspicious eyes. "Be careful? Is that all you're going to say?"

"No." He stalked toward her.

*Here it comes.*

"Now that you know what's going on, you have to remain alert. You need to keep your eyes open."

"Don't worry, Dagan. I will be aware of everything going on around me, and I'm taking this." She held up a Bowie knife.

"By all the gods," he swore and grabbed the knife by the handle. "You're going to cut yourself." He laid it on the table and scowled at her. "Where the hell did you get that? It's not a toy."

"Look, buster." She poked her finger into his chest. "I'm not a three year old. I know it's not a toy. My cousin uses it when he comes here to hang out and go fishing. I am perfectly capable of handling the thing."

He gave her that "you're crazy" look—sideways. It pissed her off more that he thought she needed to be coddled. Did she want to know Sumerian gods were running around on Earth? No. Did she want to know her name was on some demon from the Underworld's hit list? No. But she damn well wouldn't be going out without some protection.

She sheathed the knife and settled it in the bottom of her purse. Grabbing her coat and scarf, she said, "Now if you'll excuse me, I have things to do." She moved past Dagan on her way out the door. "Don't forget to lock up."

He growled or yelled or both, but the closing door muffled the sound, so she couldn't be sure.

Dagan threw open the door. "Dammit, Reese. Get your ass back here."

"No." She kept walking toward her car without looking back.

He caught up to her as she opened the door. "Look at me," he said, tugging the sleeve on her coat to stop her.

She sighed. "What?"

Dagan brushed a stray hair from her cheek with the gentlest touch. "Be careful."

"You said that already."

The barest of smiles flickered. "You're very irritating."

"So are you." She looked up into those incredible eyes of his and got lost in their concern. "I'll be careful, Dagan."

He rubbed his thumb over her lips and she hoped he would kiss her again. Instead, he dropped his hand and took a step back. His eyes bore holes into her while she loaded herself into the car and started the engine. He raised his hand in farewell then shattered into twinkling lights.

Reese put her hand over her mouth and closed her eyes. How would she get through this? With her car warmed up, she pulled out of the drive and headed to her father's house.

Dagan reappeared in Rufus's car.

Rufus put his hand over his heart. "Whoa, holy hell, Dagan. I wish you'd warn me when you're going to do that."

"Follow her, but don't let her see you."

"Not too keen on the whole bodyguard thing, huh?"

Dagan gritted his teeth. "No."

"Don't worry, I'll be on her like shit on a shingle."

"What?"

"Never mind. I'm on the case."

Dagan nodded and disappeared.

# Chapter Nine

The forty-minute drive gave Reese time to think over what to say to her father. Should she try to reason this out with him? Should she tell him the truth about the last two days in her life?

Definitely not.

She would approach him with the idea of a client party as a thank you to all their loyal customers. Maybe if he got into the planning of it like he used to, it would bring him out of the long depression.

She drove down the quiet neighborhood street and pulled into 1112 Hickory Drive. It looked like Scott, the local teenager she'd hired to shovel the drive and sidewalk had already been there.

A deep carpet of pure white snow coated the huge front yard. She and Riley used to fling their arms wide and fall backward to the ground, flapping limbs to make snow angels then go ice skating on the local pond. Frozen to their very bones they'd rush home to taste Mom's specialty, the best hot cocoa in the world.

"Don't go there, Reese, or you'll start blubbering and icicles will form on your face."

Her cold fingers rummaged through the keys on her keychain until she found the one for her Dad's front door. She let herself in.

"Dad, you home?"

"Reese, is that you?"

She heard his distant voice carry down the stairs and

entryway.

"Where are you?"

"Upstairs."

Shaking off the light dusting of snowflakes that had fallen from the roof, she slipped out of her coat and shoes. She hung the coat on the rack as she passed the wall and climbed the stairwell.

She found him in Riley's room, sitting in the closet. "What on earth are you doing?"

"Well, I didn't have anything to do today, so I thought I'd go through some of this stuff and see if I could donate it to the local shelters. Riley has grown out of this stuff and it doesn't need to be here since she's gone."

He sneezed.

She chuckled. "You need a whole crew of helpers to do Riley's room, Dad. She was a slob after all."

He tossed out some boots that had seen better days, some cassette tapes, a lava lamp, and then backed out carrying a Frankenstein mask and a pitchfork.

"Good Lord, what did she need this stuff for?"

"I think it's better not to ask, don't you?"

He smiled. "I agree. I'll put it in the get rid of pile, which seems to be growing and growing."

It had been months since she'd seen her father's eyes light up or heard his melodious laugh rumble from deep in his chest. If he couldn't bring himself to clean out Mom's stuff, attempting to clean up Riley's disaster of a room was a good step forward.

"What brings you out this way? Shouldn't you be orchestrating some massive dig or organizing a fundraiser to finance your next trip deep in the Amazon to unearth ancient pygmy villages?"

Reese burst out laughing; she couldn't help herself. She laughed so hard it made her cry and she plopped down on the floor next to her father and hugged him.

"You're crying," he said with worry in his voice.

"Oh, Dad. The last couple of days have been rather strange and intense. You caught me off-guard and I just let loose. Thank you." She kissed his cheek.

"You're welcome."

He stood, dragged her up and brushed off the dust bunnies congregating on his pant leg. "Let's go get something to drink, shall we?"

"Sounds good to me." She followed her father out of the room with a big smile on her face and an easing in her heart.

After they sat in front of the roaring fire with mugs of hot coffee, she stared at his face for a few moments, taking in the healthy color of his skin and the diminishing dark circles under his eyes. These were good signs.

"So, honey, what brings you here today?"

"Well, I hadn't seen you in a couple of weeks and I wanted to run something past you."

"Shoot."

"Christmas will be here before we know it."

"That it will."

"I'd like to organize a cocktail and dinner party for your firm and its clients."

"Oh?"

"Something along the lines of a thank you to your loyal customers, bring them in, take a look around at the inner workings and introduce them to the staff. What do you think?" she asked with hopeful anticipation.

A familiar look of doubt crossed his features. "I don't know."

"Your firm used to have one every year and the clients loved it. I think you should start doing it again. It will be good for business," she pressed on.

"Let me think on it, Reese."

Not wanting to push too hard for fear of his retreat she said, "Okay, just let me know. I'd love to help."

Standing, she stretched her muscles and wandered around her mother's favorite room. On the ornate oak mantle of the hearth and the surrounding beige walls were endless pictures of the family. She paused at one of her great-grandparents, her grandparents and her parents all together before both her great-grandparents passed. This happened to be her father's side of the family. On the other wall were her mother's relatives.

She wondered where in her family roots Enki had surfaced.

Her gaze roved over a group photo with Grandma and Grandpa Whittaker. Riley had the dark looks and hot temper from their mother's genes, but she noticed her great-grandparents also had dark coloring. Looking to her father, who sat at the table watching her, she saw familiar blond locks and penetrating blue eyes. She was her father's daughter, no doubt about that. She wondered where the light coloring originated, for she did not see it in any of the numerous pictures of the family tree. She shrugged it off. No matter, genetics were funny like that.

"What's troubling you, Reese?"

Her father's question startled her and she jumped a little. Spinning around to face him, she plastered a half-smile on her face. "Nothing really, just reminiscing."

She wouldn't enlighten him with tales of the bizarre happenings of the last two days or talk about Dagan.

"I've decided you're right about the client party."

"You did? I am?"

He nodded. Rushing over, she plopped down in front of his chair and wrapped her arms around his shoulders. "That's great."

"I'll call Tony and discuss more details and check the calendars to pick a date."

"You tell him to call me if he needs anything."

"I will. I'm sure he'll need help with some of it, although Nancy will do a fair job of getting everything set up."

Nancy, her father's secretary since he'd started the firm twenty years ago, was a gem. She would do a great job and be happy that Clive had come back to them.

"Okay, Dad. I'll leave you to it then. I've got some errands to run, grocery shopping, bank, and dry cleaners, so I'll scoot on out of here." She grabbed her purse. "If you need any help cleaning out Riley's room, let me know. I can rent a dumpster."

Her father laughed. A sound she hadn't heard in ages. Maybe the time had finally come for him to move on. Her mother would never be far from their thoughts, but Clive coming to terms with that fact meant a huge leap...a hard step to take.

With her spirits high, Reese started the car and switched on the radio. She didn't care how little sleep she'd gotten last night or what else would happen today.

The evening crackled with ice and the promise of another good snowfall before morning. Dagan liked the winter here, the frozen ground bathed in white and the trees like ice sculptures. The stiff breeze and brisk air had your lungs gulping in the clean atmosphere.

Rufus appeared like a ghost from the bush.

"I assume since you didn't call me there were no problems today."

"She visited her father for a while then went and ran errands and came home. I saw no sign of the death squad."

"Good."

"I talked to Gideon while I was there and he said everything has been quiet so far."

"I'm sure that won't last long."

Rufus threw him an amused grin. "So are you staying here tonight?"

Dagan sighed and tossed a longing glance toward Reese's house. "One never knows."

Rufus laughed. "Did she kick you out?"

Scowling, Dagan said, "Not exactly."

"What now? I need a shower and change of clothes."

"Hang loose here for a while. I've got one more place I need to go then I'll be back to relieve you for the night."

"Okay."

Dagan snapped his fingers and disappeared.

He flashed into the shop of Percilious, the grand wizard of Dilmun.

The wizened old fellow sat at a work table with his back to Dagan. "What brings you to my shop, Time Walker?"

It didn't surprise Dagan that the wizard knew he approached. "I have some questions."

"I am sure you do. You have stirred up a dragon's nest you have."

So he'd heard about the problem. "That's not why I'm here."

A black puff of smoke exploded from the beaker the old man held then it turned five different shades of color before fizzling out.

"You come about the woman nonetheless."

Percilious shifted in his seat to face Dagan. Pointing to a rickety-looking stool, he said, "Sit."

Hesitating for only a moment, Dagan sat and faced the white-haired Naruki whose life spanned more centuries than even Dagan knew. Through owl spectacles perched on the tip of his nose were youthful-looking mud brown eyes full of knowledge.

"Why have you come?"

"How powerful are the concealment wards you've cast over all of Lord Enki's descendents?"

Percilious lifted a bushy white brow. "Do you question my power?"

"With the utmost respect."

"You have balls of steel, boy, for I could change you into a bird and put you on another planet from where I sit."

Dagan chuckled. "I have no doubt, but it's the term and strength of the spells that I wish to learn about."

"For the woman?"

"Is there any way to widen the spell so it protects her all the time?"

The wizard sighed. "I have discussed this very thing with Enki; however, because there are so many, it spreads the magick a bit thin."

"Is there nothing we can do to heighten the ward for one or two individuals in a specific century?"

"I will consult my scrolls, confer with some colleagues and sift through runes and parchment. My memory is not what it used to be."

"I find that hard to believe, Percilious, but thank you."

"I would suggest you keep the *fury* in check and your

temper controlled this eve."

Dagan shifted the coat on his frame when he got up. "Have you seen something I should know about?"

The old man pivoted back to his work table. "I will be in touch, Time Walker."

Dagan knew when he'd been dismissed. Arguing with the old wizard never accomplished anything but a headache. He had more power in his right hand than most did in their entire bodies. Going up against him would be fruitless and he'd end up with scars.

When Dagan strode through the massive pearl gates of Dilmun, a hush fell over the surroundings, though people bustled around the tall, elegant buildings.

An unsettling calm.

He walked the golden streets past the towering structures of the place that he'd once called home. He didn't really feel like a part of this place anymore and hadn't for a long time. Since becoming a time walker visiting different decades and centuries, watching the humans live, he realized how pampered and spoiled his race had become. Worshipped by people they created, waited on, never having to do much for themselves, made them lazy and gluttonous. It sickened him to see it.

His mother appeared at the opening to her garden and smiled at him. She had been the first of those to refuse sacrifices. Of course, the humans did what they wanted, as he'd found out, especially since he'd been around Reese. Talk about an independent, stubborn female who tried one's patience. Foolish at times.

He'd reached the entrance of the garden. Ninmah kissed his cheek. A clouded look covered her usually bright face. He didn't know why, but it probably wouldn't be good for him. He sighed.

"Why so glum, my son?"

"You are beautiful." He gave her a half smile.

"Come," she said and led him deeper into the garden.

When they got to the center of the floral maze, he saw his father waiting. Now he knew the news would be grave.

"Father, what brings you down from Lysara?"

The men shook hands. "It seems you are creating a stir with the Pantheon."

Dagan chuckled. "Obviously, it's more than that."

"To be sure." Enlil moved away with the air of authority that he carried.

Dagan glanced at his mother, whose eyes were downcast. His parents were two of "the Four", the elders of the Naruki race here on Earth. They were part of the Pantheon and helped shape the order of their people.

"The Pantheon is discussing your situation." Enlil clasped his hands behind his back. His long robes brushed the ground as he paced. "This is something we have never encountered before. The thought of a human being your *blethred* is disturbing on so many levels."

Dagan knew that only too well.

"There is talk that maybe we should pull out, bring all the Time Walkers and Dream Walkers back to the fold and disengage ourselves from the humans for a spell. Maybe a century or two."

"No!"

Ninmah and Enlil both glared at him.

"You will do as the Pantheon orders or you may not recover from the punishment."

Dagan saw his mother flinch at Enlil's words.

"That's not the right action to take. You'll leave the humans defenseless against Kur and his army."

Enlil raised his chin. "The *nephili* and *doghume* will still be there to fight."

"And a good fight they would wage, but you know as well as I, that if we do not help them, Kur would prevail and they would all be dead."

"Their deaths would not be easy and the humans would pay an awful price." Ninmah's warm gaze fell to Dagan. "Not all of us agree with that option, and there has not been a final vote made yet."

Enlil grunted.

Dagan clenched his hands into fists. "I will not forsake my duty."

"Because of the female...Reese?"

His anger simmered. "Because it's not the right course of action. The gods created this problem and it is our duty to correct it."

"We will wage an argument before the Pantheon as will Enki, but do not hope for too much."

"I understand, Father. Thank you."

Enlil nodded, kissed his wife's cheek and shimmered away.

Dagan kissed his mother's hand before snapping his fingers. Her worried eyes were a lasting impression on his heart.

Rufus stood on the porch when he appeared. Hearing or sensing Dagan's approach, he quickly spun.

"Any change?"

"Well I haven't seen any *galla* around."

Dagan stared at Rufus, whose gaze roamed the landscape but wouldn't look him in the eye. "What happened?"

"I just want you to take a deep breath and relax, okay?"

Immediately Dagan's spine stiffened and his fists clenched. "Tell me."

Rufus stepped back. "A guy showed up about an hour ago..."

"What guy? Where is he? Is she all right?"

Dagan made to move toward the door but Rufus blocked his way. "She's fine. I've been keeping an eye on them. He's one of her co-workers."

"Is he still in there?"

"Yes." He put his hand on Dagan's chest. "Take deep breaths. You can't barge in there."

"Move." Dagan all but roared the order.

The urge to tear out the stranger's various organs battered at Dagan with relentless zeal. Percilious's words echoed in his head. *"Keep the fury in check and the temper controlled this eve."* He knew. The bastard sorcerer knew this would happen tonight and had been warning him. How much more did he know?

He turned the knob but found the door locked. As if that would keep him out, he mused. Reese obviously didn't want to be disturbed and that infuriated him. With his mind, Dagan shifted the tumblers on the lock. He fought hard to keep the rage under control. He opened the door with a thought instead of using his hand for fear he'd break the knob clean off.

Inside he heard Reese laughing and a deeper voice saying something in a soft tone. His nostrils flared and he caught Reese's fragrance, an arousal scent for him. Did it arouse the other man as well? It damn well better not. With fierce steps, he headed toward the kitchen.

Stopping at the door, his eyes first set on Reese, who wore the same clothes he'd seen her in this morning but now had her hair pulled back in a ponytail. The man sat next to her at the table drinking coffee, the aroma of which gagged Dagan, and laughing from some private joke or amusement he and Reese shared.

He ground his back teeth before saying, "Who the hell are you?"

"Dagan!" Reese jumped up from her chair as though dynamite had been set off underneath her.

The other man slowly rose from his seat and turned to face him with a surprised but curious look on his face. He crossed his arms. "Who the hell are you?"

With a ferocious scowl, Dagan crossed his arms as well. "I asked first."

"Dagan, knock it off," Reese said.

He didn't take his eyes off this newcomer.

"Reese, who's your friend?" the man asked.

She sighed. "Joe, this is Dagan, an..."

Dagan glanced her way with a smirk.

"Acquaintance," she finished. "Dagan, this is Joe, one of my co-workers and a member of my archeology team."

"Why is he here?" Dagan said.

"He's—" She stopped herself and narrowed her eyes in his direction. "Wait a damn minute." Reese stormed over to stand between them and huffed. "I don't need to explain to you why one of my friends is here. This is my house." She glared at him. "How did you get in anyway? I locked the door."

Dagan gave her his most innocent look. "Did you?"

"Ooooooh." Facing Joe she said, "We should probably wrap this up anyway. I'll work out some of the details tonight and see you tomorrow."

"You sure you want me to go?" Joe asked, throwing a side glance Dagan's way.

With fisted hands, Dagan attempted to move around Reese to get to the other male.

"Knock it off both of you," she growled. "Joe, go on home." She pointedly looked at Dagan. "I'll throw the rubbish out before I go to bed."

Joe shook his head and grabbed his coat. As he pushed past Dagan, he called over his shoulder. "If you need me, just call."

Dagan snarled and tightened his fists, imagining those same fists pummeling and bloodying the man. "She'll be fine."

Joe met Reese's eyes with silent meaning then left through the front door. When Dagan spun around, Reese had a pink blush on her cheeks.

"You have feelings for him? That human?" The thought burned him with a potent rage and he hated knowing they worked together, meaning that male would be in close proximity to his woman again.

The pink turned crimson as her temperature and anger rose. "He's my friend. I've known him a hell of a lot longer than I've known you and yes, I have feelings for him."

Dagan closed his eyes and felt his stomach—or was it his heart—drop. She cared for this human. He supposed he should be happy. She would carry on after he had become a mere memory. Why did this revelation not make him feel better? Because he wanted her, dammit. He wanted her under him, on top of him, surrounding him.

This is what the Pantheon worried about, his inability to separate himself from the human female. He'd seal her in for the night and stay outside with Rufus to keep watch. Better yet, Rufus could stand watch and he'd go back to Dilmun or Lysara, find him a willing woman and let himself go. He'd put Reese Whittaker out of his mind for the night.

Not likely, but he could try.

"Are you hungry?"

The softness of her voice broke through his barrier. He opened his eyes to find deep blue waves of emotion crashing over him, drawing him closer. Fighting the need had become extremely difficult. Her light scent grew stronger, as if to lure him to her body, securing his fall from grace with the Pantheon and his parents. She watched him with those lavish blue pools mirroring the very feelings he attempted to resist.

No words were spoken. He picked her up and headed for the living room. She didn't argue or question. Did she feel it too, the overwhelming lust and sexual power?

Dagan knew he had to be alert and steadfast as protector, but when she bit his lower lip and started running her fingers through his hair, he gave in to the sensations.

Supporting her body with one arm, he snapped his fingers and the lights in the entire house went out. Only the roaring fire provided illumination in the room where he now carried her. Without breaking lip contact, he lowered Reese to the plush rug in front of the hearth and rested himself between her legs.

Pulling his shirt up his back and over his head, Reese placed fevered kisses on his chest and shoulder. His previous assessment of her being a vixen now held true, for she would have him naked and inside her very soon. As a purebred, he should do the honorable thing and make her see reason.

"Reese, maybe we should slow down and give you a chance to think about what you're doing."

"Shut up," she said, as she threw the shirt she'd torn off him across the room. "Just shut up, Dagan. I don't want to think anymore because when I do I get frightened about what's happening. When I'm with you, I just feel and that's what I want. I want to feel... you."

He could live with that honest declaration and his purebred libido clawed its way up, refusing to be ignored. Having done the honorable thing in giving her a way out, he felt no remorse now in succumbing to the need.

As he removed her shirt and began sliding her pants down her legs, he said, "I want to lose myself in you." He bent and ran his tongue up her swollen sex, tasting her wetness.

When all obstructions were gone, Dagan settled himself between her legs and feasted on her breasts. Her soft sounds energized him. He longed to taste every inch of her magnificent body and planned to take all night doing so. Kissing her ribcage, her abdomen before tickling her naval, Dagan teased and savored each delectable spot. He planted slow, lingering kisses on her inner thighs. The torture created need because Reese reached down and guided his mouth to that place where she wanted him.

"Dagan, please."

He chuckled. "You're impatient." But he relented and sucked on her tender flesh.

She screamed in climax.

The next thing he knew the front door blasted open and Rufus stood there with a gun in one hand and a knife in the other.

Dagan turned his half-clad body around to block the view of Reese and her nakedness.

When he scanned the room and saw them on the floor Rufus immediately turned his back. "Holy shit, sorry, Dagan. I heard her scream and..."

"Yeah, I figured it was something like that," Dagan said dryly.

"I'll be going now. Are you done for the night—I mean can I go home?"

"Yes. I'll be here for the night and I'll make sure to seal the door."

Rufus snickered. "Night, Reese."

"I need to make sure I lock and seal the door next time."

That jolted her out of her embarrassment and reality came crashing down. Grabbing what clothes she could reach and holding them in front of her body she said, "There won't be a next time." *What in the damn hell got into* me?

"You wanted *me* in you."

She closed her eyes and breathed deep. "Are you reading my mind?"

"Not intentionally."

"This shouldn't have happened." She gazed into the green

eyes rimmed in black. His shadowed jaw clenched, his eyes penetrating.

"A few minutes ago you wanted to feel." He rose up to his knees and grabbed his crotch. "Feel this."

Her gaze lowered to the bulging erection he cupped. She could see the hard outline. She'd had her release and left him unfulfilled. Did he ache—for her? This was madness.

"I'm sorry," she said and ran down the hallway.

He fought the encouragement from his brain to release his ferocious hold on the *fury* and take her now. It would be explosive and virile, everything his race was made of. He stared at the empty hall then fell back down to the floor. "Damn."

A half-hour passed before he moved. After sealing them in, he walked down and knocked on the bedroom door. "Reese, are you asleep?"

"No. Come in."

She sat on the bed in a flimsy nightshirt with her knees pulled up to her chest as though she were protecting herself...from him.

He flinched.

That she thought she had to protect herself from him doused any lingering desires. "I'd like to take a shower if you don't mind."

"Go ahead. There's clean towels in there."

She didn't look directly at him. "Thanks." He needed to submerge himself in ice water for about a week. Instead, he stepped under a hot spray, hung his head and let the pulsating pressure ease the boulder-sized knots between his shoulder blades.

A sudden buzz of electricity coursed through him even before the shower doors opened. So much for relaxing.

In small soft circles, her fingertips worked their way up his spine, each one inching higher working pressure points to ease the tension. At the top, she took her thumbs and pressed them on either side of his spinal cord, and trailed them down his back.

Dagan raised his head. Reese rested her hands on his hips. Should he turn? He couldn't bear to see the hurt look in her eyes again. He liked her better angry. Her temper made his *fury* rise.

She moved her hands around to his chest and lower. The head of his cock jumped when her fingertips brushed across it. Did she mean to torture him?

"If you want to wound and torture me, plunging a knife in my chest would be quicker and more merciful."

Reese splayed her hands on his back. "Wound you? Torture you?"

He spun around and grabbed her arms. "Every time you look at me with those sapphire eyes, every time you smile at another man, every time I touch you and you cringe."

She didn't argue. Lowering her eyes and her voice she said, "I never meant to hurt you."

He released her and she stepped back. A bit of her anger surfaced. "In the last two days my life has fallen out from under me. I have creatures trying to kill me and you trying to bed me. I'm scared and—" she shot her gaze at him accusingly, "—confused."

"I didn't plan this. You draw me to you just by breathing. You crush my barriers like the walls of Jericho with one look, one touch, one smile."

He lowered his head and stroked her pebbled nipple with his tongue. She gasped and relaxed back against the wall. For the second time, he heard the drums thrumming in his head.

He knelt in front of her running his tongue down her stomach, stopping to lave slow circles around her navel. "I am a slave to your whims."

With her hand fisted in his hair and her eyes closed, Reese urged him on. Holding her hips steady, Dagan trailed kisses lower. Her desire wrapped itself around his senses and pulled him into the depths of her passion. "Open for me."

Her eyes shot open. "What?"

"Give yourself to me, Reese."

Hesitantly, she reached between her legs and opened herself, giving him a beautiful view of paradise. The ritual pounding grew louder in his skull, urging him, pressing him to take possession of the woman.

He teased. He bit. He sucked until her essence flowed over his face and she screamed. He stood and lightly bit her shoulder before claiming her mouth. Her tongue tangled with his and he pressed his body against her.

His cock swelled. He thought he would die a thousand deaths when she lightly ran her fingertips from base to tip.

He closed his eyes and ground his teeth. She gently laid her lips across his right pec, then the left, before teasing circles around his dark nipple.

He couldn't breathe. He snaked his arm around her shoulders and turned her so her back pressed against the front of him. Taking a moment, he let her arousal fill his head. With her lavender scented soap, he lathered his hands and ran them down her spine, letting his fingers slide through the crack of her butt cheeks, making it slick. She pressed both her hands against the shower wall as he pumped his hard length with a soapy hand. Leaning against her, he kissed her neck, nipped her shoulder while grinding his cock against the crease of her ass. Reese rubbed her delicious backside against him and they both groaned.

In search of her tender, pouting flesh, he slid his hand down her belly until she gasped. She rocked her hips forward against his hand and back so the slippery crack gripped his cock. He kept constant pressure on her and she increased the rhythm reaching for release.

She was slowly making him crazy. He had to stop. Now. Before he could act on that thought, she cried out. Feeling the tremor of her body set him off. Spasms of his seed spurted up her back and all over her tight ass like a raging volcano.

Dagan remained stoically silent after their shower escapade. She liked seeing the wild, out of control Dagan. It had been a refreshing change from the arrogant, sarcastic, demanding one. She didn't understand why she couldn't think straight around him. As much as she hated to admit it, coming together felt right.

He'd shut off the water, curled a towel around his waist

then bundled her in towels and carried her to the bedroom where he stood her in front of him and proceeded to slowly dry her body. He threw the towels to the floor, lifted the covers and told her to get in bed. Yep, the demanding Dagan had reappeared, giving orders and expecting her to follow them.

Closing his eyes and extending his arms with palms out, Dagan chanted some ancient words and a fire roared to life in the fireplace. Turning, he stalked to the bed, dropped the towel, and climbed in. Giving her no chance to speak, he pulled her to him to lay her head on his chest, and curled his arm possessively around her.

The contented, quiet part of her liked the warmth and hearing his steady heartbeat. The newly awakened, passionate part wanted to crawl on top of Dagan, straddle those narrow hips and ride him hard all night. A need to explore the exotic, sensual planes of this lustful man...no, not a man, but a being, a god, she needed to remember that fact. Despite his origins, Reese had never felt this way about anyone before, and she'd once thought she'd been in love with a guy in college.

Snuggling closer, Reese wondered how she could so easily set aside the fact that right outside her door someone waited to kill her. Perhaps Dagan's job included keeping the mark distracted. How many of the other humans had been female? Maybe he did this with all of them.

"Quit thinking so hard." His voice rumbled in his chest.

"I'm not."

She sensed that knowing grin. "You are. Go to sleep, Reese."

# Chapter Ten

Her mouth felt like she'd swallowed a roll of cotton and her head pounded like a base drum. A strange ringing buzzed her ears and she wished it would cease until she realized it came from her cell phone.

Reese jumped out of the bed, ran over to the dresser and grabbed the squeaking annoyance. "Hello."

"Reese?"

"Joe?"

"Where the hell are you?"

"What do you mean?"

"Well, its eleven o'clock and we were wondering if something had happened."

"Eleven?" She whirled around and looked at the clock. 11:05 a.m. "Oh shit."

"What?"

"I'll be there in a half hour." She slammed the phone down and ran into the bathroom and brushed her teeth. After a quick five minute wash, she dried off, ran to the closet.

"What are you doing?" Dagan's sleepy voice said.

"I was supposed to be at work hours ago. I am so late."

She turned and looked at the sexy man sitting with his back against the headboard and the sheet covering the lower half of his body. What she wouldn't give to turn back the clock and stay here with him in bed, but duty called. She couldn't let her team down.

Hopping on one leg out of the closet as she put her cream-colored, low-waist pants on, Reese cursed under her breath a couple of times because she almost fell on her face. She buttoned, zipped and tucked. With a brush, she bunched her hair up into a single ponytail at the back of her head before clipping her watch on her left arm and slipping the cell phone into her pocket.

Instead of in bed where she thought Dagan would be, she found him leaning against the doorjamb, fully clothed, and fully armed. She blew out a frustrated sigh.

"How do you do that?"

His brows lifted. "Do what?"

She threw her arms up, her hand flopped at the wrist and she gestured to him. "That, standing all casual, completely dressed and waiting, when I'm running around like a crazy woman trying to get ready."

He chuckled. "It always takes women longer to get ready. It's all the doodad things you have to put on and strap to yourself." Dagan shook his head.

Reese snarled. "That's the most sexist thing I've ever heard." She ran her hands down her sides. "Do you see doodad things on me?"

Her watch twisted on her wrist, her ponytail swished with her every movement and dangling earrings swung off her earlobes.

He'd lived a very long time and yet still didn't understand the mind of females. Naruki women had the most precious gems, exquisite gossamer gowns and hair that swept the ground if it wasn't fastened in some sort of pile on their heads. Reese needed none of those things. She was beauty itself with every breath she took and every smile she offered him. If it were up to him, she'd be naked all the time.

"Rufus will drive you into work."

She snickered. "I don't need Rufus to drive me anywhere. I've been on my own a long time. Besides, you might need him to—"

"No!" He straightened to his full height. "I know you are an independent woman, Reese, but now you have the shades of the dead and Kur hunting you. If I'm not with you then Rufus will be. Is that understood?"

She looked as though she would argue further. Her mouth puckered before she blew out an exaggerated breath. "Fine, but I'm already late so we have to leave now."

"He's waiting outside."

He let her precede him through the doorway and watched her lovely backside as he walked down the hall.

"Where are you going?"

"My mother wishes to see me."

She stopped and turned. "You have a mother?"

He stared at her for a moment. "Of course I have a mother. Think you I had been hatched or something?"

"No, I mean, I didn't, no. I just meant you never talk about your family or where you're from and I never thought—oh never mind." She huffed and went to the front door.

Rufus leaned his butt against a green Jaguar and had a goofy smiled plastered on his face. "Good morning," he said.

"Hi," Reese answered. "So I understand you're my guard dog today."

"Yes, ma'am, and happy to be guarding..." he gave her the once over, "...the goods."

Dagan growled a warning to the *doghume*.

Reese smiled. "Perhaps he should be the guard dog."

Rufus laughed.

They were doing it again, laughing and conversing like old friends. Dagan longed to stay, but he hadn't told Reese the reason he'd been summoned back to Dilmun. The Pantheon waited for him.

"Don't let her out of your sight," he told Rufus.

"Yes, *sahib*." Rufus bowed low before Dagan.

"Knock it off." Dagan lobbed one of his throwing stars at Rufus who caught it with his gloved hand.

"Watch the body, man."

"Exactly my point. Watch the body." He glanced at Reese.

Rufus smiled wide before saying, "My pleasure."

Dagan growled again. "Your death wish."

Rufus laughed and slid into the driver's seat since Reese had already gotten into the car.

It looked like it would be another very long day.

When she arrived at her hole-in-the-wall office, the rest of the team had already started compiling the documents they would need for a proposal. Roberta pulled up her list of regular suppliers to begin calls after they determined when and where to deliver everything, should they get permission from the Turkish government. They depended on Reese to get the money.

"Morning all," Reese called when she walked in the door.

"Uh, don't you mean afternoon?" Joe said as he looked at his watch.

"Oh, right, afternoon." She ducked her head, not wanting them to see the blush she felt creeping up her neck.

"Who's this?" Chloe asked as she eyed Rufus.

"Everyone, this is Rufus." She turned to Rufus. "Rufus, this is everyone."

He smiled and waved.

"The one scowling back there in the corner is Joe, my right-hand man," Reese said and pointed in his direction.

"Another one? Where's the badass?"

Rufus lifted a brow, but she shook it off. "You can't see him at the moment but I can hear papers rustling so I know he's there. Geoffrey, grunt or something."

He grunted.

Reese laughed. "Geoffrey Morehouse, our techno geek and researcher. You'll like him. He's a wizard with computers."

"Cool."

Reese unbuttoned her jacket and removed it. Rufus helped her then hung it on a hook by the door.

"The one on the phone is Roberta, our negotiator. She can get us anything and everything we need for a dig." She leaned over to him and whispered. "We're not sure how she does it exactly. We think she's CIA."

Rufus laughed.

"And last but not least is Chloe. She joined us for one of

her class projects and kind of stayed on. She does a little bit of everything."

Rufus walked over to Chloe and sidled up real close. "R-e-a-l-l-y."

Chloe blushed and licked her lips. Rufus took her hand, lifted it to his mouth and kissed her knuckles.

Shaking her head, Reese grabbed him by the shirt sleeve and dragged him toward her desk. "And this is my little part of the universe."

"Nice."

"We like it." She dropped her purse on the floor. "So what are you going to do while I'm working?"

"This and that."

"You're not going to tell me, huh?"

"I'll walk around, keep my eyes and ears open for any unexpected visitors."

"Okay. Now shoo, I need to get to work."

He bowed and left.

The minute Roberta got off the phone she stomped over to Reese's desk followed by the rest of group.

"Okay, spill it. Who the hell is that guy and why do you need a bodyguard?"

Stunned speechless for brief minutes, Reese stared. The hapless Geoffrey had hightailed it over for the pow-wow and she hadn't thought he'd noticed Rufus.

"Spill, Reese," Chloe said. "Who's the hunk?"

Reese sat back in her chair. What should she tell them? How should she tell them? Would they believe her when she did tell them? She rested her forearms on the desk trying to find the right words to explain how she'd spent her weekend. Well, she probably wouldn't go into every detail.

"Reese," Joe barked.

His stern face made her squirm. They were her colleagues and had studied mythology just as she had. She hoped they didn't think she'd lost her mind.

She sighed. "Okay. What I'm about to tell you is going to sound really weird and you're probably going to think I'm insane but I might as well get it over with."

"What happened?" Geoffrey frowned. "Did someone hurt you?"

Their concern warmed Reese. She knew now that she would tell them everything and they would believe her.

"Friday night after I left The Bistro, a man tackled me..."

"Damn, I knew I should have walked you to your car, Reese." Joe raked his hands down his face.

"It's okay, Joe. I wasn't hurt. Dagan protected me."

"Dagan? I thought his name was Rufus." Chloe had a twinkle in her eye.

"No, that is Rufus. I just met him Saturday."

"Why is he here today?" Joe asked.

"Let me start at the beginning."

Roberta nodded. "That would be best."

Reese rose from her chair. The others shuffled out of her way so she could pace.

"As I said, I left The Bistro and walked toward my car, when Dagan tackled me. He's a Time Walker."

Geoffrey hiked his hip onto the desk. "What's a Time Walker?"

"Well, I don't understand all of it yet, but they are able to walk through different centuries hunting Kur and his followers."

Chloe plopped down on the cluttered sofa. "Who's Kur?"

"He's a creature from the Underworld who wants to kill me."

Suddenly, the others surrounded her.

Joe got in her face. "Kill you?"

Reese patted him on the shoulder. "Calm down. That's why Rufus is here and Dagan will be back soon."

"Swell," Joe mumbled.

"Why would this Kur want to kill you?"

This question came from Roberta.

"Put your thinking caps on, my friends, and let's see how much you remember about ancient Sumerian mythology.

"It seems I am a descendent of Enki, the water god. When

123

he attempted to create a life form, he didn't do so well, and Kur is the result of his experiment."

"But why would this creature want to kill you," Geoffrey said.

"To make a long story short, Kur discovered he could suck the life force from humans to sustain and enhance his own. So, he hunts us." She held her hand up when Chloe was going to say something. "My life force has an extra something because I'm a direct descendent of Enki. It draws Kur and he wants it."

Roberta chuckled. "It is all myth, Reese. Stories being told so some guy can get in your pants."

"How did you..." She shook her head and straightened her shoulders. "At first I thought he was crazy too, until these shadow creatures attacked us at my house. I watched him fight and kill them."

Chloe jumped up. "For crying out loud, did you call the police?"

"No." Reese rubbed her hands over her now chilled arms. "Dagan sealed us in the house for the night. He has these powers and he can put a sort of shield over a small area for a few hours which nothing can penetrate."

"So you were locked in your house all night with a total stranger and a man no less?"

*He's definitely all man.* Reese thanked the heavens that no one standing around her could read her mind. She also thought better of telling them he belonged to a race of aliens.

"Who the hell is this guy, and where is he?"

Reese thought Joe's outrage was sweet. "He had to go see his mother."

"His mother?" Geoffrey laughed. "Is he a wuss?"

Reese covered her mouth to stifle a laugh. "Not exactly." She walked to the table where Joe had been sitting when she'd arrived and grabbed the edges. The knuckles of her hand turned white.

"What's wrong?" Roberta's motherly concern wrapped her up in strong arms.

She squeezed her eyes closed trying not to let the tears fall. "I'm amazed at how you guys are more concerned with the man

I spent the weekend with and not the fact that he's the supposed son of gods and fighting demons to save my life."

Chloe waved her hand in the air. "We'll get to that in a minute. You spent the weekend with this guy?"

A short laugh escaped Reese. "Yes, Dagan and I spent the weekend together."

"And?" Chloe prompted.

"And, I'm not going into all that." She bit her bottom lip and looked at her friends. "I need your help. Maybe we can find a way to stop Kur."

"I'm not saying I believe there are creatures from the Underworld about to lay waste to the planet, but the idea is intriguing and it is research into ancient culture so I'll help," Geoffrey said. "We're going to have to know everything about this Kur and the demons that allegedly attacked you."

Joe rubbed his hands together. "Roberta, how about you order us some lunch?"

"You got it."

"Give me about ten minutes," Reese said. "I need to call my dad's office."

"Problems?"

"No, Joe." She smiled at him and wiped a tear away. He knew better than anyone did how rocky things had been with her father since her mother died. "Actually things are looking much better. Dad has agreed to do a client Christmas party."

"That's great, Reese."

"Yes, yes it is. I need to call Tony."

"Okay, we'll get ourselves together while you make your call."

"Thanks." She rummaged through her purse and dug out her cell phone. It only rang once before the vice president of her father's company picked it up. "Hey, Tony this is Reese."

"Hi, kitten. How's things?"

She laughed. "Things are wonderful. I went to see Dad yesterday and I caught him cleaning out Riley's closet."

"What?"

"I know, scary, but it's true."

He sighed. "I guess if he's cleaning out anything, that's a good sign."

"I think so too." She walked to the back of the building to stand by the fire doors. "I spoke to him about a client Christmas party."

"We haven't done one since..."

"I know. I got this idea, hoping to get him talking and it worked."

"Actually, I've had several clients ask about it."

"Well, Dad has agreed to talk to you and Nancy about setting one up this December. I'm sure he'll be calling in the next day or so."

"We'll be ready for it, Reese. This is great news."

She smiled.

"I'll be in touch, kitten."

"Thanks, Tony."

A huge, goofy smile stayed on her face as she walked back toward the group.

"What's the grin for?" Geoffrey asked as he came out of the restroom.

"Today's a good day." She linked her arm through his and they skipped back in the other room.

Chloe came bebopping up. "What's this? Can I join in?"

Geoffrey winked. "Reese says it's a good day. Of course, if I were being chased by demons, I would be more concerned."

The euphoria evaporated and Reese confronted reality again, albeit a bizarre reality.

Joe held out his hand to Reese. "Come over here and sit down before you fall down. Tell us everything we need to know."

Reese took his hand and he led her over to the sofa. He brushed all the books and folders and legal-sized notepads to the floor so she could sit down. For the next couple of hours, she told them everything she knew about Kur, time walkers, and the *galla*.

At dusk, Dagan materialized outside Reese's office, his senses on high alert. Rufus magically appeared out of the darkness.

Night rapidly approached. "What's she still doing here?"

"Working."

He glared at the *doghume*. "It'll be dark soon and that will bring the death seekers."

Rufus inclined his head. "True, but she won't budge. They're working on something she says is very important."

Dagan glared through the window. Reese was smiling at the man from last night, who sat too close to her. The man lazily put his arm around her shoulders and Dagan immediately threw himself into the room and barreled toward the group.

The loud slam of the door brought the discussions to a halt. Reese looked up to see Dagan steaming straight for her.

"Uh oh," she murmured.

Dagan roared, "Get your hand off her."

Joe shot to his feet. "Not you again."

"Do not touch her—ever."

Joe marched around the table and stood toe to toe with Dagan, who towered over him by at least six inches.

"If anyone is bothering Reese, she'll tell them to leave her alone, so you can kiss my ass, Tarzan."

Dagan moved fast and had Joe pushed up against the wall, his feet dangling a couple of inches off the floor.

"Dagan, put him down," Reese yelled.

At that moment, Joe planted his fist in Dagan's face. Blood spewed from his nose.

"Joe!"

Dagan released the man, wiped the blood on the back of his hand and glared hard.

She'd had enough of the testosterone Olympics. Reese picked up the yard stick leaning against the wall, ran up to Dagan and whacked him on the arm. Then she turned and used the thing on Joe.

"Ow," Joe said.

Dagan frowned at her. "Why the hell did you hit me?"

"Because I'm tired of this crap." She shot a dirty look at

them both. "This is not Monday night wrestling and neither of you is my keeper."

She thought she heard Dagan say something about her needing a keeper, but she couldn't hear it well enough to be sure.

Reese noticed Rufus standing by the front door with his hand on the knife he had in a sheath under his jacket. This situation could have gotten ugly. Both Roberta and Chloe had their mouths hanging open and were staring at Dagan, as if he'd stepped out of a movie magazine. Geoffrey leaned back against the side door, his foot propped against the wall and a huge smile on his face. This was the most bizarre evening she'd had, well, since Dagan tackled her on Friday.

Chloe finally came to her senses and said, "So this is him, the he-man?"

Reese chuckled. "Yeah, all six-foot-plus inches of him." She eyed Dagan appreciatively. "When he's not frowning and doing that whole intimidation thing, he's actually fairly nice to look at."

"Oh, I don't know, Reese." Chloe tapped her chin as she walked around Dagan. "He's pretty nice to look at now."

Rufus laughed from his place near the door. Dagan shifted and threw laser beams of warning at him.

"What the hell is going on here, Reese? It'll be dark soon and you need to get home."

Joe readjusted his shirt and brushed off the sleeves. "You're not her keeper." He sneered.

Dagan took a step toward him and Reese put herself between the two men. "Look you two. If we are going to be working together, you need to make nice."

"What?" Dagan bellowed.

She placed her hands on his chest. "This is my team. Roberta, Chloe, Geoffrey and... Joe. Guys, this is Dagan." She looked up at him and smiled. "My hero."

Joe snickered. Dagan narrowed his eyes in Joe's direction.

"I've explained the situation to them and we have been doing research to see if we can dig up any useful information about Kur."

"Useful information? Rufus!"

She nodded. "To see if we can find a way to stop him."

Rufus slid up next to him. "You called?"

He had the most dumbfounded expression. "You let her tell all these people about us?" he whispered loudly.

Rufus shrugged. "Couldn't stop it. She opted to tell them the truth when they asked about her..." he coughed into his hand, "...bodyguard."

"Great, just great. Like I don't have enough problems already, now I have to do a *go'ras* on her whole team."

Darkness descended. Reese opened her mouth to say something else, but he raised his hand and turned. Rufus had already moved back to his position, closed and locked the door and drawn his weapons.

"*Galla.*"

Rufus frowned. "I felt the charge the minute they appeared."

"What's happening, Dagan?"

"We have company and this isn't the most ideal place to take on the warriors of the Underworld."

Reese tensed. "More of those shadow things?"

Dagan moved toward the window to gaze out at the street. The night held an eerie silence. A light mist gathered over the street. The temperature dropped several degrees in a matter of seconds.

"A large group," Rufus replied. "I count ten. Damn."

"Why did it get so cold all of a sudden?" Roberta asked.

"You're about to get a crash course in fighting demons," Rufus said.

Geoffrey ran the short distance until he stood next to Chloe. "Cool."

Rufus nodded toward the back of the room. "Come on." The rest of the group followed. He stopped long enough to inform Dagan of what he'd seen. "Two are yellow-eyed demons."

Dagan's nostrils flared and his eyes narrowed. He spoke in his ancient tongue. Unfamiliar with the language, she was pretty sure he'd been swearing.

Reese went up to Dagan. "What are you going to do?"

He rested his palm against her cheek and rubbed her bottom lip with his thumb. "Protect you." He leaned down and kissed her. "But first, I'm going to call in some help."

"Flame?"

"He's the closest." He moved away from the window to a secluded part of the tiny room.

Reese stared out into the darkness. The dense fog hung low over the pavement, curling and floating around fixtures and doorways. The temperature plummeted so much more that she could see her breath in the air. Dark beings of all shapes and sizes formed in front of her eyes. She gasped and Dagan instantly materialized at her side.

"We will be surrounded," Dagan yelled out to Rufus.

"I'm on it." Rufus grabbed Geoffrey and they headed toward the back of the building.

Dagan pulled out one of his Magnums and handed it to Reese. Moving behind her, he lifted her arms. "Stand with your feet shoulder-width apart, point and shoot. It will give you some stability. These are special bullets. If you hit the *galla* in the head they will disintegrate."

"Okay."

He kissed her neck then went to check on the rest of the group.

In her boring life, she'd never used a weapon or ever thought she'd have to, although her cousin had once shown her how to shoot.

Reese peered out to see the creatures closing in. Across the street, under a lamppost she saw Kur, tall, blond and dangerous with a big smile on his face. He waved, she shuddered.

"Can't you just do your seal thingy?" Reese called out.

"It drains me of energy." He glanced out the window. "I'm going to need all my energy for this."

"Pity," Joe mumbled as he walked by. "Seems even gods—" he looked Dagan up and down, "—have limitations."

"I don't like your friend," Dagan said to Reese after Joe

went by.

She laughed. "It seems he doesn't much care for you either."

He grunted.

"But, if we're going to work together, you two are going to have to get past it." She placed her hand on his chest. "Dagan, please. Do it for me."

He rolled his eyes. She knew that one would work.

"Fine," he grumbled. "But if he hits me again, I won't hold back."

The lights went out. Reese groped for his hand. "Oldest trick in the book."

He chuckled. "Then why are you trying to cut off the circulation in my hand?"

She loosened her grip. "Sorry, but I've had this face to face before and I don't really look forward to it again."

"No worries, Reese."

She spun around to see Rufus and her friends armed with tubes that looked to be part of metal shelving, broom handles that had been carved into spears and a large kitchen knife. They were ready to face the enemy.

"Oh my," she breathed.

"Are we set?" Dagan asked.

"As much as we can be," Rufus replied. "Geoffrey and Chloe are in the back. We've secured the doors and windows." He smiled. "That Chloe seems to know her stuff."

Dagan looked at Reese. "I want you in the middle so you're surrounded by everyone and keep your head down."

"But I want to fight." She raised her chin. "I'll not have you and my friends fighting this battle alone when I'm the one he wants."

He clenched his jaw, a familiar sight. "If you get caught then we are doing this for nothing."

"And if I let my team fight and one of them gets hurt, I won't be able to live with myself. I'm fighting."

Joe snickered. "You might as well pack it in. You can never win an argument with her."

"Besides, you already gave me this gun." Reese held it up and waved it around.

Dagan grabbed the barrel. "Watch it, would you? You're going to shoot someone."

"That's the idea. Don't stand in my direct line or it might be your ass I hit."

He threw her a devilish grin. "We'll have that discussion later."

She felt the blush creep up her body.

"All right. You are the second line of defense." He pulled her back to the desks where they had piled boxes up on top and made a cubby in between. "You stay here behind the boxes. You can point the barrel through the crack. If they get past us, it's up to you. Is that good enough?"

She had a fallen look. "It's all you'll allow anyway, isn't it?"

"Yes."

"Fine!" She plodded back to the desks and set herself down in the crevice.

"These creatures know how to use guns," Dagan yelled out to the others. "Shoot before they get too close. The demons with the yellow eyes will only go for Reese. She is their target. If you get between them and their target, don't let them touch you."

Roberta said, "How will we see them in the dark?"

"You won't have a problem. Their eyes glow a bright yellowish color."

"Any weaknesses?" Joe called from one of the windows.

Rufus nodded. "They can't stand bright light. That's why they killed the power."

"Good to know."

Roberta came out from behind the bookcase. "We have some flashlights in the storage room."

"Why don't you get those," Rufus said. "They could come in handy."

Roberta rushed past him and disappeared into the back of the building. A couple of minutes later she reappeared with three silver flashlights and extra batteries. "I'm not sure how long the batteries have been in these, so I brought extras."

Reese stood and watched her pass out the beacons of hope. "See," she said to Rufus, "I told you she's from the CIA."

He laughed just as glass rained down from the skylight.

"Reese, down," Dagan hollered and came running back to engage the enemy. "Rufus, watch the front door."

He reached behind his head and pulled out his sword. The *galla* jumped down to the floor and raised its hand toward the front door.

"'Fraid not, friend," he said in a steely voice. "Your playmates are going to have to find their own way in."

Dagan swiftly swung the sword in a wide arc and sliced through the demon's neck in a smooth motion. It turned to smoke and dissipated.

Joe ran to the spot where the creature had stood. "What happened to it?"

"Rule one." Dagan smiled. "Decapitation is the only way to totally destroy this enemy. Injuring them, even severely, returns them to the Underworld where they can heal, gain strength and return again."

Joe gave a thumb's up. "Got it, cut their heads off. Got anymore of those nice swords with you?"

"Afraid not. This one was built special just for me."

"Swell. Some help you are," Geoffrey murmured.

"Do the best you can."

The next attack came two-fold. One broke out the window where Joe stood and another rammed the back door. Chloe hid until the demons rushed in. She slid a long, curved knife from behind her back under the short-waisted jacket she wore and cleanly sliced through the creature's neck. Another appeared behind it and she pulled a small metal ball out of her jacket pocket and threw it at the black demon. The ball easily melted through its skin and a small explosion shattered it into a zillion pieces.

"Nice job," Dagan said when he ran in to help her. "We need to talk."

"Later, doll face. We're a little busy right now."

"Point taken." He frowned. "But I expect a few answers."

She smiled. "You'll get them." She ran off toward where Joe

fought off another member of the death squad.

Dagan drew his Magnum and shot the next creature trying to come through. He picked up the door and put it back in place. He pointed his forefinger at the door frame and a small beam of light extended, fusing the door to the frame. Using his power, he moved heavy boxes in front of it to give added resistance.

Others had come in the front. Geoffrey had one of the broom handle stakes jabbing at the creature who was a little on the short side. He seemed to be holding his own.

Dagan swung around when he heard a loud crash. Roberta had just broken a lamp over a creature's head. "Take that you piece of demon trash."

He smiled. Reese's friends were definitely an interesting group.

Rufus tripped over something lying on the floor and fell to one knee. One creature approached, glaring and ready to strike. Out of nowhere, Chloe appeared, stabbing it in the back.

"Thanks, beautiful."

"See me later." She beamed and ran off.

"Shit," Reese yelled.

By the time Dagan got there, a yellow-eyed *tregorian* had Reese cornered. It stood eight-foot tall in flowing black garments and a colorless, decomposed arm with long deadly fingers reached for her.

"Oh no you don't," she cried, grabbing a large, fat book that lay within reach and hurled it at the creature's cloaked face.

Dagan flew over and brought the sword down heavy across its back. When it turned, he stabbed the tip into its stomach. A horrible howl shook the windows before the thing lifted to the ceiling and turned to smoke.

"Where's the gun?"

"I dropped it and couldn't get to it fast enough."

With grim features he said, "You okay?"

"Never better."

The smile she gave him was as brilliant as the sun. He retrieved the gun, winked at her and went back to work.

Roberta turned one of the flashlights on a creature. It let out a heinous screech, the likes of which could probably have shattered glass, if she hadn't whacked it upside the head before staking it with a broom handle.

The second yellow-eyed creature snuck up behind Reese, who concentrated on the battles in front of her. It whirled her around and grabbed her neck with its scaly fingers. A slight tingling of euphoria sparkled through her body. Her arms fell loosely and the gun slipped from her fingers and clattered to the floor. She needed to fight and not succumb to the lethargy threatening to overtake her. Calling forth her rage and anger, she tried in vain to break the hold the *tregorian* slime trapped her with. "*Dagan*," she mentally called out to him.

A few seconds seemed like an eternity and she felt herself slipping away when suddenly the demon's grip loosened and vanished. Joe caught her as she started to fall.

Slowly, the haze lifted. She reached up and gently touched her neck to see if the beast had left a mark.

Looking up into Joe's eyes, she said, "What happened?"

Dagan roared, hurling his way toward her, stabbing and decapitating any demon who dared get in his way.

The crowd of *galla* thinned.

Hearing the anguish torn from Dagan, Reese crawled to her knees and pushed Joe out of the way so she could see him. Locking eyes with her, he stumbled to a stop.

"What the hell are those things?" Geoffrey's raspy voice called out.

"Another kind of demon." Dagan turned to cut down another opponent.

In a blaze of light that sent the remaining *galla* retreating, Flame appeared.

"Sorry I'm late," he called out to Dagan. "Got tied up following a swarm in the seventeenth century."

"Thanks for coming." Dagan nodded then stopped to look at her.

Sensing his need for some kind of reassurance, she called out, "I'm here, I'm fine."

Flame had dual swords hung on his hips. He unsheathed

them and roared before he and Dagan clanged the tips of their swords together then ran out the front of the building and took the death squad head-on.

"Oh my God," Reese screamed and ran awkwardly to the door.

Battered and bruised but still standing, the others rushed to the windows to watch the masters in the art of destroying the enemy. With a skill born of centuries fighting this evil, the time walkers plowed a path through the enemy toward Kur, who laughed while he watched the show. In their wake they left puffs of smoke and fiery bright lights as one by one, the *galla* fell.

Before he vanished, Kur straightened his jacket and said, "Your time is coming, Dagan."

In the next instant, Kur and his minions disappeared.

Bearing cuts, bruises, some nasty burn marks and one thick gash on his right thigh, Dagan limped into the building.

Reese ran to him. "What have you done to yourself?"

"I'm fine." Callused, bloodied fingers tentatively touched her cheek.

Flame strolled in with one sword propped against his shoulder. "Damn, Dagan, you look like hell."

Dagan shot him a nasty retort in his ancient language.

Flame shrugged. "Well you do."

"He's right, you're a mess," Reese said and lowered to take a look at the slice in his thigh.

"It will..."

Shoving his hand aside, she said, "I know, I know. It will heal quickly." She grabbed a fallen dagger and cut the leather away. "Let me look at it anyway."

Flame sidled up. "Rufus and I are going to take a look outside."

Geoffrey limped over. "You're not going out there again. It's still dark."

Chloe arched a brow. "What happened to your leg?"

"I banged into the corner of a desk pretty hard when one of those demons lunged at me."

"We work best at night," Flame assured him. He snapped his fingers as he crossed the threshold and the door reappeared in its original condition, hung in place.

"Cool," Chloe exclaimed.

Reese dragged on Dagan's sleeve. "Come on, let's go in the bathroom so I can clean you up a little."

She shook and fought the urge to crawl back into a dark hole and hide. She'd been terrified when that thing had grabbed her, locked in her mind and unable to move, until she felt nothing. Every worry and concern had floated away and she couldn't control it. If Dagan argued with her right now she'd come unglued.

"Get some of this stuff picked up, barricade all the entrances again, and post guards at the windows and doors until Rufus and Flame get back," he told Chloe.

Chloe saluted. "Right."

The lights flickered and came back on. "Flame must have fixed the power."

Reese preceded Dagan into the small bathroom. When he closed the door, he pulled her into his arms.

"It's okay, we're okay," he whispered.

With her face smashed into his chest she mumbled, "You're not okay, you're dripping blood all over the floor." He chuckled and she raised her eyes to his. "I don't think I can get used to that."

"What?"

"You running out the door and taking on the whole army."

"It wasn't a real army. There were only about fifteen of them and we had finished off more than half before Flame got here."

"Still, it's unnerving to see you do it."

"It's what I do, Reese."

She shoved him back. "That doesn't make it any easier for me."

He braced his back against the door. "I wish the mind wipe would have worked."

"Why, so you could be rid of me?" She started going

through the cabinet looking for first aid supplies.

"No." He grabbed her and turned her to face him. "Because I can't stand to see you upset like this. It would be better if you just forgot me."

"Sit."

He sat on the toilet. Reese wet a washrag and dabbed at his face. He hissed when she touched one cut along his jaw.

"Big tough guy. You can rush out to take on a death squad but get wimpy when I try to clean your wounds."

His eyes were level with her breasts so he leaned forward and nuzzled his face between them, settling his hands on her hips so she couldn't pull away.

With a small laugh she said, "Stop. Let me finish. You heard Flame. You look like hell."

"But I would much rather stay here," he cooed and nuzzled her again.

"I'm sure," she replied dryly. "Ever the man, no matter what species, but I need to clean these. And shouldn't you be guarding something?"

"I'm guarding you."

"You're pawing me."

He kissed the valley between her breasts. "Same thing."

"Not." She lightly shoved him back. "Now be still so I can do this."

"Yes, ma'am."

She lifted a brow. "I think this is the first time we haven't argued about something since we met."

"Is it?"

She nodded. "I kind of like it."

"I'm sure it will be short-lived."

Playfully slapping him on the shoulder, she continued to wash the grime and blood from his face. The smaller cuts had already started healing but the process seemed slower.

"Take your pants off."

A devilish grin curved his lips. "Be still my heart."

She rolled her eyes. "Just let me get this mess of a leg

bandaged."

He faked a frown. "Alas, shot down again."

Her hands flew to her hips. "Dagan."

"Oh all right." He stood and lowered his pants.

Doing her best to ignore the fact that he wore no underwear, Reese rinsed out the washrag using warm water then gently cleansed the area.

"Damn." He hissed.

"Should it hurt like that?"

He threw her that "duh" look. "Reese, though my injuries heal quickly, I still experience pain like any human male."

"They don't appear to be healing that quickly though."

He nodded. "It's because I'm weakened."

"What?"

Dagan grabbed her hands between his and rubbed them. "I'm a little weak from using magick and fighting demons." He smiled. "It will pass."

"But what if we go another round?" She glared at the door.

"Then I'll do my job. Besides, your team did a damn good job fighting. I'm undeniably impressed."

She lowered her eyes and smiled.

"Dagan." Rufus knocked on the door.

He jumped up and pulled on his pants. When he opened the door, Rufus looked askance at his attire.

"What's up?"

Rufus motioned for him to come out into the hall.

"I'll be right back," he told Reese.

"I got a phone call a minute ago from Gideon."

That got Dagan's attention. "What did he say?"

"That activity at Clive Whittaker's house has increased. They're not attacking yet, but they're scoping the place out."

"Damn."

"I thought you'd want to know."

Chloe strolled up to them. "Hey, guys, what's up?"

Dagan crossed his arms over his chest and in a no-

nonsense tone said, "Let's discuss your abilities and those weapons you just happened to have on your person."

She crossed her arms too.

"Who are you and what are you doing here?"

Chloe sighed. "My name is Chloestra. I was sent here by my sister at the request of Enki to protect Reese."

Rufus whistled through his teeth.

"Who's your sister and what does she have to do with Enki?"

"Ashima."

"*Shakaah*," Dagan grimaced.

Rufus looked between the two. "What am I missing?"

"Goddess Ashima." Dagan frowned in his direction. "You would know her as the Divine Fate."

Rufus smiled. "Cool." He shuffled closer to Chloe. "You have one badass spin-kick. Do you have any powers?" He wiggled his eyebrows at her.

She tickled his chin with two fingers. "That's a private conversation for later, handsome."

"Knock it off. Rufus, go check things out front."

Rufus winked at Chloe. "Later."

After Rufus disappeared around the corner, Dagan grilled Chloe further. "So why would Enki ask Fate to watch over Reese?"

"She didn't tell me. All I know is that she asked me to do it. I thought it sounded like an interesting gig, so she created a scenario where I could get on Reese's team. They have memories that say I've been on the group for over a year, but the truth is, I arrived two days ago."

Reese opened the bathroom door. "Hey, are you going to..." She glanced between Dagan and Chloe and their closeness. "Sorry, didn't mean to interrupt." She slammed the door.

"You're in for it now." Chloe smiled and took off. "See ya."

Dagan ran his hand through his matted hair. "This is turning into a nightmare, and I don't dream." He opened the door. "Reese, I—"

"Don't," she snapped. "You don't owe me anything. I'll let

you finish your clean up so I can go talk to Joe."

Dagan crashed the door closed. "The hell you will. You'll hear me out."

She spun around and jabbed her finger into his chest. "Stop ordering me around like you have the right, because you don't. No one orders me around." Her voice rose an octave in pitch.

"Maybe someone should." His rose as well.

She tried to get around him to leave the room but it was too small and he was too large. "Get out of my way."

"No." He pulled her close and crushed her mouth with his. One minute kissing her and the next hoisting her onto the sink to shove his hands under her shirt. He needed to touch her and not just in one spot, he needed to touch all of her, with his hands, his mouth, his tongue.

Reese wrapped her legs around his waist and frantically pulled at his shirt. All concern for his injuries pushed back to make room for the desire clawing at her insides.

Dagan trailed kisses down her neck and bit her shoulder blade. He caressed her breasts. She hadn't noticed he'd undone her pants until his fingers were playing with her clit and she grew wet.

A loud pounding on the door stopped them both.

"Dagan, I need to talk to you." Flame.

Dagan removed his hands from her and rested his forehead against hers trying to catch his breath and gain control again. "Give me a minute."

"Now."

A growl rumbled deep in Dagan's throat. He pulled back putting as much distance between them as he could in the small space. "You okay?"

She tugged on her shirt to put it in place. He helped her down and she refastened her pants, and ran her fingers through her tousled hair before nodding.

Disgruntled, Dagan flung opened the door. The grimace he gave his friend was met and countered with a sneer.

"Excuse me," Reese said as she rushed past them to join the others.

"What the hell?"

"Have you lost your faculties?" Flame said in a loud whisper. "I could feel it happening all the way in the other room."

Dagan averted his eyes.

"How far has it gone?"

"I'm still able to control it," Dagan assured him.

"But it gets harder each time, doesn't it?" He grabbed Dagan's arm in a vise grip. "Doesn't it?"

"Yes."

"What are you going to do?" He paced a short distance away from Dagan. "If the Pantheon finds out, you'll be punished again. Your second time will be worse. They'll not go easy on you."

"I know that," Dagan barked. "Enlil is not pleased with this development. Shit, I'm not pleased with it, but I can't ignore it."

Flame stopped and shot him a pitying look. "I'm sorry. That's punishment enough already."

What his friend didn't know was that it was already too late. He'd lost small increments of control. Touching her, kissing her, tasting her were all things he remembered with distinct clarity and hungered to do again. He yearned to feel silky strands of her hair caress his fingers as he feasted on her delicious mouth.

Dagan leaned against the wall and braced his right foot. "I'm going to need a safe place to put Clive Whittaker. Gideon says the *galla* have found him."

"I'm sure Rufus can arrange something."

"I need to see Enki again. He has sent extra protection for Reese and I want to know why."

"Extra protection?"

"Chloe, the blonde in the other room is Ashima's sister."

"Why would he do such a thing?"

Dagan put his foot down and moved away from the wall. "She's special and that means something. I need to find out what."

"I won't tell you this is foolish." He placed a hand on

Dagan's shoulder. "So I'll say be cautious. I don't know what game Enki plays but it may end with you wishing for death."

They grasped forearms.

Flame grinned. "Death to Kur and all his shit-eating demons."

"Strength to our warriors for victory over the creature."

A sweet voice called out. "If you guys are done with all the rah rah crap, daylight is coming."

Glancing over, Dagan caught the back of Chloe rounding the corner.

He had work to do.

# Chapter Eleven

While Dagan, Flame and Rufus patrolled the building and surrounding area disposing of all signs of what had taken place there last night, Reese and the others were in an excited discussion.

Geoffrey said, "I wouldn't have believed it had I not seen it with my own eyes."

"Makes you wonder what else is out there." Roberta cast a long look outside.

Reese placed her hand over Roberta's. "Let's take one thing at a time."

Joe leaned back in his chair and easily stretched his arm across the back of Reese's chair, shifting his body to get a closer look at the passage she'd been reading.

"It's best to start at the beginning. Go back as far as necessary until we find the first mention of the creature. We need any information on its origins, weaknesses and the like."

"I guess the dig is on hold, then," Chloe said cheerfully.

A steely voice came from behind her. "You won't be staying."

Reese stiffened and noticed how close Joe sat to her. She knew it wouldn't bode well with Dagan.

"What do you mean?"

Although he stood behind her, she knew his appearance must be wild, gauging by the looks on the other's faces.

"May I have a word?" he ground out.

Uh oh, quietly polite, this couldn't be good.

She got up and had to shove Joe's torso with her knee to get him to move. He grinned at her, knowing full well the effect it would have on Dagan. She owed him a kick.

"We were making plans to settle in and get to this research."

He frowned. "You and I will be leaving as soon as Flame and Rufus are finished with their sweep."

"Why?"

"We need to go see your father."

She paled, her breath caught. "My father? Has something happened to him?"

"No, not yet, but we may need to find a safe place for him until this is over."

"They found him, didn't they?" She bit her bottom lip with worry. "In the general vicinity but I've had someone doing surveillance to keep me informed."

She squeezed his hand. "Thank you for that."

He gave her a curt nod. "We need to go."

"Okay, let me grab my purse and say goodbye to everyone."

As she started to walk away, he said, "Tell Joe to keep his distance. My patience is wearing thin."

She opened her mouth to reply to that command but closed it and spun around, hugging each one. Even Chloe hugged her before Reese left them and joined him again.

Flame and Rufus came in.

"All set." Flame nodded to Reese. "Hi again."

"Hi." She smiled brightly.

Dagan shifted his stance and glared at his friend. Flame glared back.

"Are you coming with us, Flame?"

"No, I have my own duties. I'll get back to them." He lifted her hand and kissed her knuckles. "Don't fear, my lady, I'll be but a phone call away." A low rumble had him lifting his head and grinning before he disappeared, leaving small sparkles of light.

Rufus was shooting glances Chloestra's way. "Um, I think I'll stay here and help with the research." He laced his fingers together and cracked his knuckles. "I'm a wizard with a computer after all and have vast knowledge and experience where Kur is concerned." He winked at Reese and left to join the others at one of the multitude of laptops set up in the cramped space.

"Come." Dagan hurried her out the door around the corner to her car.

She hesitated.

"Don't worry. We checked it out. It hasn't been tampered with."

She breathed a sigh, unlocked the doors and got in. He slid into the passenger seat.

Kur roared his frustration and anger through Divinity. The servants scurried out of his way and the soldiers tried to meld with the marble walls in an attempt to escape his wrath.

"How can an entire squad of *galla* be defeated by one time walker and a bunch of humans? The *tregorians* are supposed to be relentless. They should have had Reese Whittaker."

Feral rolled the gold coin across his fingers. "Fleck said having another time walker show up, and the *doghume* there proved to be a daunting show of force. Even the gangly fleshies were fighting well enough to hold their own."

Kur picked up a Ming vase from its stand near the door and hurtled it to the wall, shattering the priceless piece of art into tiny pieces. "I do not want to hear excuses, Captain. I want results."

"What are your orders?"

"I must think on it a while." Kur walked over and sat on his throne. "Do we have any humans left in the holding tank?"

"Two vagrants and we picked up a lawyer earlier this evening."

Kur sneered. "Bring me the lawyer. Let the homeless have a few more hours of life."

Feral bowed. "As you wish, my king."

"And have the *galla* bring my wife to me after I've finished with the human."

Feral left to carry out his orders.

146

The *tregorians* were known to be excellent trackers. This line of *galla* was slightly different because when assigned a target, they belonged to only that target. They would do everything it took to acquire it. Perhaps he had underestimated Dagan's resolve, which was interesting. This human female obviously held some special meaning for Dagan.

Moments later, two soldiers dragged the lawyer into the throne room.

He begged and pleaded, offered money, information, even free legal representation before becoming a mass of blubbering flesh. Kur's temper boiled. The hunger reared in him. He stalked over, grabbed the human by the neck and lifted him six inches off the floor.

The human quit his wallowing and pissed his pants. Kur lowered him to eye level and stared into his eyes. He felt his gaze go crimson and watched the male's skin wither as he inhaled the life force. White bolts of energy flowed from the human's body to his, filling him with renewed vigor. When the transfer was complete, Kur flung the now empty shell to the floor.

"To coin a human phrase, 'Damn what a rush'." His body shook like a dog after a thorough bath. Already his cock pulsed and a renewed conviction to have his enemy's progeny flared.

The *galla* brought in his wife. Her hands were still in manacles. He'd made sure there were cloths wrapped around her wrists so as not to mark her skin. He took the chains from the servant.

"Take that with you." He pointed to the dead body. "Do not disturb me until I call."

The shadow creatures didn't respond. They picked up the body and closed the massive doors when they left.

"Come, wife. I need some comfort from you this night."

The gag still filled her mouth but she watched him carefully.

He pulled her along to a wall on the opposite side of the room from the throne. He pushed a small panel and an enormous door swooshed aside. The bed took up much of the room. A bed fit for a king, Kur thought. Someday soon his wife would reside here with him, willingly.

Moving them toward the bed, he felt the resistance on the chains. She began to retract her arms and try to reverse her steps.

"Now, now, Ereshkigal, I need you to be with me tonight."

She vigorously shook her head and started making keening sounds. Her eyes widened with fear. This made him angry. His wife should want to be with him, to comfort him.

He needed to calm himself. "I wish to remove the gag from your mouth and feed you. Would you like that?"

She dropped her hands and stopped retreating. He knew she hadn't eaten in days. He regulated everything having to do with his wife. She would come to depend on him for her very life and he wanted it that way.

"Do you want me to feed you, wife?"

The debate waged clear on her face and hunger must have won out because she nodded and came toward him. Kur looked down into her bronzed, beautiful, tear-drenched face. Her amber eyes studied his every move.

He had her bathed every day to be fresh whenever he felt the need to see her. Reaching up, he grasped a chestnut lock of hair, rubbing it between his fingers and imagining how it would feel to have her above him, looking down with adoring eyes and this soft hair caressing his body.

Those images caused his cock to swell. Maybe tonight he would be able to make sweet love to his wife and bring them both pleasure.

"Stand still," he said, and reached behind her head to untie the gag.

When he pulled it free from her mouth, she coughed a couple of times and rolled her tongue around her lips.

"Come over here." He moved toward a large black stone table in the far corner. "There is wine and food."

He smiled when he heard soft footfalls trailing him.

When she reached for some food, he lightly slapped her hand. "No. I will feed you."

Her hands fell limply to her sides, the chains clanging with the motion.

He picked up the goblet filled with a sweet mixture. Taking

the first sip into his mouth, he moaned with bliss and felt the power of the wine and human blood, which always gave him a buzz. Slowly and with careful precision, he lowered the goblet to her lips. She drank greedily, but he didn't mind.

"Enough," he said and pulled the cup away. "We don't want you getting sick." He set the wine down and picked up a ripe strawberry. Smiling, he dangled the fruit in front her mouth, which she opened. He watched hungrily as she opened wider, and fantasized about stuffing his cock into that hole and how good it would feel.

She made small noises, impatient to have the food. "Wait," he ordered. "Close your mouth."

She complied but narrowed her eyes at him.

He bit the tip of the berry off and chewed. "Ummmmm." Then, he took the juicy portion and rubbed it across her lips over and over. Leaning in, he kissed her, licking the juice from her lips. "So sweet," he murmured.

He kissed her five more times as he fed her food. Ereshkigal did not fight or retreat during the whole time. This pleased him and his temper abated.

"Well, now that we've had something to eat, wife, let's see what you can do for me."

Kur picked up the chains which he had dropped during their meal and led her toward the bed.

"No." Her voice sounded raspy and not quite whole.

"What, wife?"

"No," she said again and began to pull away.

Keeping a smile pasted on his face, he tugged the chains harder causing her to stumble against him. "You will do as you are told." He crushed his lips on hers, punishing. When he ended the kiss and leaned away, she spit in his face.

Anger ripped through his body. He wiped the spittle from his cheek. How dare she spit on him, the king?

Grabbing the manacles, Kur threw the chains through the rings in the ceiling and secured them to the wall.

"Let me go," she screamed.

He stormed over to the armoire in the corner and flung open the door.

Ereshkigal cried out. "Release me, release me." Yanking on her chains caused them to tighten and the cloth around her right wrist broke loose, exposing her skin to the rusted metal on the cuff. It rubbed a raw spot that began to bleed.

"Now look what you have done," Kur growled as he spun around, holding a riding whip. "I'll have to heal your wrist as well."

He pulled tight on the chains and hooked them a second time so her arms were held high above her head. "You will have to be taught how to properly act, wife," he sneered. "You will do as you are told and pleasure me when I demand it."

"Although you performed the ceremony, I am not your wife," she spat. "I am not."

The energy he absorbed from the human still had him riding high. He walked behind her, grabbed the top of her shift and ripped it off her body, leaving her naked back to him. The riding whip had tassels at the end and he brushed those across his hand.

"Some day you will acknowledge your position as my wife and queen of this kingdom. Then, you will cherish your place at my side. You are mine and will remain so."

The first lash stopped her struggles for a moment, but she resumed screaming insults and tearing the skin off her wrists. He brought the whip down harder. When one of the welts broke open, he frowned. He did not want to mar her skin that way. Walking over to the cabinet that held his tools, he pulled out a long wood plank. Returning to his position, he began to swat her bare ass. Once, twice, three times. Her naked flesh turned a stinging red. She had stopped struggling and her screaming turned to whimpers.

"You shouldn't make me angry," he told her. "I do not wish to punish you so. If you would only accept what is."

He placed the paddle on the shelf and lifted out a large golden dish adorned in expensive jewels containing a creamy salve. Releasing the chains, he pulled them down from the ceiling. "Go lay across the bed, on your stomach, with your arms stretched out in front of you."

She hiccupped and softly cried, but complied with his order.

150

When she had positioned herself the way he wanted, he dropped the chains to the floor. The weight of them kept her arms in place. The massive bed supported her entire body so that only a portion of her legs hung off the other side and he stepped between them.

Digging his fingers into the jar, he scooped the silky smooth salve and rubbed it in both palms before placing his hands on his wife's ass and massaging the balm into her heated skin.

Her crying renewed. He stared at her soft, hot skin. The welt that had bled would clear up quickly. They always did.

The blooming red color made him think of the human's blood and the rush he'd received from sucking the life out of him. He unzipped and dropped his pants, releasing his cock, which jerked out away from his body. Dipping his fingers into the creamy substance again, he took one coated hand and wrapped it around his aching cock. He moved closer to the bed and used the other hand to knead her ass.

"I want you to squirm for me, wife. Buck your ass in the air up and down like you are riding me."

She didn't move.

"Do it," he yelled. When she began to buck her pelvis so her ass advanced into his hand and then retreated, he stroked his cock in time with her movements until he exploded and ejaculated all over her back.

Smiling he said, "Soon, you will have all of this..." he rubbed his cock in the crease of her ass, "...here." He took two fingers and pushed them gently through her folds.

Soon, he would consume the life force of Enki's descendants and with the power would consummate his marriage to the Goddess and make his mark not only on Earth, but in Dilmun as well.

# Chapter Twelve

"Explain to me about those yellow-eyed creatures. How are they different from the others?"

"They are called *tregorians*. They are assigned a specific target and they belong to that one target. It is their only purpose. They will keep coming until they succeed." Unfortunately, he knew of no way to permanently kill that type of demon.

She shivered. "Great."

"Kur is getting restless."

"Why did I suddenly feel lethargic when it touched me?"

His head whipped around. "One of them touched you? When?"

"It came up behind me and grabbed my arm, but I had on long sleeves. With its other hand, it grasped my neck. I felt fine, unconcerned, willing."

Dagan leaned toward her and lightly caressed her neck with his fingertips. "Why didn't you tell me?"

"You were killing demons. Besides, he only had me for a couple of seconds and then Joe took him out."

A low rumble emanated from Dagan's chest.

"Why?" She re-emphasized her question.

"The *tregorian* sucks the will out of a subject, so much sometimes that the person will go comatose. But they have to be touching bare flesh."

"I didn't feel anything until he touched my neck." Her whole body shook from the memory. "Let's hope we don't see any more of those things."

"Yes, let us hope."

He didn't sound confident.

This time, when Reese pulled onto her father's street, she didn't notice the quiet surroundings or how beautiful the trees looked covered in ice. Her mind churned with thoughts on how to explain all this to her father, and how she would talk him into leaving his home, just when he'd begun to come out of his depressed mood and start experiencing life again. The timing sucked.

"What are you thinking?" Dagan asked.

"How this sucks."

His soft laugh made her glance his way. "Well it does. Yesterday, my father started cleaning out my sister's room and her closet. Jeez, that took guts right there."

Dagan's confused look made her laugh too. "You'd have to see my sister's room to understand the implication of actually cleaning it."

"I see." But his confused look remained.

Her voice got softer. "Cleaning out Riley's room is a start. At some point, maybe, he'll clean out my mother's stuff too." She sighed. "It's been three years and her clothes still hang in the closet. He won't allow anyone to touch them."

"It's hard losing someone you love."

His statement, laden with such sorrow, made her wonder if he had lost a loved one. "Yes. It is."

She pulled into the driveway. When she stopped the car and put it in park, she grabbed the steering wheel on top with both hands and flexed them.

Dagan reached over and laid his hand on hers. "Take a couple of deep breaths and then we'll go in together."

She nodded. "It gave me hope, but now I'm going to throw this at him." She stared at the house. "I'm not sure how he's going to take it."

"You might be surprised." He used his hand to loosen her grip on the steering wheel. "I mean look at how well you're handling it."

She threw him a droll look before smiling. "Thanks, I feel so much better."

He took her now loosened fingers and laced them with his own. "Come on, beautiful."

He met her at the front of the car and bumped her shoulder with his.

This felt so normal in a way. Taking Dagan to meet her father could be interesting. He would most likely think she'd lost her mind though.

"Dad, where are you?" she called as they went through the front door.

"In the living room," he called back.

They rounded the corner and found him sitting in the middle of the floor between two big boxes, and surrounded by stuffed animals.

She stopped short, causing Dagan to run into the back of her.

"What are you doing?"

He looked up and smiled. "Going through toys to see what I can pitch and what I can give to the local children's shelter."

When he saw Dagan, his good mood seemed to deflate. He got to his feet. "Who's this?"

"This is Dagan."

Her father walked over and eyed Dagan. She wasn't sure what he would do. She'd never brought a guy to her father's house before.

Dagan just stood there, jaw tight and hands at his side. Reese's father walked a circle around him.

In a frustrated voice Reese said, "Dad."

He stopped in front of Dagan and held out his hand. "I'm Clive Whittaker."

Dagan shook the offered hand. "Nice to meet you, sir."

"So what are you doing here, Reese?"

She pointed to the couch. "Why don't we sit down."

"Hmmm, that doesn't sound good," he said to Dagan.

Reese smiled at her father. "What would you say to coming and staying at my place for a little while?"

"Actually, sir, I would like you to consider hanging out with some friends of mine for a few days."

Clive narrowed his eyes. "Your friends?" His head whipped around to Reese. "What is he talking about?"

"Dagan, I thought—I mean you never said anything. I thought he would come and stay with me."

"How is that safer, Reese? You know what happened already."

She got up in his face. "That's beside the point. I will not let him be put with people *he or I*," she emphasized, "don't know."

He stood toe to toe with her and said his piece. "They are skilled and trained to do their job well. It will be like he's in protective custody."

"No."

"Yes."

"Enough!" Clive yelled.

They both stepped back.

"Do you want to tell me what the hell is going on? I'm not going anywhere."

Reese shot a glare in Dagan's direction before she turned all sweet to her father. "Dad, there's been some disreputable people casing your house and I—we would like to take you some place safe until things can be handled."

"Handled?" He looked at Dagan. "What people? Who do they work for? Where did they come from?" He turned around to Reese. "I don't have the mind of a five year old and I don't appreciate being treated like one. Now tell me the damn truth or get your ass out of here."

She threw her hands up in the air. "Tell him."

"Reese."

"Just tell him, Dagan."

"Great, another mind wipe. They're adding up."

Clive went to the French doors and stood with his hands clasped behind his back. Dagan breathed deep before his attempt at explaining.

"Mr. Whittaker, there is a gang out there who's trying to do harm to you and your family."

"Why?" he said, but didn't turn around.

"I know this sounds strange, but it is because of your

ancestry, your bloodline."

Clive Whittaker nodded his head. "So it begins."

"Sir?"

He turned to face them. "My father said it would come to this. I wouldn't listen to him. I loved my wife and my girls. I refused to live the life."

Stunned, Reese said, "Dad, what are you talking about?"

"Where to begin." He propped his chin in his fingers and contemplated. "I'm the son of Enki."

"What?" Dagan and Reese said in unison.

"You are the son of Enki?"

"Yes. My mother was human though."

Reese dropped to the chair. "I feel sick. The water god is my grandfather?"

"Exactly," her father said.

"How—when—oh crap."

Dagan pressed. "You have known all along."

"Yes. At a young age, Enki came to me. He explained how I would be different and needed to be careful."

Reese shot him a scathing look. "How are you different?"

He shrugged. "I have some powers, but I haven't used them in a very long time." Clive scooted over toward Dagan and leaned in. "It was a kick in my teenage years though." He slapped his knee and laughed. "I have to confess I used them a couple of times at school too, but not to cheat or anything, just to get back at somebody who pissed me off or maybe to help me get on the baseball team."

Dagan smiled. He liked this guy. "I know what you mean."

"Of course you do." Reese sneered. "It's a guy thing."

"Exactly," Clive replied then laughed again.

She growled. "What kind of powers?"

"I can move things with my mind. I used to be able to make myself invisible."

Dagan sat back and crossed his arms. "Cool."

"Used to scare the hell out of my parents when I used that one. Plus, I could sneak out of the house and back in again. Of course, it got tricky when I drank too much." He gave Dagan a conspiratorial wink. "Parts of me would start reappearing at the most inopportune times."

Dagan laughed. The look on Reese's face was priceless.

When I met your mother, I never used them again. I wanted to be a normal guy. For her, I wanted to be the world." He grew sad. "When your mother got sick, I wished I had all the powers, but I couldn't save her."

Reese went to her father and gently touched his shoulder. "Dad, she wouldn't have wanted you to do that."

"I know, but I wanted it more than anything."

"She knew you loved her."

He hugged Reese. "Yes, we loved a lifetime in those years."

Dagan watched a tear roll down her cheek and then she opened her eyes and a wave of emotion practically knocked him to the floor. He imagined loving someone so much that your life got derailed when you lost them. He never thought he would experience it, but gazing into those big blue orbs glistening with tears, he hoped.

"So," Clive said as he stepped back from Reese. "Tell me what brought you both here today."

"We have had someone watching your place after I found out you were in the area."

Continuing, Reese said, "We were attacked at my office last night."

"What? Attacked?" He ran his hands down her arms. "Are you okay?"

"I'm fine." She nodded in Dagan's direction. "Dagan, Rufus and the rest of my team were there. We handled ourselves pretty well."

Astounded, her father said, "Your team? They know about this?"

"Believe me, it was not my first choice," Dagan said and smiled at Reese who stuck her tongue out at him.

"What exactly is your part in this anyway?" Clive turned on him with interest.

He walked over to stand before Clive and bowed slightly. "I am the son of Enlil. I belong to an elite group known as time walkers."

"Time walkers? What are they?"

While he ran through a cliff note of his kind, Dagan kept his eye on Reese who wandered around the room gently touching things. She fought the sadness off with a vengeance. He wanted to cuddle her in his arms and protect her from the ugliness, but she would fight him tooth and nail if he tried. So, he kept pace but didn't overshadow. She would find her way.

"I'm protected by some pretty powerful magic, you know. And so are my daughters."

"Yes, sir, I do know that."

"What magic?" She rounded on him. "You didn't tell me anything about protective spells."

"It connected Saturday, when I took you home. So focused on the *galla* the first night," and you, he thought. "I did not pay attention to it. Saturday morning, the energy definitely got my attention and I knew something more was going on."

"You could've mentioned it."

"I did a mind wipe, not counting on you remembering anything after that."

Clive frowned. "You did a mind wipe on my daughter?" He surged forward. "What the hell is that and you better damn well not have hurt her."

"Take it easy, Dad. It didn't work." She smiled sweetly.

"And it didn't mess you up?"

"No, I feel fine."

"Well that's good." He glared at Dagan. "Isn't it?"

Dagan stared into Reese's mocking smile. "Yes and no."

"Oh never mind him. The reason we came over is to take you to a safer place. But now I'm wondering if that will help. What is this magic that you were talking about?"

"Enki had a wizard put some protective wards on all of us."

"Percilious," Dagan offered.

"Per—what?"

"Percilious, Reese. He's the wizard. Very old, very wise, a very strong sorcerer."

"Oh."

"He used his magick to protect you all, with a little extra boost from Enki. But, it only protects you when you're inside the house. Once you leave here, you're no longer protected."

Clive chuckled. "That's probably why he kept telling me to hone my skills again."

"Most likely."

Reese gave Dagan a frustrated look. "So what now?"

He directed his answer to Reese's father. "Since you are *nephili*, I'm not as concerned about your welfare. Let's face it. You have a much greater chance of fighting off the demons."

Rubbing his hands together, Clive said, "I guess I'll be calling forth the rusty powers to start using them again. I'll need to be in top form if I'm going to fight demons."

"Dad," Reese argued. "I don't want you fighting anyone."

"Of course you don't, sweetheart. Just like I would rather have you staying here with me instead of walking out that door and heading into another attack."

She started to say something, but he held up his hand. "But, I know you won't do it. You are your mother's daughter after all."

"Hey!"

He turned to Dagan. "My question is, can you protect her enough?"

"If she lets me."

"Let him," Clive said.

"Okay, we're finished here. Don't get me started about what is strange in this whole situation because there aren't enough hours in the day to go over all of them," Reese ranted.

Clive approached Dagan and stuck out his hand to shake. "She's a handful."

"You don't need to tell me. I've had the front row show."

"Stubborn, pigheaded, strong-willed."

"Yes, I've seen all that."

"They get it from their mother."

Reese marched over and shoved Dagan away from her father, turned him around and headed for the door. "That's enough fraternizing. We've got things to do."

Before she left, she hugged her father. "Are you sure you'll be okay?"

"Better every day."

"All right, I'll call you later."

Before joining Reese in the car, Dagan sought out Gideon to introduce him to Mr. Whittaker and gave him an update. Gideon would position himself inside the house. Now that he knew Mr. Whittaker was *nephili*, they wouldn't have to hide.

"I want to go back and help with the research," she said when he slid into the driver's side of the car.

"Fine, I need to do some surveillance and see if I can get a fix on the *galla*. In a firm tone he added, "I need you to stay put. Stay with the others and don't go wandering off."

Anger laced her response. "I don't go wandering off."

"Good, because the next step would be chaining you up."

Appalled she said, "You wouldn't dare," and glared at him.

He smiled. "Oh yes, I would and enjoy it."

Reese's stomach fluttered. Her indignation was half-hearted. All manner of thoughts crept into her mind about Dagan chaining her and doing who knows what. Her creative imagination could come up with many scenarios and her body ached. Staring at his profile, the strong jaw and sexy lips, she had to stifle the moan that fought to escape.

"You need to stop that."

Dagan's husky voice drifted toward her. "Stop what?" She licked her lips.

"Whatever you're thinking."

"What?" How could he know she was thinking anything? "Are you reading my mind again?"

"Purebloods have heightened senses." He whipped his head around to her and his nostrils flared. "All of them." His eyes angled down to the juncture between her legs. "I can all but taste you."

She clamped her legs together. "Oh."

He turned his gaze back to the street. "So stop it or I'm not going to be able to keep myself from pulling this car over and finding a quiet place to do just that."

Reese felt the heat building. It started at her cheeks which were flaming and inched down to her very core which now seeped. The man had an incredible way of looking at her and making her want to lie down and say "Take me". That irritated her because he was arrogant, bossy, gorgeous, hot—she really needed to stop.

Thankfully, they arrived back at her office and she jumped out of the car as if she'd been shot from a cannon.

Rufus, keeping watch, opened the door to let her in then went out to speak with Dagan.

"Problem?" Joe asked her when she all but ran into him.

"What—oh—no." She took a few breaths to slow her heart rate. "How's the research going?"

"Slow, but we're doing everything we can."

"Okay, that's good."

Joe looked past her to where Dagan and Rufus were talking. "So how's your dad?"

"Well, that's something I need to fill you guys in on, so why don't we get everyone together and I'll tell you all at once."

"Sure." He rolled his eyes toward her and then back to Dagan.

"Don't."

"Don't what?" he asked innocently.

"Don't go there."

He put his hands up in surrender and walked back to the piles of books and people.

"Hey, Reese," Geoffrey called.

She nodded to him. "Can I get you all to stop for a few minutes? I need to give you some new information."

Pulling up a nearby empty chair, she sat to calm her nerves before she let them know the truth about her family. Was she jumpy because of this new revelation or because of Dagan? Both.

"What's up?" Roberta said.

"Okay, I know this is going to be weird so I'm going to say it straight out and we'll go from there."

Everyone gave a quick nod.

"We went to see my father to fill him in on recent events and move him to a safe place until this is over. I thought that was going to be the strangest part to this plan." She leveled her gaze on each face. "You know, telling him what has been happening without him thinking I'm a candidate for the loony bin."

She slouched back in the chair and closed her eyes for a moment. "Anyway." She started up again. "It turns out he already knew about Kur and the *galla*."

"What?" a group voice rang out.

"I know, I know. That's what I said, but it's true." She got up to pace in the tiny area. "It seems that Enki is my grandfather."

"I need a drink," Geoffrey said.

"Me too," chimed in Roberta. "I'll go find that bottle of Wild Turkey from last Christmas."

Reese let a soft sigh escape and ran her fingers through her now tousled and somewhat frantic hair. "My grandmother was human but then we have Enki, the water god."

Chloe smiled. "Interesting."

"Unexpected," Rufus said as he strolled up to the gathering.

Dagan wasn't with him, but he'd told her he would seek out the *galla*. She assumed he had gone to do it. Refocusing on the others and the conversation, Reese tried to keep her thoughts from drifting to the exchange between her and Dagan earlier and how she wanted it, very badly.


Anger rolled off Dagan when he stormed toward Eridu. He held one of his Magnums and pointed it at Leotis. "I'll let myself in."

Leotis roared. "Those weapons will not harm me, Time Walker, and you know this."

"Yes, but it will hurt like a bitch."

Natalia growled.

"No offense intended, Natalia," he said, and kept going through the temple doors.

Enki lay spread eagle across the canopy bed in his great room with one slender female sprawled across his chest so he could suck on her breasts and another between his legs sucking his endowment.

"I hate to intrude but I need some answers," Dagan said angrily.

Enki pushed the woman off his chest so he could lean up on his elbows. "Dagan? Come join us. There is plenty to go around." He kissed the woman next to him.

"Sorry, no. I need to talk to you about Reese."

Enki sighed. "Yes, well I guess you ladies need to let me up." Naked, he scooted off the massive bed. "But don't go too far because we will pick this up again when he leaves."

The girls giggled and rushed from the room.

Enki grabbed the sheet and wrapped it around his waist. Coming down the steps he said, "So what is so important that you intrude on my rest period and anger my guards?"

"You didn't think to mention that Reese was your granddaughter."

"I did not see that it mattered all that much."

Fighting the urge to walk over and shake the deity by the throat, Dagan said, "Being the daughter of your son makes her blood very potent. His as well."

"So you have seen my son?" Enki walked to the food tables and picked a plump grape to toss in his mouth.

"I have."

"How did he seem to you?"

"A pleasant difference, good humored, but sad."

Enki turned and started for his throne. "Yes, this sadness because the female died. I never understood it. There are so many others to choose from to be distraught over losing one."

Dagan wasn't surprised that Enki would not understand the emotional loss of a loved one.

"Will your magick protect him?"

"Yes, and he has powers as well. He will not be an easy target for Kur."

"But Reese is not so fortunate."

"No, she did not inherit powers." He held up his hand to silence Dagan's retort. "That is why I used extra power for the protection on Reese and Riley."

"Even without powers she manages to handle herself," Dagan mumbled.

"I have been watching her and her sister over the years. They are remarkable women."

"I've not seen the sister, but Reese is..."

"Hard to put into words, is it not?"

"Yes, very hard."

"I wish to speak to her," Enki said.

"Reese?"

"Yes. This eve I will come to her house. Make sure she is there. But I want only her, no others. There are things I wish to discuss."

"I'm not sure that's a good idea. Safety in numbers would be best. Plus, you on Earth with Kur skulking around?"

"You stay with her to guard against unwelcome surprises. Kur will not sense my presence." Enki rose and strolled back to the bed. "Tonight." He stripped off his sheet and called, "Ladies." The two young women were entering as Dagan whirled around and left.

# Chapter Thirteen

Dusk settled as Dagan finished his sweep of the area and ended up at the offices.

"Did you make arrangements?" he asked Rufus.

"Chloe will be staying with Roberta and I'll be hanging with Joe and Geoffrey."

Dagan had called Rufus to let him know something would have to be done about protection for the group. They were now targets as well. Kur would use any means to get at Reese.

"I will see what other *doghume* are around and call them in for backup."

"Good." Dagan watched Reese say goodnight to the others and tensed when she hugged Joe. "Enki is coming to her house tonight, so I'll take Reese with me."

"Figured that."

He strolled up and took her coat off the chair. Stopping behind her, Dagan shook it out and held it for her to put her arms in.

Surprised, she looked up. "Thanks."

"You're welcome," he murmured next to her ear. "Are you ready?"

She nodded. "Goodnight everyone."

"What's wrong?" she asked after he'd gotten into the car.

His jaw tightened. "We'll have a visitor tonight."

She stiffened. "Visitor?"

"Enki."

"What? When?"

"Tonight, he will come to your house. It seems he wishes to speak with you."

She rolled her eyes. "Could this get any weirder?"

"Most likely," he said and sped away from the building.

"Why is he coming to see me?"

"I have no idea, but he ordered me to be your bodyguard and told me he wanted to speak with you alone."

When they arrived at her house, she stayed glued to the seat and crossed her arms. "I know, I know. Wait here," she said in a saccharine sweet voice.

"Exactly." He got out and stood several yards away from the house. His scan revealed no intruders in the area. "Come on." He motioned to her.

"Are you sure the Big Bad Wolf isn't going to jump out and get me?" she mumbled as she hurried by.

He caught up with her and slipped his hand around her waist, pulling her tight against his side. Leaning down and nuzzling her neck, he said, "I didn't say the wolf wouldn't get you." He growled softly before he opened the front door for her to enter.

Shivers raced across her skin, not from the cold.

"Could you—" Before she finished he snapped his fingers and the fire roared to life. "Thanks."

He grinned. "You're welcome."

"I guess I'll make up some dinner," she said, walking into the kitchen. She poked her head out from around the corner. "So what does a Sumerian god eat anyway?"

"Same things as you do. Make whatever you want. I'm certain he's not coming here to eat."

"Right." She whipped back into the kitchen.

"I want to take a look around before night falls. Be back in a few minutes."

She heard the door slam. Reese went to the pantry and pulled out some potatoes and her bat. "Just in case."

After washing and peeling the potatoes, she put them on the stove to boil and went to get some steaks. She figured broiled steaks, potato salad and fresh vegetables would hit the spot. Her system needed refueling, plus her nerves were jangling at the thought of meeting Enki. She pulled down the whiskey and the wine.

When Dagan came in, he shook all the snow off his coat and hair, wiped his feet and then locked the door. Reese walked over and handed him a large mug of coffee laced with whiskey.

She smiled. "To warm you up."

"I could think of other ways to do that." The fire ignited the devilish gleam in his eyes.

She stepped back eyeing him warily. There was a pyramid of reasons why getting more involved with Dagan was a bad idea. Feeling a little breathless, she put distance between them. "Dinner will be ready soon. I hope broiled steak is okay."

"Delicious," he hissed.

His gaze stroked her as if it were his large, fully capable hands. She swallowed hard.

Dagan downed the contents of the mug and set it on the small end table before he moved closer to her. He took her cup and set it aside then ran his fingers and lips in a tantalizing trail along her throat and finally landed on her mouth.

Warmth flooded her as she felt the press of his body along her length. He sucked her lips lightly, angled his head and covered her mouth with his. It felt like a tsunami had crashed over her body leaving quivering emotional turmoil. Her lips parted readily and he delved inside, raking his tongue boldly against hers. Her mind spun and her body floated on heady waves. He tasted wonderful.

"Am I interrupting?" A smooth, amused voice came from behind them.

Dagan stilled. Reese made a small sound of distress when he broke the kiss. He caught her jaw, forcing her to look at him when she tried to see the man who had interrupted their erotic interlude. And it damn sure was erotic.

He brushed his lips across hers again with an apologetic look in his eyes. "Hello, Enki."

Horrendous embarrassment flashed across her face. How did this keep happening?

Dagan moved aside.

"So this is Reese?" Enki walked over to her, holding out his hands.

When she raised her right hand, he took it in both of his and then kissed the back with a bow.

"Uh, nice to meet you." She struggled to get past the total humiliation of being caught kissing Dagan by her grandfather.

Enki tilted his head and amusement gleamed in his eyes. "Is something burning?"

Her eyes widened and she screeched. "Dinner." She ran into the kitchen to check the steaks. Luckily, she arrived in time to save them. She could cut off the charred bits.

Reese busied herself in the kitchen setting the table, dishing out the food into bowls and pouring the wine. She had managed to hear some kind of whispered, heated discussion going on between Dagan and Enki when she passed by the doorway, but she couldn't tell what they were saying.

She walked into the living room. "Let's sit down to eat, gentlemen."

They followed her into the kitchen, picked spots and waited for her to be seated before seating themselves.

"So, what do I call you?" Reese asked Enki as she passed the potato salad.

"You can call me Enki."

She shook her head. "Okay, Enki. Why haven't you visited my father, your son in his time of need?"

Dagan's hand stopped. He shot a freaky glance her way and then turned his eyes on Enki.

Enki continued to shovel food onto his plate. "You have every right to ask, Reese. As it happens, I have gone to see him, but he never knew. Sometimes, I came in dreams letting him relive moments with your mother. Other times, I made sure he slept deeply and came to talk about how he felt and why it was important to get past the debilitating emotions."

"He loved her more than life, I think." She lowered her eyes to her plate.

"Yes, I believe that too. But it does no good for you to lose both of them and I tried to get him to understand that." He smiled at her. "Actually, he had started coming out of that void."

"So you were the reason he finally began doing things around the house again."

He loaded a fork full of food into his mouth and nodded.

"Thank you," she whispered.

"I have kept an eye on all of you since you were born."

"All of us?"

"There are others to be sure."

She broke a small smile. "Of course, there would be. You are the *water* god after all."

He pointed his empty fork her direction. "Exactly."

Reese chewed a bite of food before turning her blue powered gaze on Enki. "So why are you here?"

"Of all the children, you are one of the strongest. Not just in spirit though, your blood or to be more precise, the part of my blood that flows in you, is powerful. I have placed protective wards around your home, plus added more of my own energy to make them extremely powerful. However, you are vulnerable when you are not here."

"I understand."

"Although Clive is *nephili*, you did not inherit any powers."

"So I'm told." She sipped her wine. Dagan silently watched them.

Enki loaded his mouth with more food and swigged his wine to wash it down. "I have come to offer you an opportunity."

"What kind of opportunity?"

"To come to Dilmun and train with Gilgamesh."

Dagan choked on a piece of meat. Reese got up and patted him on the back. He grabbed for his wine glass and guzzled down the entire contents. "Thanks," he finally said when he could speak.

Glaring at Enki, Dagan said, "No human has ever been brought to Dilmun before. Not in the entire history of our life here."

"You are correct."

"The Pantheon will not allow that."

"You forget that I am one of the four. I have the power to do this without their consent."

Enki looked on her expectantly. "Well, what do you say?"

"Gilgamesh? The first hero of record. The one the stories were written about?"

Enki nodded.

Dagan poured himself more wine. "Gilgamesh trains warriors."

"I'm not a warrior," she announced.

"All too true, however, you are bright, strong and have already shown you are unafraid of these creatures. Without the proper training, you fight them."

"Fight for my life." Now she downed her wine. "And who said I'm not afraid? I'm scared shitless."

"If you work with Gilgamesh, you will also have the talent to hold your own against them. You do not have their brute strength but even that can be gotten around if you have the knowledge."

She sat quiet for a few minutes, pushing the meat around on her plate, contemplating this new twist.

Dagan had quit eating, but poured more and more wine into his glass, which couldn't seem to stay full.

"I'll think on it," she finally told him. "It's a bit much for me to absorb."

"I understand, my child. The offer is open to you for as long as you need."

Enki pushed away from the table. "This was a lovely meal. Thank you for your hospitality."

Reese walked up to him, hesitant to touch his person. He gave her a wide smile and pulled her into a bear hug.

"We will see each other again, have no doubt." Enki turned to Dagan. "I will see you soon, Time Walker."

Dagan bowed to the deity, who vanished.

She turned to him. "Well, that was interesting."

Dagan grunted his response. "I'll make one more sweep of the property before closing us in for the night," he said and marched into the next room.

"Okay, Grumpy," she mumbled and began clearing the table.

"Training with Gilgamesh," Dagan mumbled while spearing his hand through the arm of his duster. "Like hell she will."

Making circuitous passes around the property in the cold night air helped cool his temper a bit. Still, he would be damned if he would let her go through that rigorous training when he could very well protect her.

But he wouldn't be here forever.

"No, she's not doing it."

Ticked that he hadn't run into any of the creatures when he was bursting for a fight to settle him down, he plowed into the house, locked the doors and windows with the will of his mind, and raised his hand while chanting the incantation that would seal the home. The concealment spells were enough, he knew, but knowing that she would be unable to leave made him feel better. He had a sneaky suspicion that what Enki offered her would be quite a draw for her curious nature.

His temper still simmered. How dare Enki offer her something like that? It was his job to protect Reese—his. He trudged into the kitchen.

Reese caught a glimpse of him as she turned to place another plate in the dishwasher. She straightened. He caught her wrists, jerking them behind her back and securing them as he spun her around to face him and shoved her back against the door, pinning her between the panel and his hard body.

"What are you doing?" she gasped.

He growled, tangling his fingers in her hair as he swooped down to bury his tongue in her startled mouth.

Reese's knees buckled but he had her pinned too tightly for her to worry about falling. One knee pressed between her thighs. She thought her body would combust from all the heat building between them.

His body quaked even more than her own. He tore his mouth from hers and gasped for air in greedy gulps. Covering her cheeks and neck with open-mouthed kisses, he melted her surprise until she clung to him with desperation.

Through the volcanic rush of hot blood coursing in her veins, she felt a cool breeze across her midsection. Dagan's thigh kept the pressure between her legs, and with determination, he lifted her shirt free of her body. Goose bumps rose on her exposed skin but were quickly chased away by Dagan's warm hands as they roamed over her arms, waist and ribcage. Her nipples pushed against her lacy bra, the cold making them stand at attention. It didn't take long for Dagan to cover first one then the other with his hands, massaging and kneading her sensitive flesh and making her sob. The delicious pressure building inside her focused on the spot where his thick thigh muscle rubbed against her core. She grabbed onto his massive shoulders and tried to move her body in just the right way against his leg to get what she craved.

He squeezed and plucked her nipples. Her inner muscles clenched. He took her mouth again, stealing her breath. She felt him slide his hand between their bodies and into the front of her pants. She whimpered when one long finger stroked her weeping cleft. She thought she would die from the sheer vibration of her breaths and his when he found her opening and slowly pushed his finger inside.

Tearing his mouth from hers, he leaned heavily against her. "You feel so good, so tight and wet for me."

Her heart stammered at his breathless words and how they made her stomach quiver and her muscles tighten around the finger still imbedded deep within her channel. She heard the sound of a zipper and anticipation kicked her heart rate up another notch.

Dagan reached behind his back and pulled out a long, thin blade. "Don't move sweetheart. I can't wait another minute."

It barely registered to her fuzzy brain what he was about to do. His hands were now steady as they cut down the front of her pants and underwear, leaving them hanging wide open. He put the knife on the counter and stared hungrily at the bold position he held her in. He cupped the globes of her ass and raised her hips. She looped her legs around his waist instinctively.

His cock felt like steel covered in silk as it eased its way into her passage. He panted and her breath hitched when he curled his hips and plunged into her. He shuddered and his hips jerked, driving him deeper into her depths. She closed her eyes and arched her back, accepting the intrusion and reveling in the feel of his thick shaft stretching her sheath. Reese cried out as her body exploded into a million sensations and rapture. Dagan pumped harder and faster until with a howl his body froze but his cock jumped inside her, spewing hot fluid to coat her womb.

It had happened. He fought his way through the blind desire screaming through his taut body. The *fury* had taken over and he was helpless against it. All his senses were now focused on Reese. Her need called to him and drove him mad with desire, the desire to pleasure her in every way, the desire to bury his cock in that luscious channel and make her scream his name for days on end.

For now, the intensity of it had settled. Still joined in that erotic position, he gently massaged her ass and ran light lips over her mouth. She circled her arms around his neck and leaned into him. Fully carrying her weight, he did an about face, walked through the hallway and down to the bedroom where he lay them on the bed without breaking the contact of the kiss or separating his body from hers.

He spent several moments kissing Reese, letting his tongue slide up the sides of her mouth, dance with her tongue and drive a moan from her. Hesitantly, he broke away and stood. He snapped his fingers, causing all the lights to go out. He waved his hand and the fireplace in the bedroom leapt to life.

First, he removed the tattered clothes from her body, kissing the valley between her breasts when he took away the bra, and running his tongue around her belly button when he discarded the remains of her pants. She watched him with such passionate longing he didn't think he'd be able to wait long enough to take off his own clothes. No, this time, he wanted to go slow and make it better, make it last longer for the both of them.

In the firelight, the sweat on her body made her skin glisten. He stretched his arms over his head, took a deep breath and tried to relax. Expelling the breath as he brought his arms down, he grabbed his cock and stroked it slowly. She licked her lips while watching his shaft jump.

Reese crawled onto her knees and came to the edge of the

bed where he stood. Lifting one light brow and with a quirk on her lips, she darted her tongue out to caress the tip. He sucked in a breath. The sensations crawling over his skin threatened to make him lose control—again.

Growling, he gently pushed her so she fell onto the bed and he followed her down, covering her body with his. Massaging the base of her skull with anxious fingers, he delved into the sweet cavern of her mouth and groaned.

She locked her legs with his and massaged his ribcage with her pussy, giving them both benefit from it. Her juices coated his skin and his heightened senses flooded with her scent and taste. The *fury* was building again. She had no idea what she could do to him during this time if he let her. Reese could make him wither into a begging mass of bulk if she put her mind to it.

He had no intention of allowing her time to do it.

Dagan tore his lips from her and rolled to lie next to her, propping his head on his hand. He plucked her nipple until it stood erect then rolled it between his thumb and forefinger. Moving his hand down to her stomach, he snuggled her closer. Finally, he ran a lazy finger in the crease between her legs. She responded by spreading her legs wider.

He spent the rest of the night letting the *fury* have free reign.


The morning came too soon in Reese's opinion. Exhaustion pulled at her to dive back into the depths of sleep, but she smelled the delightful aromas of coffee and bacon. Memories of the night came rushing back. She smiled and stretched.

Getting out of bed, she ruffled her hair, put on an oversized T-shirt and socks, and headed for the kitchen. She stopped in the doorway. The bacon sizzled in the frying pan, steam wafted off the biscuits on the counter, and Dagan stood at the stove scrambling eggs. He was bare on top and she took a moment to appreciate his broad shoulders and narrow hips where a pair of jeans hung loosely. His back stiffened.

"You make it hard to concentrate when you do that."

She smiled and walked further into the room. "Do what? Look at you like you're candy in the store window and I want to eat you up?"

He spun around, grabbed her by the waist and hoisted her up to sit on the sink. "Yes." He gave her a quick kiss. "Good morning, beautiful."

"Don't you say the nicest things?" She batted her eyelashes.

"Don't get used to it. I'm sure we'll be at each other's throats before the day is out."

She nudged his shoulder. "You're cooking."

"Looks like," he said as he turned back to the stove.

"I didn't know you could cook."

"There are a lot of things you don't know about me, Reese."

How true. They really didn't know that much about each other.

The doorbell rang.

Reese looked at Dagan. He shrugged. "The seal has expired. It's not *galla* or I would sense it."

She jumped down from her seat. Dagan grabbed her arm. "But be careful."

"I will," she said and gave him a quick peck on the cheek.

Smiling, she opened the front door to find her sister, Riley, standing there.

"Hi, sis," Riley said and pushed her way into the house.

Stunned and trying to recover from the shock of it Reese said, "Riley, what are you doing here? I thought you were in Europe."

Riley dropped her purse on the couch. "Was."

Reese waited for further explanation but none came. "And?"

"Daddy called a couple of days ago. He sounded so good and more like his old self again."

"So you decided since he seems to be dealing with his misery, you could come home?"

Riley folded her arms across her chest and took her usual obstinate stance. "I don't know what you mean. Pierre had gone back to college and Jean-Luc got a new job at the museum, so…"

"Who the hell are Pierre and Jean-Luc? What happened to Bob or Fred or whatever his name was that you supposedly followed over there in the first place?"

She frowned. "You mean Toby? He only stayed for the summer. I met and became friends with Pierre and Jean-Luc and they invited me to stay with them after Toby left."

"I'll bet," Reese mumbled.

Ready to lay into her sister, Reese noticed Riley had stopped talking and stared toward the kitchen. Turning, Reese saw Dagan leaning against the open doorway frowning.

"So, who's tall, dark and yummy?"

Reese sighed. "Riley, this is Dagan, Dagan, Riley."

Riley let out an appreciative whistle.

"What the hell is she doing here?"

"How should I know? I opened the door and there she stood."

He turned around mumbling and went back into the kitchen.

"Wow, where did you get him and does he have a brother, a cousin?"

Reese waved her hand in the air and followed Dagan.

"This creates more problems," he hissed.

"Why?"

"Because now not only do I have to worry about you and your father, who at least is more able to protect and take care of himself, I have to worry about her." He pointed to the open doorway and the other room.

She crossed her arms over her chest, a mirror of the same stance her sister had taken. "I beg your pardon, Mr. Macho He-man Stud, but as I recall, I've held my own. Enki was impressed at how I handle myself. You are being a real sexist pig. Why is it you think my father can take care of himself, but me you have to dote over?"

"Because he is *nephili*," Dagan roared in exasperation.

"Hey, kids," Riley strolled into the kitchen. "Is that food I smell?"

Dagan and Reese both glared at her. Riley raised her hands in front of her.

"Don't mind me. I'll just help myself." She scooted in

between them and started loading a plate.

Dagan stormed out of the room with Reese on his tail. "Where are you going?"

He grabbed his shirt from the floor and pulled it on. "If she is here, then Angelique will be as well."

A cloud of jealousy passed over Reese's face. "Who the hell is Angelique?"

He tucked his shirt into his pants in jerky movements. "A friend."

"I'll bet."

He stopped and stared at her. "She lives in Europe and I asked her to watch over Riley when I found out about your sister being there."

His cell phone rang. Dagan searched the pockets of his jacket to find it. "Hello."

"Yes, I know. She's in the kitchen." He listened to the person on the other end of the line and shook his head. "No, I'll come out. I'll see you in five minutes."

"So, what, you're leaving?"

He strapped his weapons on his belt and his leg then laid his coat and sword on the bed. He took her chin between his fingertips and lifted her face to his. "I would love nothing more than to stay here with you forever in that bed." He nodded in the bed's direction. "But I have work to do and so do you. I have to make arrangements with Gideon and Angelique."

She stiffened at the mention of the other woman's name.

"Where will your sister be staying?"

She sighed. "Most likely with my dad."

"Okay. I want you to go directly to your office. The others will meet you there. I'll have Rufus and Gideon on watch. I'll leave Angelique with your sister and father."

"Where will you be?"

"Doing my job. I'll come to you when I can." He slanted his mouth over hers for a long, tender kiss.

She clung to his arms and tipped into him for the kiss. His scent seemed stronger now and that it coated her skin made it more potent.

"Okay."

He slid the sword over his shoulder and put on his coat. "Straight to the office," he said and ran his finger down the bridge of her nose.

When the front door closed behind Dagan, Reese turned to find Riley standing in the kitchen doorway with a plate of food and a fork.

"So, who's Angelique and Gideon? Why would Daddy need to protect himself? And why were you so angry with that, that god?"

If her sister only knew the half of it, and she would have to know, now that she was back and in the middle of everything.

He stood outside Reese's office. He and Rufus had coordinated the watch detail since he'd be gone. He made certain someone experienced in fighting demons would have her in sight the entire time.

*"Dagan?"*

*"Yes, Mother."*

*"The Pantheon wishes to see you immediately."*

His jaw clenched. He had a bad feeling about this. *"I'm on my way."*

Dagan stepped up to the doors outside the colossal hall where the Pantheon met to debate and settle specific issues serious enough to be brought before them. He had changed into his leathers, black T-shirt and duster and carried his full time-walker armory. If he was going in to stand before the high council, he was going in armed as a visual reminder of his duty.

The doors opened and he was summoned inside. He nodded acknowledgement of Nammu, Inanna, his mother and father, and Enki, who sat off to the left with one leg hanging over the arm of his stone seat. Dagan stepped closer and bowed to An and Ki.

An said, "Dark news has reached our ears, Time Walker."

"I dare say it is not so dark for my lineage," Enki chimed in.

Leave it to him to see benefit in aligning his house with Enlil's.

Dagan glared in his direction. Enki just waved.

Ki stood. "This is a serious matter, Enki. I see no amusement in the situation. We have many time walkers and dream walkers roaming the planet. If this happens to one it can happen to others."

"Serious business for our race," Inanna agreed. She floated down the steps coming toward him in an ethereal wisp of motion. "Not the first time you've been brought before us because you developed feelings for a human."

"No, my lady." Dagan responded. The bright eyes and brilliant smile of Lila caressed his memory. Happy days until Kur and his soldiers had cut him down and forced him to watch as Lila's life drained from her body.

"You were severely beaten the last time, if I recall."

He raised his eyes to look steadily into hers. "Yes, my lady."

A delicate brow arched. "And you come here fully armed." Inanna walked a slow circle around him. "Did you plan to do battle?"

He clenched his jaw rather than say he'd do whatever it took to keep Reese safe and be with her.

"Ah, no answer. Smart of you." She moved in close and whispered in his ear. "But do not believe you can keep your thoughts from me, Dagan, son of Enlil."

Ki's artic voice toned in. "Do you wish to forfeit your duties as time walker?"

"No, my queen."

"Good. You are one of our best."

An, the king, rose from his elevated place, which looked down on the others. His stoic silence and fierce features were well-known to all Naruki. With a growl and a glower his deep, baritone voice bounced off the glimmering walls when he said, "The decision has been made."

Dagan looked up to the illustrious leader of their race with a mixture of trepidation and concern.

"You will turn over the protection of Reese Whittaker to Scion and report back here to Dilmun. It is our desire to have you back in the fold. You will assist Gilgamesh in the training of new time walkers until such time as we deem you can be put back in the field."

Dagan's fists clenched and if he ground his teeth any harder, he'd have none left. He glanced at his mother's sorrowful expression.

"It is because of Ninmah's argument that we will not order punishment by the *sukkal*. In your defense she has forced it to our attention that you cannot choose your *blethred*."

Dagan didn't feel entirely grateful at the moment. He felt as though his heart would explode and his skin would ignite at any minute.

"Should you live through the separation from this human female, if she is truly your life mate, the pain will be more severe a punishment than this council could inflict upon you for this offense."

Dagan dared not look at the king, and he couldn't face his father. Chancing a glance at the water god proved to be unsettling for Enki only smiled, which Dagan considered rather odd. When the *fury* reaches its most uncontrollable part, the thing he would need most would be the bonding of his body with Reese. If the male did not bond, a rare enzyme released causing muscle spasms, fits of rage, severe pain like every nerve in his body had been filleted and impossible cravings, none of which could ever be satisfied. Dagan remembered no story of survival in these cases. He didn't worry about surviving the holocaust because even if his body endured the separation, his heart would not.

"You are to return to the planet and turn over the protection of the female to Scion immediately."

"Do you have anything to say on this matter?" Ki asked.

With all the honor and respect he had been raised to show the Pantheon, Dagan faced the king. "By ordering me to separate myself from the woman you think you've solved your problem. I say you're wrong. Centuries of interacting and sexing with the humans have blurred the lines between our races. I won't be the last."

He whirled about and walked from the hall with his head held high and no intention of following their orders. His problem now was Scion and how to waylay him until he finished with Kur.

"You are not going to turn her over, are you?"

Dagan stopped dead in his tracks. Spinning around, he found Enki grinning like a Cheshire cat who had eaten the proverbial canary.

"I'm not sure what you mean, my lord."

Enki laughed and slapped him on the back. "Do not hand me that drivel. There is no way you will leave her. I felt the intensity in that kiss last night and I saw defiance flash through your eyes just now in that room. Do not think the others did not see it as well."

They started walking further away from the great hall.

"If I know your father, he is discussing this with Ninmah at the moment and she is fighting the good fight. How can I help?"

That took Dagan by surprise.

"Come now, you know that I would like nothing more than to have your house aligned with mine."

So true. Licking his chapped lips, Dagan said, "Can you find some way to keep Scion busy for the next forty-eight hours?"

"I cannot guarantee a full forty-eight, but I may be able to arrange something to keep him busy for a while." Enki started off toward his carriage. "Whatever you are going to do, do it quickly."

Things were heating up, which meant Kur grew antsy and needy, maybe needy enough to do something stupid. He was counting on it. He'd worry about the separation sentence later. Right now, he wanted to concentrate on how to lure Kur to him.

# Chapter Fourteen

"Damn," Geoffrey said as he pushed another book out of his way. "There isn't much here."

"I haven't found anything regarding a creature named Kur," Joe grumbled.

Chloe smiled. "He was the mistake. You don't think the gods would let it be known that they'd actually made one, do you?"

Roberta plopped down on the leather sofa up against the back wall. "If we can't find anything worth finding about this demon, creature, thing, then how do we stop him?"

"You don't stop him. We do."

That voice sent Reese's heart into overdrive. With a huge smile, she turned to where Dagan stood. The smile faltered when she saw him. His movements were terse, his features were drawn and his eyes were shadowed.

Something was wrong.

He approached her with a hesitant gait. "Where is your sister?"

She bit her lip. "I told her everything this morning. She's in denial. I thought it best she talk to Dad, so I took her to his place."

He nodded. "Good."

She placed her hand on his arm. "What's happened?" He jerked away as if the touch burned him.

"We need to go to Slow Burn again."

"Why?"

"What's Slow Burn?" Geoffrey called out.

"It's a nightclub," Reese responded.

"Cool. I could definitely use a night of drinking and carousing. How about you guys?" he asked the rest of the group.

Joe grunted and kept his eyes leveled on Dagan. Chloe winked at Rufus, whose high wattage smile sent a definite message.

"We're in," Chloe said.

Roberta cocked her head to one side. "Now's the time to be shaking this booty," she slapped her hip, "before it gets carted off."

Reese pleaded on their behalf. "It in no way means we are lowering our guard, but if we're going to fight for life, we have to be allowed to enjoy that life, don't we, Dagan?"

He glared at her and his eyes flashed to black then back to green. "Fine. We meet back here in an hour and a half. Come on." He grabbed Reese's coat, and pulled her with him to the door.

She tugged her arm free to put the coat on. "What the hell is the matter with you?"

He opened the door, subtly shoved her through it then secured her in the car before pulling out his cell phone. "Angelique, tell Gideon that we're going to Slow Burn."

They didn't speak during the drive to her house. He didn't tell her what was bothering him or why they were going to the bar again. She imagined it to be some dire situation that he felt he had to make right, at least in his mind. Being an adult left him free to do what he damned well chose to do with or without her. It's not like one night of unabashed, incredible sex meant they were a couple.

When he stopped the car in her driveway, she shoved the door open, got out and slammed it. He caught up to her as she marched to the front door. The door flew open without her touching it and she hesitated. Had he done that or was someone in there waiting to attack them?

Dagan grabbed her elbow and moved her inside. "What has gotten up your butt?" he raved. "I can hear those little wheels churning inside your head."

She jerked her coat off and threw it across the back of the nearest chair. "Nothing," she fumed. "What you do is none of my business anyway." She huffed off down the hallway.

Right on her heels, he slammed her back against the wall and ripped the front of her shirt open. She would have to stock up on clothes with him around. Leaning down, he placed soft open-mouthed kisses on the swell of her breasts.

Her breath hitched. She grabbed handfuls of his hair, holding him in place when he took her nipple between his teeth through the fabric of her bra. "What are you doing to me?"

"As much as possible in the next thirty minutes."

He picked her up, holding her aloft, kissing his way down her torso. She spread her legs and rested them across his thighs. Dagan undid her jeans and slid his hand underneath her panties to find her wet and urgent.

Slipping first one finger then a second inside and feeling her muscles tighten around them, he swallowed hard and laid his mouth on her throat, inhaling her excitement.

"Dagan," she whispered.

Reese gripped his shoulders, beginning to move. He wrapped one arm around her waist holding her against the wall while she rode his fingers. "That's right, *reskar*," he said, then took her earlobe between his teeth. "Ride me any way you can."

She screamed when her body exploded and a rush of her cream spilled over his fingers. Breathing heavy, she leaned her head back to the wall. He gently pulled his fingers from her body, sticking them in his mouth to lick away her juices.

His eyes couldn't focus and his body revved when he tasted her essence.

She opened her eyes and her gaze held his. "I love what you do to me."

She reached down to unclasp his pants, but he stopped her. "No, baby, we don't have time." He brought her hand up to his mouth and kissed the palm. "Later tonight, we'll finish this."

"But..."

"Tonight." He set her feet on the floor and pushed her back against the wall while ramming his tongue into her mouth in a sensual thrust. Promises of what would come.

He'd managed to get the *fury* under control again, but Flame was right, each time it became more difficult.

"Cool," Geoffrey exclaimed when they pulled into the parking lot and got out. "I've never noticed this place here before and believe me, my college buddies and I have hit every hotspot."

Reese chuckled and subtly glanced Dagan's way. "This is a special place."

"Special how?" Joe wanted to know. He shot a glare at Dagan.

"Let's just say otherworldly," Dagan replied. "And leave it at that."

The same bouncer was at the door.

"Hello again, Seamus," Reese said.

He smiled big. "Well now, it's nice ta' be seeing ya again, Ms. Reese." He held out his big hand to Dagan. "Twice in one week may be a record for you, Dagan."

"Probably is, Seamus, but I have more business."

"Well you'll see some others here tonight. Must be a slow night for the hunt."

"Message received."

"Who are these other folks with ya?"

Dagan glanced back to the gangly group. "Some of Reese's friends. They wanted to see how the other half lives."

Seamus laughed. "Move on up here then."

He took his time frisking and sniffing each one. Joe scowled. Roberta threatened to tear Seamus a new one if he once let his hand slip inappropriately, and Geoffrey just took it all in stride. Chloe and Rufus were the last to enter.

A couple of women passed by and Reese couldn't tell if they were humans or *otherworldly*. Rufus let his eyes wander along with them.

Chloe reached her right hand around and grabbed hold of his crotch, squeezing just enough to get his attention. "Let's get one thing straight, hotshot. I like you," she ran her tongue over his tightened lips, "a lot." She released her grip on his family jewels and massaged them with a purpose. "Keep your eyes on this form." She ran her other hand down her body. "And we'll get along fine."

When the shock wore off, Rufus's eyes heated. Chloe still openly massaged him and Reese figured they had come to a mutual understanding.

"So who are we here to see anyway?" Reese asked.

"Flame," Dagan yelled over the careening music and noise of the crowded bar.

They found a table and pulled enough chairs around to sit. Before they had their drinks ordered Chloe dragged Rufus to the dance floor.

"Come on, lover boy," she purred. He followed along like a whipped pup, but Reese didn't believe it for a second. She knew Rufus could handle himself.

"Wow, can you believe that Chloe?" Geoffrey hollered. "Who'd of thought she would turn out to be this little she-devil."

Joe sat stoically next to Reese, and Roberta bounced her head in time with the beat of the eighties music.

When the drinks arrived, Dagan whispered in her ear. "I need to go find Flame."

"Okay."

After emptying her glass, Roberta jumped up. "Come on sweet thing," she said and grabbed Geoffrey's arm. "Let's boogie."

He threw a surprised look her way and then shrugged and went along. Reese laughed.

Joe still had a sour look on his face and nursed his drink, holding it between his palms. She scooted her chair over close to his and leaned into him. "It's a lot to take in, isn't it?"

He stared down into the amber liquid warming in his glass. "I don't like it."

"I can't say that I blame you. Believe me I didn't like it at first either, too unbelievable. When my father told me the truth about him and my grandparents, you could have blown me over with a feather. Now my sister is back." She threw her hands up.

He glared in the direction that Dagan had gone. "What about him?"

"Who? Dagan?"

He nodded.

"Well, that's another thing all together." She looked off into the distance, but couldn't see him. "There's something there, I haven't figured out what yet."

"He acts like he owns you." Joe's voice had grown hard.

She grabbed his bicep and squeezed as she leaned in and rested her head on his shoulder. "You are a good friend who watches over me."

"Which has generally been an easy thing to do...until he showed up."

Reese sighed. "I can't help you there, Joe. He saved my life. He changed it forever."

"Yeah, but not in a good way."

She frowned. "You can't blame Dagan for that. He didn't start this war anymore than I did, but we are participants nonetheless."

"I don't like it."

She smiled. "I know," she said and kissed his cheek. She stiffened.

Joe straightened and faced her. "What is it?"

About that time, a tall shadow clouded their table. A finely sculpted wraith with long black hair, a bare chest, black leather pants and gold biceps cuffs stared down at her.

Joe jumped up, slamming his drink down on the table. "Who the hell are you?"

Without acknowledging Joe, the warrior looked at her again. His shimmering eyes focusing on her breasts.

"Hello, Abu," she said in the best bored tone she could muster.

"Reese." He lifted his hand toward her. "How nice to see you again."

She rolled her eyes, but raised her hand. He took it between his and kissed first the back and then placed a warm kiss on her palm. Shivers raced across her skin. She remembered what had happened the last time he sought her out.

"Reese, who's the reject from Halloween?" Joe wanted to know.

"Joe, meet Abu. He's a god of some sort."

"Please, in that getup?"

She stifled a laugh.

Abu turned angry eyes on Joe. "Who is this human?"

"Don't get me started, asshole. I've had about enough of you so-called gods."

This made Abu smile. "I guess you have been around Dagan then."

"You know it. I imagine you know him too. Hung around together have you?"

Abu snarled. "In a manner of speaking."

Joe shook his head. "You don't like him either, huh?"

"We have had our differences."

"Hmmph—differences. I'll bet."

Abu turned his attentions back to Reese. "Would you care to dance?"

"You do remember what happened the last time we danced, don't you?"

His eyes lit up and he offered her a perfect smile. "Of course. Would you care to dance?"

She shook her head but couldn't help the slow smile from appearing. "You're doing it just to piss him off, aren't you?"

Rationalizing that it would be better to stay seated, she still rose and placed her hand in his. Maybe she could find out a little more about their relationship.

"Reese," Joe called.

She waved him off.

The song changed and R&B music blared from the speakers. The tune was a slow, rhythmic combination of beat and heat. Rufus's and Chloe's bodies were so close together, you couldn't see light between them. The way her hands were roaming over his body while he gripped her ass, they would need a room soon.

Abu pulled her closer, placing the hand he held on his shoulder and rested his hand on top. Snaking the other hand around her waist, he reeled her in tight against his swarthy body. Man, he was built for sin.

A devilish grin broke across his face. "Thank you."

Confused, she said "For what?"

"It would be my pleasure to do any number of sinful things to you."

"So you read minds? I'll have to remember that." His closeness did nothing to stir her emotions or cause the turmoil in her body. Only Dagan managed that.

Across the room, Dagan squared off with Flame.

"You have to do it."

"No, I don't."

Flame surged forward. "Dammit, Dagan, they will torture you beyond measure. You can't do this."

"The Pantheon thinks in the old ways."

"And your parents? They are part of the Pantheon."

"My father agrees with the command, but I think my mother would side with me."

"What will you do?"

"Whatever I have to." He downed the tequila and beer. "Now will you help me or not?"

Flame ran his hands down his face. "What do you want from me?"

"I need you to go to Pyre and convince him to make this for me." He handed over a drawing.

Flame stared at the paper. "What is it?"

"My business."

"I can't believe you would do this without the Pantheon's approval."

"I haven't done anything yet."

Dagan motioned to the bartender for another. "Things are changing for us, Flame. The longer we stay here the more the old ways do not apply." He downed another tequila and beer. "She is mine in every way except the bonding."

"You may end up dead."

Resting his forearms on the edge of the bar, Dagan lowered his head. "My choice. Nevertheless, I need to do this. I don't want someone else protecting her."

Flame growled and downed his bourbon. "I get it." He slipped the diagram in his pocket.

"Tell Pyre I need it as soon as possible."

"I will have to ease him into it first. He won't be thrilled about this decision either."

Dagan grabbed Flame's shoulder and squeezed. "Thank you."

"Hey, what are friends for?"

Dagan's gaze shifted past Flame and zeroed in on the dance floor where Abu and Reese were cuddled too damn close for his liking. He growled and barreled toward them.

Flame spun around and saw where Dagan was headed. "Hell," he swore and took off after his friend.

The roaring started low in his stomach and worked its way up until it rushed out of his mouth. Everyone on the dance floor stopped, startled.

Rufus climbed his way out of the haze of lust he'd been in since he got there. "This isn't good."

He stepped in front of Dagan. "Don't do it, Dagan. They are only dancing."

"Out of my way, Rufus."

"Well, well, looked what stumbled in from the street," Abu's silky voice jibed.

Rufus cringed. "Dagan, think about this."

His black eyes shifted and he glared at the *doghume*. "You don't want to get in the middle of this."

Knowing the better part of valor, Rufus moved aside.

His control over the *fury* slipped a peg. Abu had one arm still draped around Reese's hips and his other hand tangled in her hair, nuzzling her neck. His gaze locked on Dagan.

Dagan roared closer.

"It seems we have been here before." His icy tone barely leashed his temper.

"Dagan," Reese pleaded. "We were only dancing. I swear it."

"Step aside, Reese," Abu said in a low growl. "She has your scent imbedded in her skin, Time Walker. Seems you have been a bad boy."

His fists clenched and released. He felt Flame at his side.

"Control it, Dagan. It will do no good to let loose. He will destroy you if you don't keep control."

"He only did it to piss you off, Dagan, and you know it."

He turned his fiery glare on her. "And why did you do it, Reese?"

"Because this is an innocent dance and you have nothing to be jealous about." Her face now marred with anger she yelled, "Plus, you have no say in the matter. I thought we had that out the last time."

Abu reached his arms around her shoulders, clasping his hands in front and pulling her back to him. "Shall we see what else we can manage that he will have no say in, little flower?"

"Ooooh, men," she screamed. Reese rammed her elbow into Abu's ribcage, causing him to release his hold on her. She turned around and punched him in the jaw. He didn't flinch.

Anger roiling off her, she stepped up and slapped Dagan hard across the face then glared daggers at Flame before storming off.

Rufus let out a whoosh of breath. "Damn, Dagan."

Flame agreed.

Rubbing his jaw, Abu came up to him and leaned against Dagan's shoulder. "For such a small female she has a powerful right hook."

Dagan let a small laugh escape before he shoved Abu off him and planted his fist in Abu's already aching face. "That's for pissing me off."

Abu stumbled back but didn't fall. He shook his head as Dagan pursued Reese.

"Abu, that had to hurt," Rufus said.

The tall warrior laughed and wiggled his jaw. "Nah, if he wanted to really hurt me, I would have ended up on the floor."

At the table, Roberta slanted a you're-too-stupid-to-live look at Dagan before saying, "She grabbed her purse and headed for the door."

He heard Geoffrey quip, "Remind me never to get her mad at me. Ouch."

Dagan flew out the door in time to see a large shadow of a man grab Reese and pull her toward the parking lot.

"Let me go. Let me go." Reese screamed as she kicked him in the shin and slapped at his chest.

"Hey," Dagan yelled and launched himself at the kidnapper. Before he landed on the guy's back, the intruder released Reese and spun around. "Oh shit."

Scion caught him mid-air and pushed him up against the outer building with his very large hand around his neck cutting off the oxygen.

"Scion," he squeaked. "What the hell are you doing?"

Reese had fallen to the ground when he'd let her go and she stared up at what looked to be a statue. He had to be at least six-seven or six-eight. His hair was long and wild down his back. The arm extending from his body looked to be the size of a tree trunk. He would definitely be scary if you met him in a dark alley.

"As I understand it, I am supposed to take over the handling of this situation." He ground his teeth. "It seems someone was attempting to keep me from doing my job."

"Scion—" Dagan tried to speak but the other time walker squeezed his neck tighter.

"Stop!" Reese got up and went over to the giant. "Please, stop," she pleaded. "Let him go."

He turned his fierce gaze on her and sneered. His other hand reached out and grabbed her arm, pulling her closer to him. "I see now why you were attempting to keep me away, Dagan. She reeks of you."

From out of nowhere, a maniacal scream rent the air. A body flew across the space and landed on the giant's back. It wrapped legs around his torso, started pulling his hair and biting him.

"Ow," he growled. "By all the gods." He removed his hand and Dagan dropped to the ground in a heaving heap. Reese ran over to him and helped him up.

"What the hell is going on?" a female voice broke through

the tirade.

With his arm around Reese's shoulder, Dagan rubbed his neck and started toward the other woman. "Angelique?"

Reese stiffened. The tall, chic woman had long, dark, curly hair and wide brown eyes. In jeans that were skintight, you could see all her ample curves. She wore stylish snow shoes, had a perfect white smile, and flawless skin, though her nose and cheeks had turned red from the cold. Another woman Reese couldn't see liking just on principle. They were crawling out of the woodwork.

"What the hell are you doing here?"

"Dagan, what is this thing attacking me?" Scion yelled. He reached around and pulled the tiny creature off his back, clamping it to his side.

Incredulous, Reese said, "Riley?"

"What?" Dagan spun around. Sure enough, Scion held Riley against him, her feet dangling several inches off the ground. She tried to sink her teeth into his arm and used some colorful descriptive words to describe his anatomy and his ancestry.

In her seductive French accent Angelique said, "She insisted on coming here." She shrugged. "I could not keep her from sneaking out, so here we are."

Scion clamped his large hands on Riley's arms, held her in front of him and shook her. "Cease, female, afore I put you over my knee."

"You wish, scum," Riley spat. She lifted her knee and forced it into Scion's ribs.

He grunted but didn't release his hold.

Exasperated, and thinking she'd had enough for the night, Reese closed her eyes and counted to ten. "Riley, what are you doing?"

Her sister was still trying to catch hold of something but her arms weren't long enough. "This brute attacked your Mr. Yummy and I saw him knock you down."

"But, I'm okay and this is a...*co-worker* of Dagan's."

Riley stilled, but narrowed her eyes on Scion. She casually glanced at the axe hung across his shoulders, lying along his back. "What is he, a lumberjack?"

A small rumble like the beginning of a thunderstorm rolled out of Scion's mouth until it turned into a full laugh. He pulled Riley close to him, wrapped his arm around her waist and held her to his side. She wound her leg around his to help hold herself up.

Scion walked over to where Dagan and Reese stood. "She's small, but feisty. I like that in a female." He nuzzled her neck and earlobe. "She smells good too."

"Hey, watch it, Jack," Riley warned. "I'm still within striking distance."

He growled and swung her to the front of him, pulling her legs around his waist. "Be still, my little meerkat, or I'll take you for a ride." He thrust his pelvis forward, making her squeal.

Dagan put his hands up. "Okay, can we focus, people?"

Patrons from the club had filtered out into the parking lot to see all the activity.

"Seamus," Dagan called to the bouncer who waded his way through the crowd. "Can you get everyone back inside?"

"Sure thing, Dagan." He turned to the onlookers. "Let's break it up, folks. Nothing more to see out here. Back inside, back inside."

Dagan swung around after all the outsiders were gone. Rufus, Chloe and the others had joined them. He shook his head and raised his eyes to the heavens. "Would you put her down?"

Scion grumbled a little. Riley kissed his cheek before he set her feet on the ground.

"We need to go somewhere and talk," he said to Scion.

Scion frowned. "This is true."

"How about my place?" Reese recommended.

"Actually, I was going to suggest that Rufus take you home."

"But..."

Dagan caressed Reese's cheek. "I have to talk to Scion. We need to exchange information and discuss strategy." He looked up to the sky. "It's getting late and with you not in your house, the *galla* and Kur will be looking to take you again. I will be there later."

Reese let out an irritated breath. "Fine!" She turned her back to him. "Come on, Riley."

Her sister ran to catch up to her, but threw a come-hither look over her shoulder at Scion. He winked and grinned.

"Angelique, since you're here now, how about you taking Riley to her father's with Gideon. Then, you can split watches with Chloe and the others."

"I'll go get my car."

Geoffrey piped up. "Joe and I will stay at my place with Angelique."

Dagan chuckled and slapped Geoffrey on the shoulder. "You'll have your hands full."

With a twinkle in his eye, he winked. "One can only hope."

"Have at it, my man, but be careful she doesn't devour you."

Geoffrey faked a shiver. "Can she do that? Cool."

Angelique pulled up in her fully loaded BMW. Reese hugged Riley then stepped back while Riley jumped in the front seat. "Come on, gents," Angelique said and blew Geoffrey a kiss.

Rubbing his hands together, he climbed in the backseat behind the driver's side and Joe slid in behind Riley.

"Rufus, I'll be by later then you can hook up with the others."

"Okay, boss." He walked over to speak with Scion and let Dagan and Reese have a moment.

"Hey." Dagan tried to coax the reluctant Reese to look at him.

"Don't." She shrugged off his touch. "Something is going on. I can tell."

He wished he could tell her the truth of the matter, but the time wasn't right. He needed everything in place first.

"I will fill you in when I come to you tonight." He moved in behind her and encircled her with his arms, laying his chin on top of her head. "Okay?"

"If you lie to me, I will so banish your ass."

A light laugh tickled her hair. "Banish my ass? And how do

you intend to do that?"

"My grandfather is a god, you know."

"Ugh, don't remind me."

She sniffled but offered him a disarming smile.

"Rufus," he yelled. "Get her home. Scion and I are going on a little hunt."

"Sure thing." He held his arm out and smiled wide in Reese's direction.

She looked at Dagan one more time, then hooked her arm through Rufus's and left.

Scion moved up next to him. "The Pantheon will burn your ass for this."

"You don't know my plan yet."

"True," Scion agreed. "But I have lived a long time and I can see that you don't intend to follow their orders."

"Can you give me forty-eight hours?"

Scion lifted a blond brow. "I imagine I could keep myself busy with demons for that length of time." He frowned. "But no more, Dagan."

"Agreed." He smiled at the large man. "Besides, you might have to help guard Riley while you're here."

Scion tilted his head in contemplation. "Hmmm, did you say forty-eight hours?" He rested his fist over his heart. "Are you sure that will be enough time?"

All Dagan's senses went on alert. He closed his eyes and focused trying to locate the *galla*.

"Dagan?"

"I feel them." His eyes popped open. "They're at Reese's father's house."

Scion turned concerned eyes his way. "The females were heading there."

"Come on, we have work to do."


Kur was in a foul mood. The evening with his wife had not gone as planned and he fumed at the thought of not being able to bury his throbbing cock into his willing wife. She persisted at denying him his desire, which meant more conditioning. He tired of the game, eager to begin that part of his plan. For centuries, she had kept him at a distance, forcing him to punish her over and over again. No matter, it was destined to happen. It would take time.

Feral came strolling into the throne room.

"This better be good news," Kur spat out to his captain. "I do not wish to hear of another failure."

Feral bowed. "I understand your disappointment, my king, for it rivals my own."

Kur liked the sound thinking of his second-in-command. The demon knew his place and knew how to placate his boss. "What is it then?"

Feral stepped forward. "I thought you would want to know that we have located another of Enki's descendents for you to consume."

"What?" Kur rose and hurried down the steps.

Feral smiled. "It seems that Reese Whittaker's sister has come back to town and is now staying with their father, who it also turns out is a *nephili*."

"A *nephili*?" Kur smiled. "It seems that the tides have shifted our way."

"I hoped you would review our plans to see if you have any suggestions."

Kur clamped his hand down on Feral's shoulder. "You are correct. I plan to win the next round."

# Chapter Fifteen

Reese and Rufus pulled up to her house. He put on his night goggles to check for the *galla* energy signature, but found none. He signaled her to get out and hurried around to walk next to her toward the house. The whole time he scanned the area for any intruders.

Within seconds, a red flash of light denoted the arrival of something and Rufus fell to the ground. Reese swung around to find a tall, beautiful blond woman. She looked normal enough, even with the whole Goth fashion.

"Who are you? Rufus!"

"Stay where you are." The woman sneered.

Reese glared at the newcomer. "What do you want?"

The woman hissed. "I want you."

Reese tensed and got ready to fight.

The other woman laughed. "It will not be that easy." She held up her left hand. Her fingers lengthened and grew long fingernails. Her right foot planted square on Rufus's back. "I have a proposition for you."

Her smile grew sinister.

"You come with me or I'll rip his throat out." She slowly bent toward Rufus.

Reese didn't know what to think of this. "How do I know you won't kill him anyway?"

The demon snarled screwing her pretty face into something ugly. "He is insignificant. It is you I want."

"I'll give you insignificant, bitch," Rufus said and rolled over, grabbing her leg and tossing her to the ground. "Run,

Reese."

Before Reese got two feet, the blond flashed to her, grabbed a handful of hair and twisted her around, putting a long thin blade at her throat.

Rufus stilled.

"You tell the time walker that Vile has his little plaything. If he wants her back, he will come to the place where they first met by dawn."

Before Rufus could respond, the demon flashed them away.

Dagan and Scion materialized inside Clive Whittaker's home. Gideon jumped.

"Holy hell," Gideon swore. In baggy jeans and a partially tucked-in flannel shirt, Gideon walked over and looked up at the towering Scion. "Who is he?"

"Gideon, Scion, Scion, Gideon."

"Another time walker."

Dagan nodded.

"Sweet."

"Have your sensors picked up anything, Gideon?"

"It flutters every now and then, but nothing major."

Just as the words left his mouth, the gauges started waving wildly.

"We've got company," Scion said.

"Has Angelique dropped Riley off yet?"

"Yes, she's upstairs taking a shower or something."

"Where is Mr. Whittaker?"

"I'm here," Clive Whittaker called out from the den. "What's happening?"

Dagan lifted his head and sniffed the air. *"Zulies."*

Scion frowned. "I smell the filth."

Gideon's gaze passed between them. "Smell what? What's happening, Dagan?"

"We have some real nasty visitors."

Clive inhaled. A foul odor wafted the air. *"Galla?"*

Dagan moved toward the window to gaze out at the street.

"Worse," Scion replied. "The *zulies* are one step up from the *galla*. They are bigger in size and have a nastier disposition."

"Gideon," Dagan barked. "Call Angelique and let her know what's going on. And, call Rufus and make sure he and Reese got to her place."

Gideon whipped out his cell phone and started making calls.

Scion's determined gaze met Dagan's. "I'll go secure all points of entry as best I can, and check on Riley."

"What can I do, Dagan?"

Dagan held out his hand and a large canvas bag appeared. "I happened to bring along more weapons this time."

Gideon rushed over and helped them unload the bag. "I got ahold of Angelique, but I haven't been able to raise Rufus."

This news lay heavy in his stomach, eating a deep hole into his heart. His first instinct driven hard by the *fury* told him to rush out and find Reese. The warrior in him reigned supreme for now, knowing he would be out-numbered.

The entire house shook as though an earthquake had hit and they were experiencing the aftershock.

"What the hell is that?"

"They're being neighborly and knocking," Dagan replied dryly.

"But I thought with all the protection, the *galla* and demons couldn't see my house."

Dagan frowned. "Normally they wouldn't be able to." He had a feeling that Kur had either coaxed or threatened a sorcerer to work with him. It was the only explanation for how the demons and *zulies* would be able to get through the wards. More unexpected surprises.

Another force shook the entire house. Scion and Riley rushed downstairs. Clive hurried over to his daughter. "Are you all right?" He looked Scion up and down.

"Yes."

"Everything is as secure as I can make it," Scion told Dagan. "This feeble structure will not hold up to their barrage much longer."

"They're not going to raze the house down. The *zulies* will want close contact, hand to hand. They are too uncoordinated for weapons."

"What *is* that terrible stench?" Riley asked.

"*Zulies* are those who are dead but have been taken control of by something else," Dagan offered.

"What do you mean taken control of?" Gideon asked with a complete look of horror on his face.

"A demon or wizard or god will summon them up from the grave to do their bidding."

Aghast Riley said, "You mean zombies? These things are zombies?"

Dagan exchanged a telling look with Scion. "They will be coming."

"Don't they just sound like loads of fun," Riley replied hotly.

"I think staying together is our best defense," Dagan said to the others. "Grab some weapons from the bag and we will position ourselves here in the great room."

They all nodded. Riley liberated a massive sword but found it hard to handle.

"I think I should hold on to that, little lady." Scion appeared beside her and relieved her of the weight. "You stay close to me," he ordered.

She retrieved two funny looking guns. "Look, bub. I'm not going to cower while all you big macho men fight the battle."

Scion turned his impressive frame to her, grabbed her by the shoulders and shook her none-too-gently. "Reckless. You stay by my side."

Her teeth clattered when he shook her. "All right, all right. Stop shaking me, dammit."

Clive started toward Scion, but Dagan waylaid him. "He is her best chance at getting through this."

"Does he have to be so rough with her?"

Dagan gave him a quizzical look. "Have you spent much time around your daughters lately?"

"I see Reese all the time. Riley has been in Europe for the last couple of years, but I talk to her on the phone."

"Right," Dagan snipped. "They are stubborn, irrational and do not do what they are told."

A slow smile crossed Clive's face. "They get that from their mother too."

"Well if you want Riley to survive this little encounter, Scion is where he needs to be and will handle her the way she needs to be handled."

All the windows in the room blew and they were pelted with flying glass. Gideon, nearest the windows, dropped to the floor with his hands over his head until the storm passed. Dagan pulled him to his feet, making sure he had no debilitating injury then handed him a gun. "Pyre made special ammo. Aim for the chest or the head."

Scion completely surrounded Riley until the danger had passed. He kicked the sofa over and shoved her down on the floor behind it then pushed it back toward the corner, so she was covered on all sides. "Keep your head down. If the creatures get anywhere near you, you scream for me."

Clive had a few cuts and one sliver sticking into the back of his leg. Walking over and placing his hand on Clive's shoulder, Dagan grabbed the piece of glass with his bare fingers. He met Clive's eyes with his own, an unspoken assurance passed between them. "Count to three."

"One, two..."

Dagan ripped the sliver out. To his amazement, Reese's father didn't cry out or fall to the floor in pain.

"Daddy," Riley cried.

"I'm okay," he assured her.

All this happened in a matter of seconds. Before Dagan could turn toward the glassless windows now offering free entry for Kur's soldiers, they were pouring into the house and the battle began.

Calling upon his inner energy, Dagan slashed through the small force. He kept aware of the others and fought back to back with Scion a couple of times.

The gunshots reverberated in the room and the smell of gunpowder filled his nostrils, but he kept at it until there were none left, or so he thought.

He saw Riley come out from the hidey hole Scion had put her in pulling a gun from the waistband of her jeans. A *zulie* lying by her feet opened its eyes and grabbed her ankle. On reflex, she screamed and squeezed the trigger of the gun she held, shooting the *zulie* in the head.

She yanked her ankle out of its hand. "Damn zombies."

Scion crowded in on her. All Dagan's senses lit up again when a tall, lanky figure phasing in and out strolled through the now shattered door. Once inside, it solidified.

"Hello, Venom, what brings you here?" Dagan asked in a wary tone.

"I heard a *nephili* had been found." The creature glanced at Clive Whittaker.

Dagan chuckled. Venom was the leader of the *Anuna*, those who had fallen from grace with the Pantheon many centuries ago. Banned to the Underworld, they roamed, searching for a way to lay low the Council and take their place as rulers. "I guess that answers the question of who made the *zulies*." He shook his head. "I thought you abhorred Kur. Why would you be working with him?"

The demon sneered. "We came to an agreement."

"Oh?" The movement of other demons didn't escape Dagan. His hand tightened around the hilt of his sword, still dripping with dark ooze. He sensed Clive tense as well.

"I told him I would waste no more than one Earth-bound hour on this venture. If I manage to get the *nephili*, he is mine."

"And what did Kur get in return?"

"He would not say, but it seemed very important to him."

Dagan's stomach churned. This day continued to suck. The *Anuna* were fallen gods stripped of their rights, most of their powers, and kicked out of Dilmun. Banished to the Underworld they were to walk there for eternity. When Kur went to the Underworld, he brought with him certain knowledge about thin layers between the realms that shift and will open to certain frequencies. That is the only way this *Anuna* was able to be here now.

They could not be killed because they were gods, but in Venom's current state, the *Anuna* could experience pain. If Dagan hurt Venom enough, he would return to the Underworld to heal.

He pointed the tip of his dripping weapon toward Venom. "Shall we begin?"

Bowing, the fallen god said, "Yes, as I have wasted ten minutes already explaining that which was not necessary."

"I'm sorry to delay your fun," Dagan said and made a courtly bow.

Venom laughed and attacked.

In solid form, *Anuna* made easy targets. He carried no weapons, but did have the ability to blast an opponent with a bolt of energy containing enough voltage to incapacitate if hit directly.

If taken, Clive would spend a lifetime in the Underworld being tortured as revenge on the gods who had banished them. Or, they would try to use him to barter their freedom. Either way, it wouldn't be good.

Venom charged him, swinging a fist toward Dagan's head. He deflected the blow with his left forearm, curled his fingers and put his fist in Venom's face. The creature stumbled back, roared and came at him again, extending sharp blades from its fingertips. Dagan spun away but not before Venom raked his bladed fingers across Dagan's stomach.

Clive was doing the Ali shuffle with another demon and getting in some great upper cuts and jabs, sparring for his life. When the *galla* scratched his face very close to his eye and let loose with a wail, Clive reached behind his back, produced a *Khukri* knife and sliced both arms and the *galla*'s chest in a big X motion.

Dagan ducked as a wooden chair from the dining room set came hurtling toward him. On the way up, he landed his fist into the midsection of the creature Clive battled. It grunted and stumbled back. During that exchange, Dagan lost sight of Venom.

To his left he saw Scion with his battle axe clearing a wide path and not allowing any of the demons near Riley. He grabbed the handle, spun around and planted the end into the head of one of the *zulies*. It fell to the floor unconscious.

Riley had her hands full with the guns and popped off some rounds into the stomach of a demon rushing in from the right.

He rose several feet into the air, holding his stomach, before crashing back to the ground. Something between a groan and a whine came out of the thing before it sagged, dead.

Riley walked over and kicked the thing in the face.

Gideon had a chair in one hand with its legs pointed outward poking at the *zulie* who concentrated on him. A long chain swung from the other hand, the length of which wrapped around his forearm. Dagan didn't remember having a chain in the bag. Maybe Gideon had brought his own arsenal.

The five of them were holding their own against the onslaught. It made Dagan uneasy. The *Anuna* were masters at strategy and warfare, especially Venom.

From behind him, Dagan heard Venom yell "*Searci.*"

All the remaining demons and *zulies* stopped and joined Venom where he stood.

Dropping his gaze to Dagan, Venom said, "The hour is up."

"Already? Damn, I was just getting into it."

Some kind of vortex opened and the enemy stepped through and disappeared.

Scion stormed over. "What the hell?"

"Yeah," Gideon laughed. "We kicked their butts."

Scion and Dagan shared glances.

"What is it?" Riley asked, having noticed the concerned look.

"It was too easy." Dagan flipped his phone open and pushed three.

"Dagan?"

The voice on the other end of the line sounded woozy and out of sorts.

"Rufus, where's Reese?"

"She's gone."

"What?" he roared. "Are you at the house?"

"Yes."

"I'm on my way." He shoved the phone back in the holder on his belt. "Scion, can you take care of everything here? *Rufus says Reese is gone. I have to get there.*"

"Has something happened to Reese?" Riley asked. "I'm coming with you."

"No," both Dagan and Scion replied.

"Riley, you need to stay here and see to your father. Scion and Gideon will take care of the clean up. When I know more, I'll call."

He snapped his fingers and appeared in Reese's front yard. Rufus sat on the porch steps holding the right side of his head. Blood had matted his hair.

"What happened?"

"We'd just arrived. I scanned the area and there were no signs of anything. When we got out, all of a sudden, I'm struck from behind and I went down. I came to long enough to see a blond witch telling Reese that if she didn't go with her, she'd kill me."

"So Reese went."

Rufus shook his head, then regretted it. "Not at first, but the bitch—Vile—pulled a knife on her." He shifted uneasily. "I knocked her to the ground but she was too fast."

"Was she alone?"

"Yes." He looked at Dagan, but then cast his gaze downward. "She told me to tell you that if you wanted to see Reese alive again, you were to go to the place where you met, before dawn."

"That's not much time."

"What are you going to do?"

"The only thing I can do—go to her."


Dagan materialized at the corner where he'd met Reese a few nights ago. So much had happened in that short time.

No snow fell, but the bitter wind cut through him. Though he had changed his clothes, the icy air pricked the still healing cuts.

Across the street, a tall, lithe blonde stood wrapped in a fur coat. She crooked her finger at him. Obviously, this was the bitch who had taken Reese and he would do whatever it took to get her back.

When he jogged toward the woman, she turned and started walking, only stopping when she'd reached a huge warehouse at the end of the block. Going inside got him out of the icy blast and it took him all of a few seconds to adjust to the deeper darkness.

"Come with me," Vile said in a gently accented voice.

He followed her to the back corner of the cavernous building. As he slowly closed on the location, his attuned senses picked up the faint heartbeat and the severe smell of blood. His heart pounded against his chest wall. Was he too late?

Coming around a stack of boxes, Dagan saw Reese. Her wrists were manacled and the chain hung from the ceiling. Her head hung forward and she slumped in a thick pool of blood.

His heart skipped and the *fury* in him bellowed, but before he could move, Kur stepped into the light next to Reese's still body.

"It seems I have to be more specific next time I give Vile instructions." Kur indicated the woman who had led Dagan there. "I told her to toy with the prize, but she got a bit carried away."

It was all Dagan could do not to lunge at Kur and rip his throat out.

Reese was still alive.

Dressed in jeans, a knit cap and a long shoreman's jacket, Kur looked like a dock worker.

"I deplore the cold," he said conversationally. "But I thought keeping it this way would help slow the blood flow, thereby keeping her alive longer. I had so wanted you to be here when I drained my prize."

Dagan clenched his teeth.

"It doesn't matter what condition she's in when I take her life force. The end result is the same."

"So what's the plan?" Dagan finally spoke. "Surely you didn't bring me here just to watch."

Kur laughed. "You're trying to be so nonchalant when I know it's killing you to see her life slipping away—drip, drip, drip."

Dagan lifted his hand over his head and unsheathed his sword. "Come on, Kur. Let's do this again, only this time, just you and me." He swung the sword across his body. "Are you man enough?"

An insane fire burned in Kur's eyes. Kur cocked his head, considering Dagan's proposal. "I will take you on, Time Walker. I should have finished you properly the last time. But, I have the greater advantage," Kur snickered. "I devoured two life forces before I came here." He licked his lips. "You were expending your energy fighting Venom."

"He sends his regards."

Kur scowled at Vile. "Don't let her die before I'm finished here."

"No worries," she flicked him a kiss and tossed him a blade.

Kur raised the blade up in front of his face and bowed to Dagan. *To the death* had never meant more to Dagan than at this moment. He had to stay focused. The woman he loved hung in a pool of her own blood but he couldn't let it distract him, or he'd likely join her and the creature would win.

Kur advanced bringing his sword in a high arc toward Dagan's neck. Holding the hilt in both hands, Dagan did a one-eighty and blocked the move. Kur faltered, a little off balance. Dagan's sword crisscrossed his body in a figure eight, aggressively backing Kur up until he pressed against the wall. Raising his blade at the last minute, he deflected the fatal blow. The hard contact reverberated up his arm and Dagan sliced into his forearm when he retracted.

Kur hissed. "I'm impressed."

With a glint in his eye Dagan said, "I live to fight."

Kur's face screwed into a mask of hatred. "Not for long."

Dagan and Kur performed their deadly dance across every inch of the warehouse floor. Each swing and stab, thrust and parry took chunks of skin and dotted the floor with blood.

On one lunge, Kur slipped in some blood, skidded forward and fell to his knees cursing. It presented Dagan with the chance he'd been waiting for, so he stuck the tip of his sword through Kur's extended knee, wrenching a scream from the dark lord. Dagan quickly spun around and brought the blade down, slicing deeply at the point where Kur's neck connected to the shoulder. Unfortunately, he missed the jugular. Blood spurted from the wound.

Vile raced over and sent a knife hurtling toward Dagan, who deflected it. Quick as lightning he sailed two metal stars at her, lodging one in her shoulder and the other in her hand. She screamed and dropped next to Kur before pulling the metal objects out, letting them fall to the concrete floor. Blood oozed from the wound on Kur's neck, his fingers bloodied from stemming the flow. With a lethal glare, Vile wrapped her arms around Kur and teleported them back to the Underworld.

Dagan rushed to Reese.

Using the sword, he pounded the chains, cutting them from the wall, letting it fall to catch her weak form. He rested two shaking fingers against the pulse point. Her skin was pale and her lips were turning blue. She wouldn't last much longer. Hopelessness coursed through him, stabbing his heart with its vicious attack.

He wanted to see those blue flames glare at him and threaten to banish his ass again, needed to see her smile and feel her warmth. One more time to lie next to her and hear her sighs when they made love. One more kiss.

"Nammu," he cried. "Nammu, I need you."

The air around him grew humid and moist, a drastic difference from the frigid clime just moments before. Nammu, the mother of all the gods, shimmered to life. Her raven hair swept away from her face, showcasing her turbulent sea-green eyes which reminded him of a tropical storm, and her wide, generous mouth wore the color of a sunset. The emerald colored gown she wore was simple elegance, the bodice fitted, the full skirt sweeping the floor. Fine white lace edged the neckline and her ample bosom. A delicately arched brow hiked as she looked on him from her regal pose.

"Why have you summoned me?"

Fierce and wild, Dagan cast his tear-filled gaze in her direction. "She is dying. I need you to save her."

"You know it is forbidden to change the course of events."

"This wasn't supposed to happen," he screamed through the anguish twisting his heart.

"How can you know this?"

"Because I didn't do my job, if I had, she wouldn't be lying here on death's door."

"If you were lax in your duties..."

"Not lax," he countered hotly. "I defied the Pantheon. Instead of turning her over to Scion, I thought to cleverly have my way, and in doing so, I put her life at risk. This is my fault."

He brushed a stray hair from Reese's face and watched her chest rise and fall in shallow breaths. "I failed her," he whispered.

Her noble features sternly assessed him as she floated slowly toward them. "If what you say is true—"

"It is."

"Then I will save her." She raised her hand before his gratitude spilled forth. "But, it will cost you, Time Walker."

"Anything."

Lifting her hands toward the sky, Nammu chanted in the ancient language. A soft glow radiated from her palms until it encompassed Reese's entire body. The warm light exuded energy which it siphoned into her still form.

Dagan felt the swell and reluctantly moved away from Reese's body, not wanting to interfere with the rejuvenation. In his desperation, the minutes seemed like hours. Slowly, the color returned and her breaths grew stronger. He placed his unsteady palm over her heart and felt the strong, hardy beat.

With deep sincerity Dagan said, "Thank you, my lady."

Nammu lowered her arms and smiled at him. "She will be fine, Dagan." In a motherly gesture, she stroked his head like one would a small child. "It is you I am concerned about."

"I care not for myself. That she is alive and well is enough for me."

"She is your *blethred*."

He slowly raised his eyes to her. "I know, my lady."

"The *fury* has everything to do with your decisions on this matter."

His jaw clenched. "I should have handled things better." He lifted Reese's head to cradle it against his chest.

Nammu crossed her arms. "Tell me more about the

Pantheon's orders regarding the female."

Dagan explained everything, including his intentions to defy their order, at least until he could dispose of Kur. Lastly, he informed her of the punishment imposed on him, to return to Dilmun and work with Gilgamesh training new time walkers, while trying to live through the separation.

She growled. "This is most cruel even for the Council. They know what toll the *fury* can have on our kind."

"They are afraid of change, my lady. While I don't agree with their thinking, I will accept the punishment." Nammu faded away.

Reese gasped. Dagan kissed her forehead, her cheek, the tip of her nose.

She opened her eyes. "Hi."

"Hi." He had to fight the urge to scream to the heavens with joy.

"What happened?"

"Don't you remember?" His voice was thick and husky.

She closed her eyes briefly. "No, I don't remember anything after that demon bitch latching on to me."

Blessed be Nammu. She must have erased the torture and near death from Reese's memory.

"Thank you, my lady," he whispered under his breath.

"What about Rufus?" Reese asked anxiously.

"He'll be fine. Got a bit of a headache, but he's fit and ready to fight again."

She smiled. "That's good."

"How do you feel?"

"I think I'm all right. I guess I got knocked out or something because I dreamed of this beautiful angel with green eyes and black hair, telling me to rest and heal and come back to you."

"I'm glad you listened." And forever grateful that Nammu had heeded his call.

"What happened to Kur and the wicked old witch?"

He cocked his head. "Wicked old witch?"

"You'd have to know the *Wizard of Oz* story."

"I'm not familiar with this story."

"Never mind, just tell me what happened to Kur."

"We dueled. He lost."

Reaching her hand up, she caressed his face. "You're my hero, you know."

Lowering his head, he captured her mouth in a tender but needy kiss. Her warm breath against his skin sent shivers of pleasure coursing through him.

Dagan made up his mind. He would perform the *démarr*, the ritual that would bind him and Reese in mind, body, and heart forever.

# Chapter Sixteen

Dagan called Rufus, knowing he would worry until he reported in. After Dagan had filled her in on what had happened, Reese insisted on seeing her father and sister, so when Rufus drove up in a snazzy gray Jaguar, they went to her father's house.

Riley sat on the floor between Scion's legs. Clive and Gideon recounted the attack by Venom and the *zulies*, and Riley filled in bits and pieces that she felt were necessary to get the full effect.

Dagan stood behind Reese, kneading her shoulders. "Tomorrow, I'll go to Enki and let him know of Venom's involvement, and that there is a sorcerer or sorceress helping them. Percilious will set a new, stronger magick on this place for protection."

"Tell him I'd like to see him face to face this time, would you?" Clive asked.

"I shall. I'm sure he'll be pleased to hear it."

Riley leaned forward, putting her elbows on her knees. "So what will happen now?"

"The danger is far from over. Now that Kur knows you're all here, in this time and place, he'll continue to send the *galla* back until he gets what he wants."

"Does that mean you're going to stay here as well?"

He felt Reese's shoulders tense. "Measures will be taken to increase the magick surrounding you. Some of the *doghume*, like Gideon and Rufus, will be assigned to keep an eye out. Kur is recovering but he'll be planning. He doesn't like being defeated."

213

"And I will start learning and re-learning everything about my powers so I'm prepared should we be attacked again," Clive offered.

"What about the time walkers?" Riley persisted in her quest for answers.

"We go where needed. Kur has his minions searching different time periods for more descendants.

Riley sat up and curled her arm around Scion's leg. "So." She slipped her hand under his pant leg and massaged his calf. "That means you can come back here sometimes?"

Dagan watched Scion give a lazy smile and his eyes darken. Something told him that Scion would be visiting here when his duties permitted it.

"Yes, that's true."

Reese still had not relaxed.

A short time later, they loaded into the car that Rufus had secured for them and headed back to Reese's house.

He drove. She sat quietly watching the landscape whiz by, like the night they'd first met.

Something had happened. Her clothes had been bloody and she didn't like the fact that she couldn't remember anything. Had he done another mind sweep? Why would he only take those few memories and not everything? It had to be bad.

Part of her was angry because he wouldn't fill in the missing time. He'd told her, "All that's important is that you're here, whole and safe. Nothing else matters."

But it mattered to her.

"Dagan, why did Scion show up tonight?"

"He came to help."

He hadn't looked at her in a while. She knew by the way his hands gripped the steering wheel and his jaw clenched that he wasn't telling her the whole truth. She wanted to punch the big jerk. How could she love someone who lied to her?

Should she rethink that question? No, she knew it to be true.

She loved Dagan.

Although it had been a short time rout with demons trying to kill them and gods showing up on her doorstep, she loved him. She had fallen for him the first night when he'd cradled his body against her to keep the chills and the boogieman at bay. Then, bringing her donuts and coffee the next morning. Noble, courageous, compassionate, incredibly sexy, and the son of gods; what more could a girl want in a man?

"Why are you lying to me?" She twisted in the seat to look at him.

His dark eyes sought her out. "I'm not lying, Reese. Scion came to help protect you."

What would happen now? All the reasons she'd fallen in love with him were the same reasons he couldn't stay. Their occupations, if that's what you could call what he did, an occupation, were too different for them to be together. She stared at his stoic profile as he concentrated on the driving. Should she tell him how she felt? Did he feel the same way?

Dagan wondered what was going on in that pretty little head of hers. He hadn't lied to her about Scion, not really. He left out the part about turning her protection over to Scion and going away...forever. A minor tactical move on his part. He would rather bask in the brief time they shared than dwell on what manner of punishment Nammu and the Pantheon would deal him when he returned to Dilmun. The dictate to work with Gilgamesh, if he survived the separation from Reese and enduring whatever flaying he would receive, meant nothing compared to spending a few precious moments gazing into her beautiful eyes. Over the centuries, that memory and the warmth of her smile would stay with him.

*"Dagan, I have the item you requested."*

Flame's voice communicated clear in his mind.

*"In Reese's living room by the hearth you'll see a glass box mounted on the wall with a sacred chalice inside. Please place it on top of the box."*

*"How the hell did she get one of the Naruki chalices?"*

*"I didn't ask."* Dagan glanced over at his life mate and smiled. *"I'm sure she dug it up somewhere."*

*"No doubt. It'll be there when you arrive."* He paused briefly.

*"Are you sure about this?"*

*"Absolutely. Thanks."*

Bonding with Reese would unleash the *fury* he'd fought so hard to contain. This course of action guaranteed a painful separation and increased his risk of dying. Of course, once the Pantheon learned that he'd bonded with a human female without their consent, they may very well execute him, saving the pain of separation altogether. Either way, he was damned.

"Will you tell me something about yourself?" she asked.

He inclined his head.

"Where are you from?"

"Originally, my home is Lysara. It's a city in the clouds where Enlil, the air god lives."

"I've never seen anything about Lysara in my studies nor heard about it in any teachings."

"Nevertheless, it is there."

"Is it beautiful?"

"It's the most peaceful and pleasant place." He smiled. "My father does enjoy the opulence of deities."

His feelers were out before they pulled up to the house. He helped her out of the car and used his body to shield her from any attackers. Upon entering the house, he locked the door then went through every room to tightly secure it before putting the seal up for what would most likely be the last time. Prior to chanting the ancient spell, he secretly willed the items he would need for the *démarr*.

She barely had her coat off before he slid his arms around her and kissed her. No words, just actions as he picked her up and headed for the bedroom. She didn't argue or question. Did she feel it too, the overwhelming lust and sexual power? He could no more walk away now than he could the first time they had come together, only tonight would be different.

He needed to prepare everything for the ritual. Laying her on the bed, he touched his fingertips to her temples and she fell instantly asleep. He shed his coat and shirt then went into the living room where he found the item Flame had delivered on top of the glass case. He removed the case and wrapped his fingers around the Basco chalice. In their beliefs, the four chalices were created by the original Naruki gods, Aradumas, Basco, Parsimion, and Gartyemar, to bond the brethren. When the females were created, lust ran rampant until the first male experienced the *fury* and died. First, they thought it an isolated incident, until the next one broke into the frenzy followed by death then the next and the next. It took thousands of deaths to the point of near extinction before his people discovered similarities in each case and started conducting massive studies. Each new discovery brought them closer to a process that eventually worked.

One such epiphany was that the *fury* came upon a male when he found his life mate. Through ancient ritual, using the sacred chalices, the Naruki males bonded to the females, unleashing the *fury* to consummate the joining, sometimes lasting for days. The intense drive subsided, or at least diminished to a more reasonable level and life moved on.

Of course, those were only legends. Who knew the real reason bonding rituals had started? One certainty remained. When the *fury* set upon a male, if he did not bond with his female, the consequences were severe.

The drums and raised voices of his ancestors and their gods thrummed in his head, stronger with every second that he held the chalice. He needed to hurry and complete the necessary preparations.

Quickly he moved through the house, placing the required items in the appropriate places. When that was done, he took the chalice into the kitchen, washed it with warm water and soap then rinsed with clear, cool water to set in motion the chain of events that would, this night, bind him to Reese forever.

Setting the chalice on the counter, he retrieved the chilled bottle of Merlot and filled it nearly to the top. With a large knife, he sliced the palm of his hand and dripped his blood into the wine. Within minutes, the cut had healed. Confident, he went back into the bedroom to begin.

Dagan lifted Reese's slumbering form against him and as he released her from the sleep, fell onto the bed with Reese under him. He kissed her hard. Grabbing the neck of her almost nothing shirt, he ripped it down the front to bare her breasts. He latched onto her nipple with his teeth, gently tugging it. Reese put her hands on either side of her breasts and pushed them together, offering them up to him. Shifting, he ripped apart the pants that covered her sex. Keeping one hand flat against her stomach, Dagan kissed his way down to her wet core where juices flowed and he lapped them up.

Her scent intoxicated him and his eyes rolled back in his head when he swallowed. She would soon be his...forever. The *fury* swelled in him. He watched the heavy-lidded beauty as she lifted her hips and he tongued her. His hands slid beneath her to grab the sensual globes of her ass and squeeze them gently. Reese cried out as the orgasm rocked her. He purred against the sensitive button as she rode the climactic ecstasy.

Dagan brought his arms along either side of her and crawled up her torso, keeping contact, skin to skin. His bulging erection caressed its way toward her most intimate place. She licked her lips and her exquisite eyes followed his movements with anticipation. As the tip of his cock reached her opening, Reese bit down on her bottom lip. He rocked his hips forward and back entering her a little further each time. She moaned and lifted her hand to brush the hair back from his face then she smiled and his heart took flight. The *fury* slacked long enough for him to appreciate the radiant look of his woman in sexual bliss.

The night grew hot from two overheated bodies straining against each other. Dagan knew he would love her many times before the sun rose, but he must mount her from behind and fill her with his seed while saying the sacred words for the ceremony of *démarr* to begin. Using great restraint, he ceased, wrenching an aggravated moan from Reese.

"Don't worry, my love, I'm far from being done with you this eve."

"That's good to know, sweetheart, but where the hell are you going?"

He chuckled. "Not far, I promise you."

Dagan rustled around in the darkened room, placing ceremonial cream candles in a semi-circle around the bed. He snapped his fingers and the candles came to life.

Reese gasped. "What's this?"

"I want to see you come apart in my arms by something

other than moonlight."

"You do say the sweetest things." She patted a place on the bed next to her. "Now come over here, big boy, and finish what you started."

He inclined his head. "As the lady wishes."

"Ummmm," she said. "I like hearing that."

Before he joined her again, Dagan faced to the left and bowed toward the silver candlesticks, murmuring words in what she knew now to be the Naruki language she didn't understand. The words were eloquent and rolled off his tongue like a song. He then turned to the foot of the bed, bowed to the place where candles in artistically designed stone holders flickered and murmured more words. Last, he acknowledged the weathered wooden candelabra.

She wondered why he'd done this but when he slid between the sheets and nipped her shoulder, she didn't question it.

"Now, my lovely, I want you on your hands and knees."

He threw the pillows off the bed and rolled her to face the mattress. He lay atop her back, propped up by his muscular arms. His hot erection surged and probed against the crease of her ass in an erotic rhythm. She wanted to reach around and dig her fingers into him, but he kept her from it by the way he positioned his arms next to her.

Dagan eased back and rose onto his knees. His large callused hand smoothed down her spine, and his mouth brushed fluttery kisses on her hips before gently biting her bottom. He pulled her up and settled her weight on all fours, smacking her buttock when she barked for effect.

She turned her head around to look over her shoulder. Dagan's eyes had gotten darker in the flickering light. He stared at her sex and then glared at her with some primeval gleam in his eyes. He moved in close and with one hand guided the tip of his erection along the opening. She wiggled her bottom side to side then did a couple of pelvic tilts, giving him the hint that she was ready to be fucked, but Dagan seemed to be prolonging the deed, to irritate her no doubt.

"Dagan," she pleaded. She went down on her forearms, which thrust her butt in the air and she shook it. "Don't make me wait."

"Say you give yourself to me, Reese," he whispered against her back in a husky voice. He pushed his hips in tight, shoving his arousal straight between her legs. "Say it, now."

Exasperated, she said, "I give myself to you freely, without hesitation, and with every expectation of not regretting it." She glared at him. "Now are you going to finish this or do I have to throw you down and ride you?"

His nostrils flared and his hair flew back from his face as he entered her, going deep with a powerful surge. A strange scent permeated the air, something like cinnamon, almond and vanilla all mixed together and a slight breeze blew through the room though the windows were sealed. The wild rhythm he started pushed her up toward the pleasure horizon. Through the roar of blood in her head, she vaguely made out Dagan's voice chanting some kind of poem or song, but she couldn't concentrate. His fullness stretched her wide and the gliding friction took her in a frenzy, but she rode the cosmic tide right along with him until they both exploded in an atmospheric cataclysm of light. The fires on the candles flamed high and it felt as though part of her lifted from her body. She swore there were fireworks going off in her bedroom as Dagan grabbed her hips and pumped in and out at an urgent pace, faster and faster until his body grew rigid and she felt hot liquid pulsing into her. She screamed.

The room returned to normal darkness. The candles extinguished themselves when Dagan fell next to her in a heap of sweat-covered, satiated male. She fell down to her stomach and he gathered her close to his heated body. He smelled wonderful.

"What were you saying? I couldn't hear it very well."

"*Wyle karecel démarr.*"

"*Wyle karecel démarr.*" She felt his smile.

"Yes."

"The language is very beautiful. What is it?"

She grew increasingly tired, as though she'd run a marathon or been awake for days. The drugged feeling dragged her lids closed.

"Sleep, my *reskar.*" He kissed her temple.

Reese felt a heaviness across her thigh and realized it to be Dagan's leg. His hand massaged her breast and when she opened her eyes, she saw him propped up on one hand, staring at her. It was still dark outside. She didn't know how long she'd slept, but she felt rested enough.

"Hi," she said.

"Hi."

"What are you doing?"

"I think you know what I'm doing and what I want."

She smiled. "I think I probably do."

He leaned down and kissed her, a gentle brush of the lips. Reese wanted more. She wanted the desire, the hunger that he'd had when he'd made love to her before. Lifting the hair off his nape, she nipped his neck and then licked the spot, blowing soft warm air on his heated skin. Her desire wept from between her thighs readying for his entry. The passion flared within her and she found it hard to breathe when his fingertips rode enchantingly along her shoulder, down her stomach, to part her entrance.

Dagan kissed her long and sweet. She'd never tire of kissing him. Two of his fingers pushed inside and she hissed. Each time he shoved his fingers in, his thumb tickled her clit, driving her wild. She waited desperately for him to fill her. Her breaths came in short gasps as the sexual pressure built. Yes, she wanted to come all over him and it grew closer.

Just as she reached the precipice of pleasure, Dagan stopped. She growled. "Dagan?"

"Careful, *reskar*, I don't want you peaking yet."

"I need it. I need you inside me."

"And there is no place else I want to be except deep inside you, but I have other plans for your body right now."

His sexy grin warmed her.

"Trust me, you'll like it."

A frustrated sigh escaped her lips. She'd been so close that now her body hummed with anticipation.

Sitting back on his haunches, Dagan hooked his arms under her knees and lifted her so her thighs lay against his. For the *démarr* to be completely binding, he had to take Reese three times before sunrise and fill her with his seed each time. There were no specifications on how this was to be done so he used his imagination.

He scooted close and slid his cock between the folds of her pussy, intimately stroking her clit. It drove her crazy with desire and made her come apart. When she screamed her climax, he eased away enough to release her legs and lower them. With his hand, he rubbed the tip of his erection against her pulsating flesh before entering her. The candles flared to life in time with his passion. He used a rocking motion at first, but soon the *fury* took over and his thrusts became hard and fast, burying deep within her softness.

He roared, "*Wyle karecel démarr*," as he ejaculated inside Reese.

They lay side by side, trying to slow their hearts and breathe regularly.

"You're right," she told him. "I did love it."

He'd had many women over the centuries of his life. Some were familiar with the acts of sex and made good bed partners, others not so experienced and more work. This had never been a problem for him because he'd made pleasuring women an art and excelled at it. What had transpired between him and Reese over the last two days was different from anything he'd ever known. The intensity of their joining each time increased in magnitude until he was sure he would physically combust.

Others who had found their *blethred* told stories and, obviously, there had been talk amongst the males of how the *fury* took over the Naruki mind, body and soul until they acted irrationally and without reason. He now understood what they'd meant, for he definitely wasn't acting like himself.

Slowly, the candles dimmed and the room grew dark again. As his mood tempered and his energy calmed, so did the symbols. The silver candlesticks represented the light of Heaven, the carved stone holders represented the permanence of Earth, and the worn wooden piece represented the constant transition of the Underworld. These items had been passed down in his line for centuries and used every time one of them found his or her mate.

Reese rolled against him and rested her hand upon his

chest. His hand clasped hers, dwarfing it. They were so different and yet some cosmic jester had thrown them together. He didn't know what would happen next, but after tonight, whatever happened in Reese's life would include him, although he would not be here to see it.

She kissed his neck. "You'd think after all this incredible sex that I'd be flying high and running on a huge rush of hormones and adrenaline, but like before, I'm totally exhausted and hardly able to lift my arms."

"In a marathon of sex, Reese, one is bound to get exhausted." He chuckled. "Rest, I'm not going anywhere and neither are you."

"I couldn't if I wanted to."

She closed her eyes and snuggled into the crook of his arm, rolling the front of her delectable body against his side. She was undoubtedly the most beautiful woman he'd ever known in any century.

# Chapter Seventeen

He awoke an hour later when soft fingers roamed down his chest and back up again. Crooking one eye open, he saw passion-laced eyes staring at him, uncertainty warring with desire.

"You are worried," he said in a sleep-laden voice.

She sighed. "This won't work, it can't." She rolled away from him and got up from the bed to silently pace the floor.

"What are you talking about?"

"Us." She gestured, pointing first to him and then her. "I love what I do, relationships never work for me. I'm gone all the time and most times I'm out in the field on some dig, very hard to reach."

He calmly watched her nervously explain her thoughts. She pulled on a robe. "And the thing is, I'm falling for you in a big way and now I'm worried about where that will lead."

Dagan rose from the bed and pulled on his pants. He stared out the window at the darkened sky. "Kur and I have a destiny. At some point, we will fight the final battle and it will be I who puts him down."

"Noble rubbish," she said.

He inclined his head. "Perhaps, but my duty just the same."

"I'm sick of hearing about duty. How did you get caught up in this nonsense anyway?"

He sighed. "When Ninmah discovered what had happened to the village, she called a session with the Pantheon. All the gods were present to hear the news." He began to pace. The thirteen-inch color television that sat on her dresser came on by itself. On the screen were what looked like an angry mob in a large coliseum. It was a bright day and the sunshine fell across the landscape with white, fluffy clouds suspended weightless in the sky.

A tall brunette stood in the center of the room. Calm chocolate eyes full of compassion and patience scanned the entire crowd. Her earth-tone coloring included the full-length toga that dragged along the pristine floor as she circled the room. Her hair fell to below her knees and a delicate crown of beautiful flowers encircled her head. She held her hand high, signaling for everyone to be quiet.

"A great catastrophe has befallen mankind. Because of his impetuous foolishness, Enki has doomed the humans to be hunted and used to further the creature's agenda."

The woman's voice purred like a contented cat and her gaze raked over Enki who sat perched on a stone-white chair on the next level.

"I curse your thoughtless act. For being the Lord of Wisdom, your wits had certainly abandoned you the day you created this menace."

The crowd roared its agreement.

"What can be done, Earth-Mother?" a stately-looking gentleman asked.

An ethereal woman slowly made her way through as the crowd parted and each member bowed. When she reached the place where Ninmah stood, she turned to address them.

"My Lord Enki, do you think we have anything to offer the creature which will appease him?"

With all his regal stature, Enki rose from the stone seat. "I have attempted to give him whatever he wishes, Inanna, but he refuses everything. His heart, such as it is, is filled with hatred, and vengeance is what he craves."

"Kur will not stop until he has had vengeance, and even then, there is no guarantee he will not kill every human just for spite," she said. "We have no choice but to call forth an army to fight this beast until it is defeated."

Reese turned to Dagan, who stood quietly watching the television, a frown creasing his handsome face.

"What is this?" she asked, pointing to the screen.

"My memories," he whispered.

A striking young man stepped forward. His green eyes flared with anger and something else hard to name. "I offer my services and my life, Earth-Mother, to hunt the creature until it or I am dead."

Inanna reached her hand out to him, but he moved away. He bowed to Ninmah and strolled toward Enki.

"How brave," Reese whispered.

"Brave, yes," Dagan said. "He is one of the most honorable and courageous men I know."

"I sense there is more to this story. Who is he?"

"Shara, Inanna's first born."

"Why didn't he let his mother touch him?"

His jaw clenched for only a moment. "She didn't want him to do it, but how could she refuse her own son of taking on the task when she had called for warriors to fight?" He sighed. "Although he was the first, many others accepted the challenge to hunt the beast."

"Like you."

"Yes."

He faced her. "I can't give up what I do. It's too important. Kur has killed too many and he will continue to do so until he is stopped."

"So we're left with nothing."

Dagan pulled her into his arms. "Not nothing. We can have tonight and memories." His tender kiss undid her. She melted gladly into his embrace.

When he broke the kiss she said, "I need something to drink and a power bar."

"It so happens that I have prepared a special wine for you."

"You did? For me?"

"Come, let us partake in some refreshment."

She grabbed his hand and linked their fingers, walking him down to the kitchen. "Did you...is that the goblet from my case?" she said incredulously. "That's an ancient artifact—"

He touched his fingers to her lips. "It is Basco's chalice. It belongs to my people, my race. The chalice has been around long before the oldest of us."

She lifted his fingers from her mouth and kissed his palm. "Oh. But why did you take it out of the case? If it's that old, don't you run the risk of damaging it?"

He chuckled. "Not likely." He lifted it to her lips. "Taste the sweet wine."

She drank. The rich taste was so intoxicating, she tipped the goblet to drink more. Her body felt invigorated, flushed. Her heart beat at a rapid pace and the need for something grew. What was going on?

"What kind of wine is that?" Her lips tingled and her eyes closed as a barrage of desires flowed through her. She urgently needed to taste Dagan's lips, inhale his breath, and lay her head against his chest to hear the pounding of his heart. Reaching out she lightly ran her fingertips along his bare arm, his torso, but that wasn't enough. Feeling all her inhibitions melt away, she smiled and crooked her finger.

"Come with me my Sumerian god. I want to see your mighty scepter."

He grinned wickedly.

She raced into the living room and when he rounded the corner, she had already thrown herself onto the plush rug.

Divesting himself of the pants he'd put on earlier, he dropped to his knees at her feet. Slowly, he inched his way up her body, straddling her until he had a knee on either side of her head. Since he had such long legs, he knew her breathing wasn't restricted nor was she uncomfortable. Her eyes were wide and wild as she rubbed her hands up and down his buttocks and back.

Grabbing his cock in one hand, holding it up for her to see he said, "Come now, my servant, will you please your god?"

The twinkle in her eyes and the smile that graced her face made his stomach drop.

Beautiful.

He leaned forward so the tip of his cock reached her mouth.

No female had ever touched him thusly. None would think

of doing so, yet this woman, this human, gave him the unexpected. At that moment, Reese ran her fingertips through his legs and caressed his tightened balls.

After snapping his fingers to light the candles he'd set up in this room, he extricated himself from Reese's potent mouth and repositioned himself between her thighs. With strength of will, he pushed into her at an excruciatingly slow pace. He swore he would explode.

As before, the candles on three sides represented three things. At their heads sat the white candles which represented the soul, to the right were the red candles representing the heart, and to the left were flesh-colored candles to represent the body. Gazing deeply into Reese's half-lidded eyes, Dagan murmured the sacred words.

When his cock was fully imbedded within her and they were one, she moaned.

"You are a god."

On his knees and holding her thighs over his arms, Dagan watched as he pumped into her luscious body. If he hadn't been turned on already, seeing that would have done it.

His desire and the *fury* now overrode everything. He no longer wanted slow but needed to fill her, love her, possess her. He lowered her legs and with her under him thrust hard and fast.

"Dagan," she screamed. "I'm going to—I can't..."

She cried out and her ecstasy squeezed and milked him until he growled and convulsed, spurting his seed within her to coat the walls of her womb.

"I need to catch my breath," she murmured after several minutes.

Slowly she rose, turning her back to him. He stared heatedly at the line of her spine and her sumptuous curves. Quickly, his cock filled, so he picked Reese up and hauled her to the couch.

"What are you doing?"

He plopped down on the furniture with her in his lap and turned her to face and straddle him. With a wicked grin, he guided himself to her opening.

"Not again, I can't, not yet." But the minute he filled her, Reese sighed and rode him hard. She needed little coaxing as she rose and lowered herself like a piston. His hands massaged her ass and he blew when she did.

Reese gently fell to the side. "I've never, I mean, not like this." She peered at him through a thicket of hair that had fallen in her face. "What did you do to me?"

"Which time?" he said with cocky satisfaction.

She punched his arm.

He laid his head back. Each of the Naruki had one *blethred*. They could have many lovers but only one true life mate. He'd known the time would come for him, but he never suspected she would be human.

Reese slowly opened her eyes. She'd fallen asleep again, but at least they'd made it back to the bed. Dagan lay still and blissfully sleeping, so she rolled away from him and scooted out of the bed. She fished around in the dim light to find her robe and slipped it on. She needed food.

She flipped on the small light over the sink and added a new filter and coffee to the coffee maker then switched it on. The rich aroma filled the room. Her stomach grumbled. The clock above the counter said it was 3:45 a.m., a little early for a big breakfast, but she could make some cinnamon rolls. From the cabinet by the stove she pulled out a glass pie dish. Rummaging through the refrigerator, she found the cinnamon rolls and opened them, placing each one cinnamon side up. She turned the oven on four hundred and eased the rack with the food in before closing the door.

The long island counter stretched across a portion of the kitchen giving her ease to walk around the room. She placed a knife next to the icing cup and grabbed a mug out of the cabinet. Taking a moment to deeply inhale the air as she poured the coffee, Reese thought about tomorrow—or was it today?

She needed to get to her too confined, cramped office downtown where her team would be waiting. They had a lot of work to do to get the ball rolling on this new project. If she could get enough interest, she may be able to entice a couple of the private collectors to team up and invest in the dig. The Turkish government may be a snag though. She'd have to see who she knew at the Department of International Affairs. Maybe Professor McClanahan would have some contacts she could tap.

She knew by the time she got to the office at nine o'clock, Joe would already be there working on the proposal and examining the aerial topography to determine the best place to start digging. He was her eager beaver, always willing to give up sleep and whatever girlfriend he had at the moment, to work. Joe loved it as much as she did.

Reese placed her hands on her head, the heels of the palms at her temples and pressed before rubbing her eyes. What would she do about Dagan? She'd grown too used to having his arrogant ass around. In such a short time, she knew there was something more to their relationship than just sex. She felt it inside her, squeezing her heart, filling her lungs. When she pictured his cocky smile and mesmerizing eyes, she also thought of waking up next to a hard muscled body tucked against her.

"What are you thinking? He's the son of gods and you're a small town archeologist. How would that work?" But she wanted it to work.

She thrust her hand into the mitt and removed the rolls from the oven. Setting them on the stove, she turned to fetch the plate and icing when she saw Dagan standing gloriously naked in the doorway. Her mouth watered, she couldn't help it.

"I love that smell," he said as he moved toward her. "It reminds me of you."

He reached up to twirl a lock of her hair around his finger. The light created sharp angles and planes on his features and he looked like the fierce warrior she knew him to be.

Dagan leaned down and took her mouth with his demanding lips. She opened and he swept his tongue inside. He growled low in his throat and it made her tingle. The vibrations sent shivers across her skin. It was primeval and the barest hungry emotion.

Putting his hands on her waist, he picked her up and set her butt on the island counter. Her robe fell open, baring her chest. His next kiss was long and ravenous which allowed him time to pinch and flick her nipples. The rough skin on his fingers caused such sweet friction and elicited a moan she couldn't suppress. Placing his large hand in the valley of her breasts, Dagan eased her back onto the counter so she lay with her legs dangling over the edge.

"Hmmmm, what's this?" He picked up the small, sticky cup.

A certain gleam danced in his eyes when he tilted the cup and the liquid sweet dribbled over her already sensitive nipple. She watched as he moved to the second nipple and repeated the torturous procedure. He bent forward and took the first nipple into his mouth, using his tongue to lick all the sugary substance from her before taking it between his teeth and rolling it.

Reese cried out. The painful pleasure was too much. Her heart raced and she lifted her hips to rub herself against his washboard abdomen.

Dagan shifted to the other breast and sucked the icing into his mouth. When he took that nipple between his teeth, she ran her fingers through his hair.

He massaged the nipple with his lips and put pressure on her pussy with his stomach. When he again took the nipple in his teeth, she had the most incredible orgasm. Her body quivered for several moments from the force of it.

Dagan wasn't in a hurry. They still had at least another hour before sunrise. He could take her over and over again and would like nothing more, but, he needed to get her back into the bedroom so they were within the semi-circle of elements.

He wrapped her legs around his waist. Filling his hands with her ass, he walked back to the bedroom. It felt right lying there between her thighs and playing with her breasts. She was ticklish on the outer sides of her flawless mounds, around her belly button, and behind her left knee. These were things he would always remember.

Fairy kisses and soft sighs led up to the point when he eased his cock into her wet passage. He penetrated her womb so deep that his pelvis slapped against her pussy, exciting them both even more. Watching his cock slide in and out of her body fueled the *fury*. He knew the time would come when he would dominate and control the joining, but right now, he wanted to savor the gentle loving.

Her arms wrapped around his neck and she lifted up to kiss him. She curled her slim legs around his hips and dug her heels into the backs of his thighs. Her need escalated. It was time.

Dagan ravished her mouth with his tongue, thrusting it in and out. His cock performed the same dance as it entered her body. He pumped faster, harder, going deeper every time. Her inner muscles convulsed around him.

"Oh God, Dagan. I'm coming now, now!"

Dagan roared and shot his water of life into her waiting pool. One day, their son would grow inside her.

He rolled off her and slammed face down. His right arm lagged across her waist. The *démarr* again stole his energy and hers as well. She'd already drifted to sleep.

A ray of light appeared through the window. The candles had extinguished. Dawn would be breaking soon. In mere minutes, the seal would disappear. He knew he should be up preparing for the day's battle, but he couldn't manage to move.

# Chapter Eighteen

As the sun rose quietly in the east and its rays touched the seal, it shimmered and faded away. The gas giant shone brightly, making the icy exterior glisten. Dagan had taken his shower and summoned fresh clothes. Reloaded and checked, his weapons were secure on his body. Sitting at the kitchen table sipping scalding hot coffee, he waited for Reese to finish her shower and dress.

He'd already called for Scion to meet him so he could take over the next few days of watching Reese. The *fury* raged at the thought of leaving Reese and not seeing her, being with her, again. He needed to tell her about the *démarr*. The telling would show how much he loved her. They had already come to the decision that she wouldn't give up her archeological job, which she swore was the reason for her failed relationships. In truth, Dagan knew it was because she had been waiting for him. He could not give up his job as a time walker. Kur was not only a threat to mankind but his people as well.

Reese strolled in a short time later, yawning. "Umm, coffee. Do I smell coffee?"

He rose, walked over to the counter, filled her mug and placed it in her hands. He bestowed a long kiss on her lips.

She leaned back against the counter and blew into her cup. His groin ached. He fisted his hands and ground his teeth together, fighting the *fury*. If it unleashed, Reese would be naked and panting on the floor within minutes. This generally was the case for the first week after the *démarr*. The initial bonding would wear down to a tolerable level until the next cycle when he would need to be with her again. But that would not happen now. The time had come for him to appear before the Pantheon and confess to his actions.

"I'm exhausted." Reese graced him with a sweet smile. "I guess we should have slept some."

"As I recall, we did sleep briefly."

"That wasn't sleep. I was unconscious."

He laughed, but didn't speak of what he knew. The melding of two bodies, minds and hearts used massive amounts of energy. She would recover. He was not so sure about himself.

Having tamped the *fury* back, he sauntered over and grabbed her around the waist to kiss her the way he needed to for the last time.

She set her cup down and wrapped her arms around his neck, pulling him close.

Dagan broke the contact when he felt the *fury* surfacing again. "Reese, I need to talk to you for a moment."

A worried look passed over her.

He pulled out a chair. "You might want to sit down."

"I don't like the sound of that," she said but complied.

Uncertain of the best way to begin, Dagan searched for the right words. "Last night, when we were together..." He had to move around and relax. "There is a ritual that is used by my race."

"A ritual? What kind of ritual?"

He took a deep breath and dived in. "The chalice that I told you belonged to my people is used in the ritual."

"You had me drink wine from it..." Her eyes narrowed on him. "What kind of ritual, Dagan?"

"My people go through the *fury* which is an intense drive, a need, to bond with their *blethred*. When we experience this, it cannot be denied for the primal instinct takes over and forces the bonding."

"Bonding?" She stood. "I need more coffee."

"I performed it last night."

She gulped. "The words in that language you spoke all night. That was part of it."

"Yes."

"And the candles and the wine?"

"Yes."

She gave him a thoughtful look before a troubling frown. "So what happens now?"

"Nothing for you will change. It is done and once I'm gone, you'll be the same as you have always been." Again, the *fury* swelled and he had to battle it back.

"So you're telling me that because of this *fury*, you performed a ritual on me, without my knowledge or consent, so you could fulfill your primal needs?"

"Exactly." She had to see now that he did it because he loved her.

"And, you are leaving now to continue on as a time walker and I will never see you again."

"Most likely, you won't, but Scion will be here for the next few days to make sure that Kur doesn't come back and you are well."

"I see."

He didn't like the tone in her voice. Why did she sound angry? Didn't she understand what this meant? Didn't she realize that this was his ultimate gift, his sacrifice?

"Well don't think you need to stay around." She trounced over to the door and opened it. "Why don't you go—now."

"What?"

"Go—now!" She pointed outside.

"Scion hasn't arrived yet and I'll not leave you unprotected."

"Thanks, but I've had all the protection I can stand. Leave."

He heard the catch in her voice. She was angry.

Walking to the door, he stopped long enough to caress her cheek until she turned her face away. When he went out the door, she slammed it behind him. As he turned to go back inside, Scion showed up.

Her heart fell. With her back against the door, Reese slid to the floor. "How could he? How could he do that to me, to us?"

She knew that he wasn't going to stay and there would be no future for them, but to demean what they had, what she thought they had, to something as low as getting his rocks off. "That bastard."

Tears fell down her cheeks. She used the heels of her hands to furiously wipe them away. It served her right. She allowed herself to become too attached, to fall in love with the arrogant jerk.

She couldn't sit here all day crying. She needed to work. Crawling to her knees, she grabbed onto the counter to pull herself up. First, she needed to fix her face, then she'd drive into the office and start working up some specs for the dig. As far as she was concerned, this Kur nonsense could be pushed to the back burner while they concentrated on getting the necessary information for the new find.

Dagan's steps were heavy as he walked up to the gates of Dilmun. He hadn't appeared inside because he'd wanted the time to go over everything before he went before the Pantheon and his mother and father.

The way Reese had acted hurt most of all. He thought explaining would make her understand that he would be with her forever—in spirit. While he would know and feel every moment, she would go on with her life, most likely forgetting him, for she was free to love another. His gut wrenched and the *fury* surged.

"Perhaps time away from her will prove that you are mistaken," Ninmah offered.

"I'm not mistaken, Mother, and I can't be away from her for long."

Enlil marched toward him and garnered his full attention. Dagan had not realized his father had come upon them. "The *fury?*"

Dagan nodded.

"Then it is good that you were ordered back here. Since we are not certain how this will play out, perhaps distance will help you resist the urge. You must not go back."

Dagan prepared himself for the blow that would come. "It's too late for that, my lord." He only used the formal address when he knew he was in trouble.

Enlil gritted his teeth. Ninmah stood by Enlil with worry in her eyes.

"Last night, I performed the *démarr*. We are one now for eternity."

"Oh no," Ninmah breathed.

Anger filled Enlil's features. "Do you realize what you have done? The Pantheon did not sanction this. You have signed her death warrant and your prison."

Dagan's rage blew full force. "If the Pantheon does anything to Reese, they'll have me to face. Whether they warrant it or not, Reese is mine and I am hers. They cannot change this. I didn't expect it but it's there nonetheless. You know as well as any of us, we cannot pick who our life mate is and we can't deny the *fury*." Dagan sighed. "I had no choice," he said in a softer tone.

Both his parents were quiet for a time before Ninmah said, "Perhaps the fact that she has Enki's blood can make a difference."

"What do you mean?"

"You said yourself that the draw was powerful even for you."

"True, from the moment I drew near her it latched onto me."

"He is one of the four and there is obviously something special about this female."

Dagan couldn't argue with that point. There was definitely something special about Reese.

"I will speak with Enki on this matter before you go before the Pantheon again."

"Thank you, Mother."

She graced him with one of her heartwarming smiles and disappeared.

"Do not get your hopes up, my son. Remember it is Enki we are discussing here."

Dagan laughed half-heartedly. "If I didn't know any better, I'd say you just made some kind of joke."

Enlil looked affronted. "I would never." He braced Dagan's arm. "Be careful and tell no one about the *démarr* until we get this straightened out."

"I won't."

His father shimmered away.

Maybe there was a ray of hope in this dismal situation. Sweat beaded on his brow and his blood began to heat up. The *fury* rose in him again. There were a few more steps to take to deal with these bouts of insanity. He hurried down the streets of Dilmun, not paying any particular notice to the beauty there. His only concern being to reach his dwelling before the need surfaced again.

"It's coming. Weld them tight, Pyre."

His friend said, "I don't like this, Dagan."

"It must be done." He gritted his teeth. "I need to fight. If I don't stay away from her, the Pantheon will kill her."

"The episodes are getting more violent. The beast in you is desperate for his mate."

He threw Pyre a droll stare. "That's why I asked for the chains. Weld faster."

Sparks flew into the air for a few more seconds.

"Done," Pyre said and blew out a breath. "I can't make them any more secure."

Dagan gave his friend a generous smile though pained. "Well done."

Suddenly, Dagan's body lurched and twisted, writhing in pain. A maniacal scream ripped from his chest, lasting a couple of excruciating minutes before he passed out. His vision blurred and his mind grew weary of the fight.

Flame appeared next to his brother. "He will surely die. None of us is strong enough to resist the *fury*. If he manages to survive, he won't be the same."

"No, he will not." Pyre faced Flame. "Dagan won't live through this, Flame. You must resign yourself to that fact."

When Dagan awoke some time later, his mother sat on the edge of his bed cooling his face with a rag. He no longer saw Flame or Pyre, but his father brooded in the corner.

"You should leave this place, Ninmah. I do not wish you to see this."

Her beautiful smile beamed down on him, and she did not face her mate when she said, "He is my son. I will stay with him."

She continued to dip the rag into some cool liquid and drip it over his heated skin. It refreshed his will so he could endure yet another round of hell. Another bestial scream roared from his body. Enlil grabbed Dagan's mother and jerked her away from the bed. The last thing Dagan saw before he fell unconscious was his father hugging her and turning her face away from the horror.

Someone dropped a book and the loud thud brought Reese back from her daydream. Her mind continued to wander off at all times of the day and night. It had only been two days since Dagan had gone but it felt like a lifetime.

In a sarcastic tone Joe said, "So, are you going to be working here on this planet today or do I need to get a direct satellite feed for my cell phone?"

"Ha, ha." She blew the stray strands of hair out of her eyes and tried to remember what she was doing.

"Reese, seriously, are you okay?"

"I'm fine." She hoped he bought the lie.

"No, you're not fine. You're a basket case." He plopped down in the chair in front of her desk. "Don't think I haven't noticed that you aren't eating, you have dark circles under your eyes from the lack of sleep, and in the last two days, you have done little to nothing about this dig." He leaned forward resting his elbows on his thighs. "That is so not like you."

Shuffling a few papers around on her desk, she picked up a pen, making the show that she worked. "I'll be okay. My body is catching up."

"Bullshit. It has to do with the asshole, right?"

"Don't call him that."

"Why not? He saves your life, does you, and then hightails it out of town, or should I say off the planet?"

"Let's get something straight. Dagan did save my life and yours. What else we did is none of your business, and I don't know where he went." She rubbed her eyes. "Just drop it, okay?"

"Fine. It's getting late, we're heading home. Do you want me to stay around and walk you out?"

"No. Scion is still here, but thanks." She met his gaze. "For everything."

He flashed a smile. "What are friends for? I'll see you tomorrow."

"Goodnight."

Reese finished stacking papers and made sure the coffee maker and radio were turned off before deciding to go back to her empty house. It seemed more empty than usual over the last two days and she didn't try to deny that it was because Dagan wasn't there.

She screamed when she opened the door and Flame appeared. "Stop doing that." She shook her head. "Dagan isn't here."

"I know," he said. "I came to see you."

"Me?"

"Yes. We need to talk."

"Come in then." She motioned for him to enter and closed the door behind him. "What's up?"

Flame paced the room, but didn't say anything.

Reese sat at her desk. "Flame, you said you wanted to talk."

He stopped in front of the windows. "The last night Dagan was with you, what happened?"

Confused she said, "I'm sorry? What happened?"

"Did you have sex with him?"

She felt her face heat up. "What happened or didn't happen," she emphasized, "between Dagan and myself is private and no one's business but our own." She had been angry with him after and had thrown him out, but heat rushed through her every time she remembered the way he'd touched her and loved her. No, not love.

He stormed over to where she sat. "Reese, it's important. I must know."

Grabbing her purse, she rose. "I don't think I really feel

comfortable talking to you about this."

Flame gripped her arm. "He's my best friend, like a brother."

"I know, that's my point."

"Did he tell you that you are bonded?"

Pissed now, that Flame would intrude on her personal business. "He mentioned something about a bonding. He performed some sort of ritual to fulfill his primal urges, okay? Are you happy now? He used me to get what he needed. Is that what you wanted to hear?" Tears stung her eyes and she turned away from him.

"Is that what he told you? He used you?"

"I don't remember everything he said." She pulled a tissue out of her pocket to wipe her eyes and dab her runny nose. "Something about a *fury* and primal urges." A bitter laugh escaped. "Primal urges, every species has those." She finished wiping away the evidence of her emotions. Stuffing the tissue back into her pocket, she dug out her keys. "I'm going home, you can pop yourself out."

He caught her at the door. "Reese, if I know Dagan, and I do, he didn't tell you everything and he most likely didn't explain it very well." With a droll look and a smile, he rolled his eyes. "He's got a bit of arrogance to him."

"That I had noticed. Why are you really here, Flame?"

"The *fury* is an overwhelming force with my race, more so for the males."

"I remember him saying something along those lines, but what does it have to do with me?"

He began to pace again. "With our race bonding is the ultimate sacrifice."

"Sacrifice? What are you talking about?"

"When a Naruki finds their *blethred*, they bond with them, give themselves over to them."

"What is a *blethred*?"

He stopped and looked at her. "*Blethred* means life mate."

Skeptical. "Okay."

"Did Dagan tell you what happens to a Naruki, especially

the males, when they are not with their *blethred?*"

"He said there is a time of a kind of separation anxiety, but it would pass."

He snickered. "Separation anxiety?" He looked down at her. "He can die, Reese."

"What?

"In our race, the *fury* is worse in the males. If we are separated from our *blethred* for lengths of time, we go through incredible pain, sometimes are given over to madness, and can very well die from it."

She bit her bottom lip. "He didn't tell me."

"I didn't think he would. He won't force you to be with him. He needs to know you want to be with him."

"I did want to be with him, but I couldn't see how it would work. He will not stop being a time walker."

He grabbed her hand. "No, he feels strongly about his duty."

She threw her hands up in the air. "Don't start with me and this duty crap. It irritates me."

"I understand." He turned toward the door.

"Wait." She followed him. "Why would he not tell me the truth?"

"He won't sway you." He placed his hand on her cheek. "He loves you deeply and has given his very soul to you for keeping. When he bonded with you without the Pantheon's permission, he invoked a punishment."

"What will they do to him?"

"They may need to do nothing because even now he goes through the separation with a fierce battle." His eyes held concern when he spoke. "This has never happened before. A Naruki does not choose their *blethred*, but never has one of us been bonded to a human. That is why the Pantheon ordered him to turn you over to Scion."

"What?"

He nodded. "I can't say what they'll do if he survives. It's different all the time. He defied their orders then bonded with you." He shook his head. "He knew the consequences."

"Do you know where he is?"

"I know they have summoned him back to Dilmun to await his punishment. I know he has been ordered to work with Gilgamesh to train new time walkers until the Pantheon decides what they will do."

"He's with Gilgamesh?"

Shaking his head, Flame moved to the door. "I have said too much already. I will tell you one thing more." His jaw tightened and his hand gripped the doorknob so hard, his knuckles turned white. "When I left, he was on the verge of death."

"No," she gasped. "Take me to him."

"I cannot."

Reese shoved him against the wall. "You bastard! You claim to be a brother, come here to give me all this news and then won't take me to him?"

"I can't do it. We don't have the ability to take someone with us. We can only transport ourselves. It is one of the restrictions of being a time walker." He looked at her with pained eyes. "I thought you should know what he did and why."

With that, Flame faded away.

Reese fell to her knees. *This can't be happening.* Was she supposed to sit here knowing that up there, somewhere, Dagan tried to survive hell and do nothing about it? He needed her and she needed him. The rest would work itself out.

"I know what to do." She pulled herself up on wobbly legs.

She locked up the office and headed for the car. It wasn't that late, her father should still be up.

Scion popped into the passenger seat of her car.

"Holy hell," she screamed and hit her head. "Are you trying to give me a heart attack?"

"Where are you going?" he asked calmly.

"I'm going to see my father."

"It's late and you should be going home, Reese. It has only been two days since we rid ourselves of Kur's presence. There is no telling when he will show himself again."

"I don't care," she growled.

"It's my job to protect you."

"No." She glared at him. "It's Dagan's job to protect me." Her voice caught and she couldn't look at him until she got her emotions under control.

Scion sighed. "It's no longer his duty, but mine."

*Breathe, just breathe.* She licked her lips. "As I understand it, it is Dagan's duty for eternity because I am his *blethred* and we are bonded."

"*Shakaah,*" he swore. "You must not speak of this. How do you know of these things?"

"It's true, isn't it?"

He snapped his mouth shut and didn't answer her, which was all the answer she needed.

"Scion, he performed the *démarr* before he left. I'm bound to him." She looked at him. "I need *him.*"

He rattled off several strings of words she did not understand because they were spoken in the Naruki language. She figured he was cursing up a storm.

"I need to talk to my father."

"I'm still your protector, despite what you say. You go nowhere without me."

"Fine," she huffed.

She drove faster than she should have, because not only were the roads icy but the cops would surely be out. Her heart hammered. All the things Flame had told her circled around in her head. Why would Dagan not tell her the truth?

Pulling into the drive of her father's house, she threw the car in park, got out and stormed up to the front door. Scion marched right behind her.

She unlocked the door and went in to find her father and sister in the kitchen eating dinner. Gideon sat in the living room, staring at the computer.

"Reese," her sister cried and jumped up to hug her. "What are you doing here?"

"Dad, I need to speak with you."

"Uh oh," Riley said before she noticed Scion standing off in the background. "Hi, handsome." She sauntered over, grabbed him by the hand and said "Let's go chat."

"What's up, honey?"

Guilt stole over her when she saw her father's concerned face.

"I need a big favor."

"You know I'll do anything for you. What is it?"

It was a lot to ask of him. She bit her bottom lip, warring with herself about why she'd come here.

"Reese?"

It was the only way. She knew she had to do it.

# Chapter Nineteen

His dry mouth felt as if he'd swallowed a huge fur ball, and someone had taken sandpaper to his eyelids, making them gritty. His body wracked with aches and pains as though he'd been tossed off a fifty-foot building.

Dagan rolled to his side and groaned. "Damn," he said but it came out in a whisper, his vocal box tattered from the screaming. He needed some water and a long hot bath. Fighting demons was infinitely better than this. Coming away from a vicious battle with cuts and gashes in his flesh felt far better than the broken heart and shattered soul.

Trying to move, he experienced extreme weakness to the point of barely being able to lift his hand off the bed. Why were his hands not chained as he'd instructed? He looked up and saw the cuffs Pyre had welded closed around his wrists dangling from the bedpost.

"I made him remove them."

His comatose sleep obviously hadn't helped. The insanity had kicked in. Through slitted eyes, he scanned the semi-darkened room. A form moved out of the shadows. He shook his head, adding to the already intense headache. Clearing his throat, he said "Am I delusional?"

"No, I'm here." The soft tone sounded husky to his ears. Reese sat on the edge of the bed and caressed his cheek.

Closing his tired eyes, Dagan turned his face into her hand. The sight of her brought comfort, the smell of her brought yearning. Having her near settled his body into a lull.

"You should not be here," he croaked.

"Shh, don't speak. Let me get you something to drink."

She rose and walked a short distance. He heard her pour something into a cup then she appeared back at his side, touching the moisture to his lips.

"Drink this, but only a little at first."

He let her tilt the glass so cool liquid ran down his parched throat. Immediately, he suffered a jag of coughing.

Again, he felt her soft hand caress his cheek and a cold rag lay across his forehead. She hummed some quiet tune as she rinsed out the rag and placed it on his chest.

"You've been out a long time. I didn't think you would ever wake."

He stilled the hand she used to touch his face. "What are you doing here? How did you get here? No human can enter Dilmun."

She again helped him drink some of the water. He felt a little stronger.

"I came here to be trained by Gilgamesh. Enki brought me."

Anger washed over him. "Damn him. You can't stay."

Reese stood and perched her hands on her hips. "You can't make me leave, Dagan. I'm here to learn to protect myself, since it appears that I'll need the knowledge."

He glared at her. "You have protection."

"No, I do not. Scion will only be around for a short while, I don't live with my father anymore, and my *blethred* would rather die than be around me. Therefore, I need to learn to protect myself." She turned away from him.

He watched her shoulders shake and her hands move to hug around her waist. Her angry words sent shivers across his damp skin.

Dagan rolled his face away from her. "How did you find out?"

"What, that you'd rather die than tell me the truth?" Her muffled voice was scolding.

"It's not like that, Reese."

"It very well looks like that to me."

"Look at me." He used his flagging energy to grasp the denim on her leg with his fingertips. "Reese."

Haltingly, she turned. Tears glistened on her lashes in the dim light coming through the window. The sight of her wrenched the breath from his lungs. He opened his fingers and left his hand open wanting her to reach for him.

"I did it to protect you." He let his hand flop to the bed.

"You ran away."

The accusing tone made him wince. He would much rather have her anger.

"I had to leave. The Pantheon had ordered me to turn you over to Scion and come back here."

"Why?"

"A Naruki has never had a human life mate. It breaks rules and boundaries that should never have been broken."

Words of the Pantheon spilled from his lips though he himself did not believe them. He wanted Reese to believe and go home. He needed to finish this.

A slow burn, starting in his stomach and crawling up his ribcage, his chest, his neck warned him that the *fury* built and soon another attack would engulf him. Reese had to be gone before that happened.

"It is wrong—forbidden. I broke the rules and will be punished. After that, I won't be fit for anything for a long time. You need to go now!"

She grasped his hand. "Does this feel wrong?"

He inhaled. The heat from her touch enflamed the *fury* and it consumed oxygen desperately needed to breathe and argue and push her away.

His body spasmed and jerked wildly on the bed.

Reese screamed and slapped her hands over her mouth. She watched his body writhe with pain.

Dagan used the last of his strength to fight a losing battle. He knew in the end he would die. He was vaguely aware when Flame appeared by Reese's side.

"What can I do?" she cried.

"Go to him, Reese. It's the *fury* that is claiming his life. You must get it back."

"How?"

Flamed grabbed her by the arms and turned her away from the bed. "Do you love him?"

"Yes."

"Then show him. Don't let him push you away or it will kill him."

With one last look, Flame left.

Dagan's agonizing scream reverberated into the depth of her soul. She climbed on top of him and straddled his waist. He tried to buck her off. His hands came down hard and shoved at her chest making her fall backwards slightly. She grabbed his hands and righted herself but he continued to throw her off him.

"Get out, Reese," he managed through tight lips. "Go home."

She knew she couldn't hold him for very long, even in his weakened state, he was too strong. She was running out of options and she didn't know how long the fit or seizure would last, so she did the only thing that came to mind. She kissed him.

Reese bolted forward and planted her lips on his. Dagan stopped writhing. She slid her hands forward and clasped fingers with him, lying on his chest. He heaved deep breaths and held on tight. When his eyes opened, she eased back.

"I love you, Dagan."

"Stop," he huffed. "You have no idea what you're saying."

"I love you."

He bucked his hips, trying to dislodge her. He stared at her with tortured eyes. "Get out of here, go away."

Now she was just pissed. "Fine," she growled. Getting up and standing by the bed, she looked down at him and said, "You don't want me here. I get it. I'll go stay with Enki and work with Gilgamesh until my training is done."

She had only taken a couple of steps before Dagan roared and flew off the bed. He wrapped his arm around her waist and pulled her against his naked body, then pushed her up against the wall. She flattened her hands against the smooth surface and pushed away but his body held her in place.

Placing both hands roughly on her hips, he inched them

up, taking her shirt with them. When he got to her breasts, he cupped them in his hands and squeezed. He shoved the flimsy material aside to pluck her nipples before lifting the shirt over her head and tossing it away.

"Reese," he whispered against her neck.

"Oh, Dagan," she sighed.

He coaxed her around but still kept her plastered against the wall. His lips captured hers. The kiss became ravenous, a dying hunger. She shivered from the forcefulness of it.

Pulling away, he laid his forehead against hers and breathed heavily. "If you don't go, I'll not be able to stop the *fury*. I'm too weak."

"Will it hurt you?"

He chuckled. "No, but I fear it will consume you."

"And if you don't let go, it will kill you."

"My choice," he rasped.

"Not gonna happen," she retorted.

Easing back, he raked a searching, desperate, hopeful gaze first across her exposed breasts then into her eyes. "You know not what you're doing."

"Kiss me."

He growled low in his throat. "It'll be rough and hard and very long."

"I already knew that." She ran her fingers up his gloriously naked length.

A faint smile twitched at his lips. "I'll have no control once I let loose. It may not be pleasant for you since I've held it off so long. I don't want to hurt you."

"Will it hurt more than when you left and never told me the truth of it, Dagan? If you love me...kiss me."

He clutched her hips as he leaned forward and pressed his lips to hers, the tension in his body like a bow string ready to snap.

"Dagan," she murmured against his lips.

"What?"

Reese ran her hands up his spine to his shoulders and back down again, squeezing his butt cheeks. Slowly, she felt some of the tension leave his body. His mouth lit a path of wetness down her neck to her breasts where his teeth lightly bit her nipples. She cried out.

With a strength she thought he no longer possessed, Dagan lifted her up. She circled her legs around his waist. He sucked one nipple into his mouth, bit it then licked the pain away. He moved to the next and repeated the wonderful torture.

His eyes darkened and a pained expression marred his features.

"What is it? What's wrong?"

He didn't speak. She noticed how hot his skin became. She somehow knew that meant the *fury* was coming.

"Don't fight it. Don't fight this." She laid her hand against his heart.

Again, his mouth took hers. He grabbed at the button on her jeans and ripped them open. Roughly, he set her feet on the floor and tore the pants from her body then ripped the panties away. He spun her to face the wall, lifted her high.

"Dagan, what are you doing?"

"Wrap your legs around my waist," he ground out. "Now!"

She awkwardly encircled his waist with her legs. He quickly lowered her so she could feel the tip of his shaft at her entrance. He plunged inside.

It wasn't pain she felt. She braced herself against the wall for each thrust. Dagan had been truthful when he'd said hard. He entered her with a hungry, driving force.

With his hands at her hips, he lifted and lowered her body in time with his thrusts, going deeper and deeper. She felt her muscles tighten and the release violently convulse around him.

Reese shook from the explosive passion. How could Dagan still be standing and holding her weight in his weakened state? Dagan leaned into her, lightly compressing her body to the wall with his own. He kissed her shoulder blade.

"I'm sorry, baby. Did I hurt you?" he murmured.

She gave a soft chuckle and lazily tilted her head back to meet his heated gaze. "Are you kidding? That was incredible."

A smug smile curved his lips. "I'm glad you thought so." He slid her legs down to the floor, then picked her up and carried her to the bed. "That was only the beginning."

Hours—or days—later, Reese awoke wrapped in Dagan's arms in the middle of his enormous bed. She felt weary and pleasantly sated. Dagan had been right when he said she didn't know what she was getting herself into. She'd lost count of how many times he reached for her through the night or day. Over and over, he eagerly made love to her. When she thought she couldn't take anymore, he produced a soothing lubricant to ease her body for his invasion.

She lightly stroked his chest, making circles around his taut, brown nipples.

"What are you thinking?" he asked in a husky, sleepy voice.

Her hand stilled. "I didn't know you were awake."

"You expect me to sleep when your exquisite fingers are stoking my body?"

"Surely, you can't—I mean after all that—again?"

He answered her question by brushing his lips against hers and grasping her hand to move it lower. She felt the hard ridge of his erection through the thin sheet.

She breathed a faint sigh. "Is it always like this?"

A crooked smiled curved his lips. "Yes and no."

"What does that mean?" She snuggled closer.

"If you mean will I always love you with such ferocity? Yes, because I can't help myself." He rolled them so she lay beneath him. "If you mean will we have these relentless bouts of sex, not unless we want them. Generally, the consummation is the most ferocious of the joining. It will taper off over time."

Reese wrapped her arms around his neck as he settled himself between her legs. "So what happens now?"

He laid his head on her chest. "I go before the Pantheon to receive their punishment."

"No." She framed his face and brought it up to see his bright green eyes.

"I must. It is our law, Reese. I have defied them more than once. It's time."

She clutched onto him. "What will they do?"

"I don't know." He rose up to look into her eyes. "I want you to go home, Reese."

"I'll wait."

He rested his head between her breasts. "You're an exasperating female."

"So I've heard."

She snuggled him closer, liking the way it felt to have him here like this.

When Reese woke, she knew she was alone. A sick dread filled her. Dagan had gone to face the Pantheon for their punishment. Jumping up, she retrieved her clothes from the floor and hastily put them on.

"Flame," she called out.

Nothing happened.

"Flame!"

Dagan's friend appeared before her. "You called, my lady?"

"He's gone. He was gone when I woke up. He told me he had to go before the Pantheon for punishment.

"It has begun."

"Yes," she retorted hotly. "I need you to get me there."

His face sobered. "I cannot."

She grabbed his shirt in fisted hands and pulled him to her face. "You can and you will."

"No one is allowed, especially humans."

"Look, buster, I've recently found out my father is a *nephili*, I've faced demons, Kur, and the man I'm in love with is a demigod who walks through time. I can face the Pantheon."

He chuckled. "Technically, he's not a demigod because both his parents are gods. Now, Gilgamesh, on the other hand..."

"Flame. Don't care. You can give me the politically correct version later. I need you to get me to the," she waved her hands above her head, "wherever we need to get to, right away."

He crossed his arms over his chest and raised a blond brow. "And how will you get in?"

She gave him a faint smile. "I have a plan."

*"Yea though I walk through the valley of the shadow of death..."* Dagan had always liked that particular human verse. He thought it appropriate under the circumstances. His entire body felt as though it had been plowed over by a herd of the *mredí*, a form of elephant indigenous to his planet, and his head felt ten times too big because his brain had swelled and would break out of his skull any minute. It took the last vestiges of his strength to drag clothes over his bruised body and all his willpower to do it without waking Reese and making love to her again.

As before, he appeared fully armed and in his general time walker attire, not wanting to give a quarter in this battle. A show of strength if nothing else.

The members of the Pantheon were seated in their proper regal positions when he arrived. Strolling forward to the bottom of the arena, he bowed before them as was proper.

"So, Time Walker, again you come before us well-armed. Is that to suggest that you will fight our decision?" Ki purred.

He stayed silent. She would not bait him into a scene of insolence to add to the pile of charges the Pantheon already held against him.

A soft chuckle from somewhere behind him announced the presence of Inanna.

"You are bold, Dagan. I will give you that. Still, you disobeyed orders to relinquish the protection of Reese Whittaker." She stopped in front of him. "Do you deny this?"

"No, my lady."

"No," An stated. "As well you should not since we are fully aware that you performed the *démarr* without our sanction. And with a human."

"And I would do it again, my king."

"You are insolent," Ki offered.

"He is my son," Enlil announced.

His father's outburst stunned Dagan.

Inanna said, "We know his bloodline, Enlil. But this deed cannot go unpunished. This matter had been discussed and still he chose to ignore the order."

"To perform the sacred ritual with a human is unheard of

and will not be allowed."

"Well it's too late and you better damn well get used to it."

Her voice bounced with the acoustics in the arena. What the hell was Reese doing here?

The king stood. "How dare you enter this hall, *human.*"

"Don't give me that human crap," Reese threw back. "I'm not your servant and neither is he."

Reese came to stand by his side. She grazed her fingers across his.

"How did you get in here?" Ki asked.

He noticed the sideways glance Reese cast at Enki, who sat silently in the upper tier watching the scene with interest.

"What matters is that I am here and I'm not going away. I'm his mate. We have performed your ritual, done the deed, and now we're bound together as per your customs."

Reese paced before the gathering. "I love Dagan and he loves me. Why is that not enough for you? Because I'm human. You say it as if the word sticks to your tongue." She glared at Inanna. "I'll tell you this. We were good enough to do everything for you when you could not do for yourselves. We tended the fields, brought sacrifices so you could sit on your lazy butts and rake in what humanity toiled." She lifted a brow then frowned at them. "Not to mention, at least some of you have taken it upon yourselves to dally with humans over the ages, but that's okay, even if children are produced." Reese shook her head. "I must say, that's a poor example you so-called gods present."

Dagan had to fight to keep the smile from curling his lips. Her chin rose in defiance.

"Get the guards," Ki roared. "Have this female thrown out."

Dagan grabbed Reese's arm and pulled her to his side. Facing the Pantheon he growled, "No one will touch her."

Inanna's temper flared. "Are you not in enough trouble already? You would stand against us? Surely you know you cannot win."

"He would not stand alone." Enki finally stepped down. Enlil and Ninmah stood with him.

"We have made our decision," Reese said.

He tried to keep her behind him, but she shook her head

and squeezed his hand before stepping in front of Enki.

"Dagan feels very strongly about his duty as a time walker. I respect this as should you. I won't ask him to give up his duties and he hasn't asked me to change my life for him. He chose to take the risk of giving up his life to protect me and has done this time and again for all other humans he protects against Kur and his army."

Nammu moved forward and everyone in the room lost some of the bluster. "What are you saying, my child?"

Reese blew out a breath. "I'm saying that he wants to continue as a time walker and he's a damn good one. You need him."

"And what of you?"

"I'll continue to do my work as an archeologist on Earth."

The mother of them all floated toward the center. A frown captured her brows and lips. "You would separate yourself from him, your *blethred*?"

A strand of hair had fallen into her bright eyes. "We haven't worked out all the details yet."

"Dagan, have you not explained to your woman about the *fury* and how it affects our race?"

Dagan bowed low before Nammu. "We were otherwise engaged." He straightened and sent a devilish grin Reese's way. She blushed.

Turning his attention back to Nammu he said, "First, I had not planned on ever seeing her again. We haven't had time to discuss the rest for I was uncertain as to what would happen when I came here."

"That is sound thinking on your part." She walked over to Reese and framed her face in both hands. "You are so beautiful, with quite the temper." Winking, she said, "Keep a leash on it. Control is what you will need to handle this one." She pointed to Dagan.

Reese smiled and shot him a quick glance.

Nammu stood regally before Enki, Enlil and Ninmah. "You three seem to always manage to have ruckus surround you." Moving closer to Enlil, she scolded. "He has your traits engrained in him."

"That he does, Great Mother."

"Enki, you created this problem so long ago, and now, in a roundabout way, you bring us a new weapon to fight against it."

"Only too happy to help, Great Mother," Enki offered, his lips twisting in wry humor.

"An," Nammu called.

"Yes, Great Mother." He appeared instantly at her side.

"I have witnessed the pain and agony Dagan has suffered not only over the last couple of days, but before. I decree that it is more than enough punishment for his crime."

"But..."

She held up her hand. "We must come to terms with the facts. We created then interacted with the humans. Lines get blurred, laws change; it is the way of things." Nammu faced the rest of the Pantheon. "However, this does warrant close attention. We have no idea what other surprises await. Mankind is an evolving species and no longer limited to our rules."

An bowed. "Yes, Great Mother."

"Dagan, take your woman from this place. Explain to her the extent of our race and the *fury*."

"As you wish, Great Mother." He grabbed Reese's elbow and escorted her toward the door.

"But..." Reese protested.

"Not now, sweetheart," he whispered in her ear.

Dagan scurried Reese as quickly as he could back to his dwelling. He closed and locked the door.

"Well that was interesting," she said as she moved farther into the room.

"Quite." He followed in her wake, dropping his weapons along the way.

She turned, recognizing the all-too-familiar look in his eyes. She squealed and took off running with him in chase.

He caught up to her in one long hallway, wrapping his arm around her waist and pulling her against his rock hard body. He inhaled her incredible scent and rubbed his already swollen cock against her behind.

"Did you mean what you said?" His hot breath sent shivers

across her skin.

"What?" She groaned when his hand caressed her breast through her shirt.

His free hand unbuttoned her jeans and then unzipped them, sliding his hand down the front and into her panties. "That you would be willing to find a way to make this work...us?"

"Yes," she breathed.

She gently rocked her pelvis.

"Good," he murmured against her neck. *My woman.*

Easing his fingers from her, Dagan picked Reese up and carried her to his bed where they stayed for the rest of the day and well into the night.

Hours later when Reese woke, the darkness swelled and the bed was empty. "Dagan?"

"I am here." His voiced drifted from the dark.

She scooted up to rest her back against the headboard and pulled the covers over her nakedness. "What are you doing?"

He moved into the dim light coming from the windows. "Watching you sleep."

"Oh." She grinned, liking the thought of him watching her in slumber. It was kind of a turn-on. "Shouldn't you get some rest?"

"Soon enough." He sat on the bed. "I've been thinking about us...our situation."

She bit her lip. "So have I."

His brows shot up. "You have?"

"Yes." She grasped his hand.

He sighed. "I do not want to stop being a time walker."

"I understand that and would not ask you to."

Laying his forehead against hers he said, "I will be gone for long periods of time."

"When I'm on a dig I'm gone for months and months. It's no different." She cupped his face in her hands. "Maybe I can stay here for a while. I can do as Enki suggested and take some lessons from Gilgamesh."

He shot her a disgruntled frown. "No."

"But..."

"No, Reese. If there is any teaching to be done, it will come from me. He will not touch you."

She heaved a sigh. "Dagan, he will be teaching me to fight, which would involve touching, but not groping."

"The Great Mother told me to teach you our ways. One thing you should learn about bonded males is that we have little tolerance for another male touching our mates."

Irritated she said, "And you should get used to the fact that I don't take orders well, nor do I hold to that jealousy crap. I love you and we are married, in a sense, but if I want to hug Joe or Geoffrey or some of my other male acquaintances, I will do it."

He absently toyed with a strand of her hair. "I carry weapons."

She batted his hand away. "Let's get one thing straight, big boy. The rules that dictated the Naruki lives are changing. You should realize when you've lost an argument and you've lost this one."

"So we are at an impasse."

"No, we're at a turning point. We'll take it one day at a time and see where that leads us."

"Here, angel." He pulled a solid gold, beautifully hand-carved bracelet out of nowhere and presented it to her.

"It's gorgeous."

"Since we have agreed to try and work this unusual relationship out, I had it made for you."

She lifted it into the faint light to see it better. "These stones are extraordinary."

"They mine them from deep in Mount Cradacus."

"What is Mount Cradacus?"

"It's the most active and volatile volcano in existence."

She tilted her head. "I've never heard of it."

He chuckled. "It's unseen by the human eye. It lies here in Dilmun. It's where Pyre forges our weapons."

Reese slipped the bracelet on her wrist. "Oh." The bracelet

grew warm and set off a humming vibration. "What's it doing?"

An odd smile touched his lips before he clutched her hips and shifted her back down to the bed and settled his body atop hers.

"It has been enchanted and attuned to me. When I have to be away from you, it will let you know I'm coming back. When it gets warmer and starts to hum, you'll know I'm not far."

A smile curved her lips. "Really?"

He interlocked his fingers with hers and kissed her gently, tenderly. "Wear it always, *reskar*."

# About the Author

To learn more about Sloan McBride, please visit www.sloanmcbride.com or www.myspace.com/sloan_mcbride. Send an email to Ms. McBride at SloanMcBride@aol.com or join her newsletter:

http://groups.yahoo.com/group/SloanMcBrideNewsletter/join

*In their fight for survival, the layers come off—body and soul.*

# Parallel Fire
## © 2008 Deidre Knight
### *A Midnight Warriors story.*

Anna Draekus is a soldier wrapped up in secrets, one of which has just been blown. As a member of the shadowy Madjin Circle, she was marked and trained from childhood to protect the king, even without his knowing. And now that her superior officer Nevin Daniels has discovered her allegiance to the Madjin, another secret is in serious danger of exposure.

The one where she fantasizes about cracking the taciturn Refarian's composure and making him scream her name in passion.

Nevin has tried everything to exorcise Anna from his mind and body, once and for all. Nothing works. He's long lusted after the free-spirited and plainspoken soldier, but her mere presence ties him in knots and drives him to the brink of insanity. Something a man in his position can't afford. Something a man of his maturity could never hope for.

Then a routine patrol finds them wrecked and marooned deep in the Wyoming backcountry. And Anna unwraps Nevin's deepest secret of all: Beneath his tightly controlled exterior beats the wild heart of a tiger.

*This book has been previously published.*

*Warning: This title contains explicit, rutting-like-a-stallion sex and graphic language.*

*Available now in ebook from Samhain Publishing.*

*Can love tame a jaguar god?*

# Treasure Hunting
## © *2008 Jenna McDonald*
### *A Hunting Love story.*

A good tromp through the jungle fending off giant bugs and hunting for long-lost ruins in South America is exactly Meg's idea of a great vacation. She takes the sudden appearance of a wounded jaguar in stride, thinking it'll make an interesting story. But when she wakes up to find a man in place of a cat, she wonders who's going to believe it!

Santiago has learned the hard way that he and human women just don't mix. When you can change into an animal at will, it tends to upset people. But despite his best intentions, he finds himself falling hard for the little blonde who saved his life.

It'll take a leap of faith-and of love. Or this treasure will slip through his fingers.

*Warning: This work contains graphic m/f sex, bad language, and terrible humor.*

*Available now in ebook from Samhain Publishing.*
*Available now in the print anthology* Hunting Love *from Samhain Publishing.*